"So tell me what th...

"He w... ...d you
were a...

"R... ...across
the oc... ...wait,
you ju...

Ka... ...could
kiss it ...s spot
on. Bu...

Sh... ...d sis-
ters o...

"B... They
were ... ...was a
sort o... ...ought
maybe...

If ... ...t, she
woul... ...ace.
And ... ...uld
have ... ...But
beca... ...arm
to a... ...p in
the ... ...re.

"Fresh and fun. . . . Hot sex and snappy repartee flourish."
—*Los Angeles Times*

Also by Lauren Henderson
My Lurid Past

Don't *even* think *about it*

Lauren Henderson

doWn tOwn press

New York London Toronto Sydney

DOWNTOWN PRESS, published by Pocket Books
1230 Avenue of the Americas
New York, NY 10020

First published in Great Britain in 2003 by Time Warner Paperbacks

Library of Congress Cataloging-in-Publication Data

Henderson, Lauren, 1966–
    Don't even think about it / Lauren Henderson.—1st Downtown Press trade
pbk. ed.
      p. cm.
    ISBN 0-7434-6469-9
    1. Triangles (Interpersonal relations)—Fiction. 2. Dating (Social customs)—
Fiction. 3. London (England)—Fiction. I. Title.

PR6058.E4929D66 2004
823'914—dc22

                                                                    2004055122

First Downtown Press trade paperback edition November 2004

10 9 8 7 6 5 4 3 2 1

DOWNTOWN PRESS and colophon are
trademarks of Simon & Schuster, Inc.

Designed by Jaime Putorti

Manufactured in the United States of America

For information regarding special discounts for bulk purchases,
please contact Simon & Schuster Special Sales at 1-800-456-6798
or business@simonandschuster.com

To my mother and my sister Lisa, my number one fans (tied first place), who are probably in a bookshop somewhere at this very moment sneaking my books from obscurity on the shelves to a prominent place on the front display table.

Acknowledgments

This book is specially dedicated to Aaron, the only friend of mine ever to say that he wanted to be in one of my books and—most importantly—didn't care what I wrote about him. Aaron, I hope you meant it, because it's too late to change it now . . .

Thanks also to Wilma Carroll for working out Katie's tarot reading for me.

Prologue

Katie had never been to a fortune teller before, but she knew what to expect. Too much black eyeliner on a hard, wrinkled face; lots of cheap jewelery; an abrupt, seen-it-all-before manner; and a hand upturned for cash. Oh yes, and one other thing. Fortune tellers were definitely women.

A soft voice behind her said: "Katie? You wanted your palm read?"

She turned round to see a young man in his late twenties with calm dark eyes and long black hair pulled back into a ponytail. Like all the other barmen, he was dressed in black.

"Yes, that's me," she said, slipping down off the bar stool. She met Michael's eyes, and he smiled at her encouragingly as she followed the barman over to the quietest corner of the bar, behind a couple of pillars. Her heart was pounding. She had never had her fortune read before. And she had particular reasons, tonight, for wanting it to turn out wonderfully.

The young man led her over to a small table and indicated a chair. She sat down, and he did the same, facing her at the table. It was only then she realized that this unflamboyant, quiet young man was actually the psychic with whom, on a wild impulse, she had booked a session.

Taken aback as she was, Katie was determined not to lose face. She had only been in New York for a couple of weeks, but she had learned almost immediately that New Yorkers prided themselves on their ability not to show surprise at anything. She wasn't going to come across as some dozy British chick, too traditional to imagine that a man could tell fortunes too. Actually, she should have expected that a psychic in this particular bar wouldn't fit the usual stereotype. Earlier, she and Michael had seen a very fat man go into the women's toilets and emerge, half an hour later, in a flouncy dress and blond wig. He was over at the bar now, handing out bingo cards and announcing himself in a loud campy voice as the "Bingo Bitch." The weirdest thing was that she could have sworn he went into the loos a black man and came out white—at least his hands and face, which were all the dress revealed.

Katie focused on the young man. His face was smooth and round, his serene dark eyes the only feature that caught attention. That, and his air of tranquillity. She found herself relaxing, and warned herself to be on her guard. These people always elicited as much personal information from you as they could, to help them along. You were supposed to stay quiet, not to react too much, giving them as little help as possible.

"My name's Armando," the young man said. "And I know you're Katie. So, what are you here for? A general reading?"

Not knowing what the other alternatives were, Katie nodded. The table was covered in a black cloth. A pack of cards was placed on the far side, close to Armando, but that was all the paraphernalia she could see. No crystal ball, no incense, nothing. Perversely, she found herself being rather disappointed.

Armando reached for the cards and slid the pack across the table to her.

"Cut them three times with your left hand and put them back together however you want," he said.

Katie obeyed. Her hand shook with nerves as she stacked the cards back on top of each other. Behind her she could hear the Bingo Bitch hoisting himself onto the stool he had placed in a small cleared area of the bar, and saying into the microphone: "All right, boys and boys—and of course our fag hag friends—bingo time is here again! Let's hear it for me, the Bingo Bitch!"

Armando took the pack again and dealt several cards off the top, laying them out on the table in a pattern. Two in the center, on top of each other at ninety degrees—a cross—four surrounding the cross and then a vertical line of three to each side.

"Wow," he said, pointing to the cross. "The Lovers, with the Tower on top. Not only love, but great sex too! The Tower is very explosive. It can mean premature ejaculation in other contexts, but in this one I'd say it was very positive. Right?"

Katie couldn't help grinning smugly.

"And the Two of Cups on top. Everything is going really well for you. As if we didn't know that already!" He slid his finger to point out a card below the cross. "The World. Travel. This is your job—it's connected with traveling. Either that, or you travel a lot for work. Then there's the Sun. You are very happy right now. No surprises there! Hmn . . ." He indicated the card above the Sun. "This is your friends, your home, your environment . . . the High Priestess. Some kind of secret there. Maybe you know it already?"

Katie shook her head.

"A secret to be revealed, then. And above this, the King of Wands. The only man in the spread. He's charming . . . maybe a little unfocused. Look. He's sitting on the throne, holding his staff, as if he's ready to stand up. And do you see the little lizard at his feet? He doesn't even notice it. He's looking away from it, onto the next thing."

That was Michael all over, Katie thought. Always keen to have the next experience, always wanting to try new things, new bars to go to, new people to meet. She loved that about him. It felt as if life with Michael would never get stale.

"From the position," Armando continued, smiling at her, "I'm assuming this must be the boyfriend."

Katie couldn't repress a surge of excitement at the word "boyfriend." She and Michael had only met a week before, and though they'd been inseparable ever since, it was much too early for words like that to be introduced. It was the first time someone had said "boyfriend" in relation to Michael. She felt as warm as if she'd just drunk a double shot of bourbon.

"But these are a little more confusing." Armando touched the two cards on either side of the cross. "Past and future. Hmn." He reached for his glass of water and took a sip. "The Queen of Pentacles in the past. A brunette, well-groomed, very elegant. And then in the future, the Queen of Swords. An angry woman, dark too—is that you, I wonder . . . ?" He glanced at Katie's dark hair. "And then below this, the Wheel of Fortune.

Reversed. Which suggests a circularity, obviously, looping round. Do you have sisters, perhaps?"

"No," Katie said.

"Cousins? Friends, even? It's quite a strong pattern—I thought it might be, what's the word, familial? Because there's a resemblance between the Queen of Swords and the Queen of Pentacles . . ."

"Not really," Katie said. "Well, my mum."

"Is she often angry?"

"She can be."

And she wouldn't like me getting off with some strange bloke I met in a bar in New York, Katie thought, let alone moving into his hotel room the night afterward. Plus she's elegant and well-groomed . . . She pulled a face.

"I think I know who that might be," she admitted.

"OK."

Armando still looked a little puzzled.

"Past and future," he said. "These dark women . . . the resemblance . . . I really thought you had sisters. Ah well." He smiled at her. "Do you have any questions?"

Katie blushed. "Will it—" she started. He was a tarot reader, she reminded herself, he must be asked this sort of thing all the time. "This love affair you're seeing—will it last?"

Armando studied the cards again. "I would have to do a much bigger spread for that," he said. "Right now all I can tell you is that you are both equally in love. The central cards, the pairing of the Lovers and the Tower . . . it's completely mutual."

Mutual, Katie thought, the warmth still flooding through her. She'd never known a man who loved intimacy as much as

Michael did, who didn't pull away for space after they'd have sex. Michael had happily hung out with her practically all day and night since they'd met. And he was so interested in her; he'd asked her a million questions about herself. It wasn't just a holiday thing. She'd known that after a couple of days, when she'd been waiting for him to get that twitchy, strained look men get when they're desperate to get away from the closeness they have with you, even just for a while. But Michael hadn't withdrawn. He hadn't kissed her goodbye the morning after they'd had sex for the first time, saying he'd phone her. Instead he'd reached for the phone to order room-service breakfast, and then they'd had sex again. Katie's face cracked into a huge smile.

Katie paid Armando twenty dollars and practically danced back to the bar. She wanted to cover Michael with kisses, hang herself around him as if she were a cloak round his shoulders. Catching sight of herself in the bar mirror, she knew she had never looked better; she was positively glowing with happiness, cheeks flushed, eyes bright. If she remembered an article she had read in a magazine on the plane coming over, about the symptoms of love being very similar to a drug high—over-stimulation, poor control of emotions, and of course, addiction— she banished it from her mind immediately.

"Hey!" she said, wrapping her arms around Michael's wide back and planting a kiss between his shoulder blades, the highest she could reach.

"How was it?" he said abstractedly.

Climbing onto the stool next to him, Katie realized that he was doing bingo.

"It was great," she bubbled happily. "He's really good. You should try it."

"Bingo!" Michael shouted.

"Ooh, we have a winner," the Bingo Bitch cooed. "Come up here, sweetie, and show me your . . . tally. *Oooh,*" she added, taking in Michael. "Look, girls, he's a big one! Maybe a little straight round the edges, but I'm sure someone could bend you up—or over—a little, darling!"

The rest of the bingo players whooped in appreciation while she cast an eye over Michael's bingo sheet.

"Yes, it's a bingo! Collect your five bucks or two free drinks at the bar . . . mine's a Cosmo, since you ask . . . oooh, look at this great big head!" She stroked Michael's shaved scalp, which, Katie had to admit, was unusually large. It gleamed in the lights. The Bingo Bitch had a hard time taking her hand off it.

"I *love* a big head," she cooed. "Well, don't we all? Right, enough dirty talk, back to our balls . . ."

Michael came back to Katie, laughing. He was so cool, she thought proudly. How many straight men would be OK with entering a gay bar in the first place, let alone not blinking an eye when a Bingo Bitch stroked their head and teased them about bending over?

"Five dollars or two free drinks," he said. "The drinks are a better deal, but I've suddenly been swept by an urge to demonstrate my heterosexuality . . ."

Outside the bar Michael kissed her, properly, long and deep and wet, their whole bodies pressing hard into each other. His big waxed coat hung around them like a cloak, as if he were a magician making Katie disappear into its folds. Katie had always liked big men; they made her feel small and dainty by contrast. She ran her tongue down his throat and licked into the hollow of his collarbone, pulling aside his T-shirt and sweater, sliding her hands around his strong, thick neck. He was so warm, like a furnace under her palms.

I love you, she thought. This is mad, but I really think I love you. And you love me too, that's what Armando said, so maybe this isn't so mad after all . . .

Michael raised one arm and a cab screeched to a halt. He bundled her in. She climbed onto his lap immediately and started pulling up his T-shirt.

"Well, that's confirmed. I'm definitely heterosexual," Michael said, taking one of her hands and placing it firmly between his legs. Katie thrust her palm down and stroked hard. Michael moaned in her ear and started sliding his hand up her skirt.

Suddenly the taxi screeched to a halt. The driver had tried to run a red light and lost his nerve at the last minute. Katie crashed back into the partition, bumping her head.

"Ow!" she yelled.

Thrashing around trying to get her balance, she accidentally kicked Michael's crotch with her boot.

"Jesus!"

"I didn't mean to—"

"Aaah . . . No, no, it's OK—here—"

He pulled her back onto the seat again.

"How's your head?"

"Sore. How's your willy?"

"Ditto."

They looked at each other and burst out laughing.

"Come here," Michael said, slipping his arm round her shoulders and pulling her into his chest. With his other hand, he stroked her hair. "So tell me what the fortune teller said."

"He warned me off you," Katie said happily. "Said you were a serial killer with a freezer full of body parts."

"Right so far. What else? Are you going to make a trip across the ocean and meet a tall, dark, handsome stranger? No, wait, you just did that, didn't you . . ."

Katie pulled his hand down so she could kiss it. "It was very good," she said. "He got lots of things spot on. But there was one thing . . ."

She told Michael about Armando's thinking that she had sisters. Or cousins.

"Because they all looked like me. You know, brunettes. They were surrounding me, and there was this card saying it was a sort of pattern . . . We couldn't work out what it was. I thought maybe it was my mum . . ."

If Katie hadn't had her head resting on Michael's chest, she would have seen a very strange expression come across his face. And if the taxi hadn't hit a pothole at that moment, she would have noticed that the arm around her tensed up in shock. But because she was in love, she attributed the tightening of his arm to an atavistic male impulse to steady her against the bump in the road. And—ironically—it made her love him all the more.

Chapter
One

"So, latest news—Michael has a new girlfriend," Sally announced. "Guess what she's called?"

"Hmmn," Jude said. "Have we had this one before?"

"No, it's a new name. I think . . ." Sally ran quickly through a mental list. "Yes, it's a new one."

"OK," Jude started. "Jenny? Rachel? Daisy? Or is he having one of his foreign phases?" She stalled for a moment, then came up with: "Marie? Or Cherie?" triumphantly.

"Nah, this one's English. He met her in New York, but she's English."

"Brunette . . ." Jude began.

"Sparky . . ."

"Pretty . . ."

The two of them were almost chanting this together now. It was a long-established ritual.

"And, of course, she's twenty-four," Sally finished.

"That's older than the last one," Jude pointed out.

"Yeah, but she was just a fling. He likes them about twenty-four if it's going to last a bit."

"Is this going to last a bit?"

"He sounds serious."

Jude rolled her eyes.

"No, he does actually sound quite serious," Sally insisted.

Jude shot a glance sideways at Sally, to see if her expression belied the tone of her voice, which was as easy and unaffected as ever. Sally seemed perfectly relaxed, though. A dress she had just bought lay in her lap and she was holding up the bodice against herself, measuring the length of the straps. She marked off one of the straps with a pin and started to unpick the stitches holding it in place at the back.

"Why am I so short-waisted," she said, more as a lament than a real question. "Every single thing I buy, the straps are always too long . . ."

No reply was needed. Sally had voiced this complaint many times before. Jude registered it absently with a tiny part of her mind; her thoughts were somewhere very different. Every time Michael found a new girlfriend, Jude expected that this time, Sally would crack. No matter how long Jude had known Sally and Michael—five years now, was it, since Sally had moved in next door, and cast her whole exciting, rich, charmed life out so generously before Jude, like a glittering net in which Jude had been only too happy to entangle herself? But even if it had been fifty years, instead of five, Jude would never understand the way Sally talked about Michael and his constant pursuit of girls who all, to Jude's unprejudiced eye, looked like younger and younger versions of Sally herself. Sally really seemed not to care. If anything, she was amused, even flattered, by the resemblance. Maybe it was just that Jude had never been able to stay friends with an ex, let alone turn one into a sort of brother whose relationships she watched over as Jude imagined a sister might. Maybe Jude was simply envious of the kind of closeness Sally and Michael had. Jude had struggled with this question long and often and never arrived at any conclusions.

"When does he get back from New York?" she asked.

"Next week."

"With the new chick?"

"I think so. She lives in London, anyway, so we'll meet her soon. You know how Michael likes to bring them round for approval. Oh, I never told you her name. Katie."

"Perfect."

Jude held up her glass. Sally, pins in her mouth, stretched to the coffee table to retrieve her own, and they clinked glasses in a toast to Katie.

"She sounds nice," Sally said through the pins.

"Young," Jude said from the elderly heights of thirty-three.

"Well. . . Nice but young."

"Do you ever think you should warn them?"

Sally's head jerked up and she stared in surprise at Jude.

"You're not *serious?*" she said.

"Well—" Jude hedged, suddenly embarrassed. "I just mean, we've seen so many of them go by . . . you've seen more, of course . . . but sometimes I look at the latest pretty little sparky brunette and wonder if it's mean not to tell her. Give her a bit of a hint, at least. They're all so excited. You know, lit up by Michael as if he's turned on a bulb inside their heads."

"Yeah," Sally said reflectively. "I saw this ad on a bus stop the other day, for a mobile phone. It was a couple kissing, and the guy was holding up his phone above their heads, with the light switched on so it cast a sort of spotlight over them, like a kiss in the movies . . . and it did make me think of Michael. That way he has of making you feel so special."

Michael had never been sexually interested in Jude, who was tall, stocky, quiet in company, and above all, mousy blond. But she could still understand exactly what Sally meant. Even if Michael weren't chatting you up, he had an extraordinary ability to focus entirely on you for the time he spent talking with you—before he shot off to meet the next new person. Michael was the most charming person Jude had ever met. You forgave him almost everything; you forgot his awful habit of collecting people, catching up with them and then moving on to the next one, keeping hundreds of plates spinning in the air. Because he wasn't false. He meant everything he said. And no one could help responding to that genuine, high-beam level of interest. Jude compared Michael to a celebrity interviewer. While you were featuring on his impromptu talk show, he was all yours. And you were all his.

"But you don't honestly think I should have a talk with Katie?" Sally said, still incredulous. "What am I supposed to say? 'You know, Mikey never stays with anyone very long, he'll probably break your heart and leave you in a few months' time for another version of you, get out now while the going's good'? She'd just think I was a bitter old hag. Besides, even if she did believe me, she'd think she was the one that could change him. People have to learn from their own mistakes."

"Yeah, fair enough," Jude admitted. "It wasn't that I really thought you could do anything—it's just watching all these little things just put their heads into the lion's mouth, you know . . ."

Sally was standing up and taking off her toweling dressing-gown. Pulling on the dress—a delicate swish of red crêpe—she went across to the mirror to check how it was hanging now the straps were shortened.

"Mikey doesn't do any major harm," she, or rather her reflection in the mirror, said to Jude. "He's loads of fun, he makes you feel wonderful, he knows a lot about all different kinds of things, and he's brilliant in bed. All those girls ten years younger than him—God, he must be a revelation. I know they get their hearts broken when he dumps them, but they learn an awful lot too. I bet they go away and start teaching their new boyfriends all the amazing things Mikey does. It could be a lot worse. I mean, he's not a bastard or anything, he's just incapable of having a relationship that lasts any longer than a year."

"A *year?*" Jude said. "The longest I've known him to go out with anyone was six months, tops. Oh." She looked at Sally. "You two went out for a year."

"Yup. Well, fourteen months, actually. Then he broke my heart, etc., etc., and then I realized that was just the way he was, and after a while we managed to be friends. Does this look OK from the back?"

"Fine. I don't know why you bother, though. If it was me I'd just tie knots in the straps."

"*Jude.*" Sally was genuinely horrified. "On a nice dress? You wouldn't!"

"No, OK, I was just teasing," Jude said evilly, watching Sally relax in relief. "I'd safety-pin them to my bra."

"Stop!" Sally pretended to cover her ears. "I can't listen to this!"

She took off the dress, put on her dressing-gown again and settled back into the corner of the sofa, threading a needle.

"So how are things with Scott?" she asked companionably, following the unspoken rule of all good girlfriends: each girl's love life (past or present) must be given equal discussion time over the course of the evening.

Jude's heart sank. Thinking about Michael and Sally always lifted her spirits; their lives were so cool, so packed with drama and incident that her friendship with them transported her away from her own life, which she considered deeply boring by comparison. Whenever Sally asked her about her secretarial jobs or boyfriend traumas, Jude felt embarrassed by her own comparative dreariness. Well, the Scott thing wasn't that dull; but it wasn't going anywhere, which was almost as bad.

"He's working really hard right now," she muttered. "I haven't seen him in a while."

"You brought your mobile," Sally noted.

It sat on the coffee table, a nasty pale blue plastic rectangle, mocking Jude by stubbornly refusing to ring.

She pulled a self-deprecating face and fiddled with a strand of hair.

"He said he might ring . . . you never know. He might. But he warned me he'd be out of commission this week. He's got a big deadline."

"What's this one?"

"Oh, he hates it, but it's good money. He's doing a lot of stock shots for an online image service. One of those photo catalogues. It's completely mindless but it pays the bills."

"OK, but I don't see why he can't pop over and see you in a

break, though," Sally said, echoing Jude's own thoughts on the subject.

Jude shrugged. "He did warn me. He said he'd definitely ring me next week, and he usually does what he says he'll do."

"Men do have this way of disappearing into their work," Sally said consolingly. "I wish I could do that. If I like someone, I can't stop thinking about them, and seeing them actually makes me feel better, even if I'm working really hard."

She looked quizzically at Jude. "But does it matter that much? I mean, how much do you like him?"

Sally had a way of getting right to the core of the problem. Jude loved to watch her analyzing other people's emotional traumas, but it was a different matter when the laser was trained on you.

"I really don't know," Jude said, shrugging again. "Sometimes I wonder if it's just that I haven't met anyone else. You know what it's like. You make a big deal out of some bloke because he's the only thing going, and then when someone else comes along, you can't imagine why you wasted all that time on someone when you've obviously got nothing in common with him. But Scott . . ." She paused, trying to corral all her confused, messy thoughts about him into one neat statement. "Scott's different. He's very—deep. I don't know what he's thinking half the time."

"He's not a big communicator," Sally agreed tactfully.

There was a subtext here: Scott, when introduced to Sally and Michael, as all Jude's new acquaintances were, had not made the best of impressions. Sally and Michael were usually high-spirited, and particularly when meeting new people; they bubbled with all those social skills, the articulacy and openness trained into them by their confident, arty, middle-class parents, who had taken them everywhere from an early age and expected them to be able to hold their own in conversations with their parents' adult friends. Scott, by contrast, didn't give much of himself away at a first meeting—or even a fifth. Watching Sally and Scott try to get on had been like seeing a wave repeatedly dance and break against a stone wall. Of course, the wave would eventually begin to wash away the wall, but that would take centuries of effort. It was one reason why Jude was unsure about Scott: not being able to get on with her friends was a big black mark against him.

"Oh well, see what happens, eh?" Sally said, tying off a knot in the thread. "Plenty more fish in the sea. That's what Mikey said."

"Michael doesn't like him either?"

Sally looked horrified at what she had let slip. "It's not that we—I—don't like him!" she said quickly. "We just don't know him that well, that's all. He's not around that much. You should bring him out for another drink some time, when he's a bit less busy."

She cut off the thread from the second strap.

"That should be it," she said, standing up and slipping on the dress again. She went over to the mirror. "Are they even?" she said doubtfully, half-swiveling around. "Does the left one look shorter? God, I wish I were taller. I'm so sick of having to take things up all the time."

Sally was looking particularly pretty that evening. Her dark hair had just been cut in a short pixie style which made her brown eyes look even bigger and her cheekbones more sharply defined. All her features seemed angled, even the straight dark eyebrows which rose slightly at the outer corners. She only needed the pointy ears to make her resemble a very pretty elf. Sally was the kind of girl for whom words like "gamine" and "petite" had been invented.

Jude, staring at herself and Sally in the mirror, decided that her own adjectives would be "clodhopping" and "hulking," if only by comparison with the small, delicate Sally, who barely came up to her shoulder. Sally's dress was charming on her, making her look like a poppy come to life. Jude, in the same dress three sizes larger, would have looked like a giant water-injected tomato.

No man would ever approach Sally and Jude in a bar with the line, "So, are you two sisters, then?" Jude was tall and blond, which sounded good in principle. But she was big-boned, which always sounded like an excuse for being fat. Jude wasn't fat, but she stood five foot nine in her stocking feet, with big shoulders and widish hips, and she was well-upholstered. Sally always made Jude feel like a farm girl. Or the maidservant in a play, with Sally as the fragile heroine and Jude, red-cheeked, pulling the mistress's corsets even tighter to achieve an eighteen-inch waist.

The sight of them together was too depressing for Jude, even though she knew perfectly well that anyone but an anorexic fifteen-year-old would look hulking next to Sally. She sighed, turned away from the mirror and reached for her glass of wine. More comfort was needed. Food, she thought. Complex carbohydrates. Those always cheer me up.

"I'm starving," she announced. "Shall I put the pasta on?"

"I'll do it," Sally offered.

"No, it's my turn," Jude said. She wanted to keep busy, to stop herself from reflecting unproductively about both Scott and her own unfeasible enormousness. "Anyway, you did the sauce."

"We are *such* an old married couple," Sally said as Jude went through into the small kitchen. "Need any help?"

"No, just find us something decent on the box."

"What d'you feel like?"

"Nothing too deep and meaningful."

"Oh, and I was *so* looking forward to watching that Channel Four documentary about the dysentery epidemic during the First World War . . ."

Jude put the kettle on and took out a box of pasta from the cupboard. It was always a slightly surreal experience for the girls to be in the other one's home, no matter how long they had hung out together, since their flats had exactly the same configuration. Sally's was considerably nicer, however, which was why they tended to hang out there. Sally had bought hers, with help from her parents, when the council started selling off unoccupied flats. Jude had illegally inherited the lease when her mother retired to Cornwall. It was effectively hers for life, but she didn't own it, and without the generous injection of cash for redecoration that Sally's parents had also kicked in, and probably because it lacked that atavistic thrill of possession, she had done little to improve it. Perhaps it was also because she had grown up there, and had a sort of sentimental attachment to the grotty bathroom floor and chipped old kitchen fittings. Or, more likely, she was just lazy and poor. Either way, Sally's smart little fitted kitchen always stirred her envy.

"God, did you put the entire contents of your fridge in here?" she said, noticing how thick the sauce was with ingredients. "Mushrooms, carrots, onions, peas, peppers, corn, and is this chicken?"

"I had some leftover roast chicken from the deli. I thought it would be nice. You know I hate not to use things up."

"Do you have a screwdriver and a wrench?"

"In the toolbox—" Sally started automatically. "What do you need a *wrench* for?"

"I just thought I'd put the kitchen sink in here as well."

"Piss off. Just because I try to keep us well-nourished—"

The doorbell rang.

"You expecting anyone?"

"No. If it's those bloody kids again," Sally said, getting up from the sofa, "I'm going to pour boiling water over their heads. Yeah?" she said into the intercom, her voice unfriendly. It buzzed back at her.

"Oh, my God!" she exclaimed in excitement, her tone altering completely. "When did you get back? Come on up!"

Jude appeared at the kitchen door.

"Michael?" she said. It wasn't really a question. No one else would have prompted that level of enthusiasm.

"Yes! He's back!"

"Well, obviously."

Sally ignored the sarcasm. "Oh, this is so nice! I've missed him!"

"How Michael always manages to come round when we're

eating is a mystery to me," Jude commented, just as happy at the prospect of seeing Michael, but feeling obliged to be cool, if only to balance Sally's excitement.

Sally opened the front door. Normally, if a visitor was on their way up, the girls would open the flat door and then retreat to the sofa and TV again, as the lifts took longer to arrive than a bus in rush hour. But Sally hovered around the doorway, listening out for the terrifying series of creaks and groans that indicated the ancient car was hauling its weary way up to the fifth floor. It had the attitude of a crabby pensioner complaining endlessly about its bunions and hip replacement to anyone who would listen. Finally it whined and came to rest, making even the faint beep as its doors opened sound resentful, and Michael's unmistakable heavy tread could be heard in the corridor.

"Mikey!"

"Sally!"

They hugged, Sally almost disappearing into the folds of Michael's big waxed coat.

"Ah, I've missed my girls!" Michael was beaming with happiness, his big dark eyes—his best feature—bright as they looked down at the top of Sally's head. Michael wasn't conventionally good-looking, and he had taken to shaving his head years ago, when his hair started receding, but his features were strongly defined—he had a large nose and jaw—and he actually looked better shaven. His big, well-shaped head was even more imposing bare; the whole effect, with his height and breadth, made him look noble and rather intimidating, until you noticed the friendly gleam in his dark eyes. He planted a kiss on the top of Sally's head and held her back so he could look at her, his face lit up with pleasure. "Is Jude here too?" he asked.

"Present and correct," Jude called, waving from the kitchen door. She tended to hold back a little, not wanting to assume that Michael was as happy to see her as Sally, to whom, after all, he had much closer ties. But Michael always said "my girls," and he immediately strode over to the kitchen to fold Jude in an equally enthusiastic embrace.

"Excellent! Dinner! What are we having?" he said, taking off his coat and throwing it in the direction of a chair. He smelled of airline travel, a musty, cold odor, as if he had traveled across the Atlantic in a cargo hold.

"Pasta alla Sally," Jude said. "Leftovers in a spicy tomato base, served on a bed of delicious spaghetti."

"Yum, my favorite." Michael flopped heavily onto the sofa. "I hope there's lots. I'm starving. Those airline meals are so tiny. Like those calorie-counted TV dinners you used to eat, Sal. Piece of chicken as small as your thumb, two slivers of potato, and three green peas."

"God, I remember those. I always ended up sneaking to the fridge at midnight to eat a whole pint of ice cream, I was so hungry."

"Depriving yourself never works," Michael said comfortably, patting his domed, upturned belly. "Women are never half as fat as they think. Besides, I keep telling you girls, men like women with some flesh on them. No one likes making love to a bag of bones. I wish you girls would realize you're both gorgeous exactly the way you are."

"Aaah," Sally cooed. "But you always noticed when I hadn't shaved my legs, you hypocritical bastard. Here."

She put a glass of wine down in front of him.

Jude carried in a plastic container of grated Parmesan and deposited it on the coffee table. "Check out this presentation!" she said. "Fine dining at its best!"

"I can add to the tacky atmosphere," Michael said. "I brought some extra wine." He fished in his capacious leather rucksack and pulled out five mini-bottles of airline wine.

"Chatted up a stewardess, did you?" Sally said cynically.

"More or less." Michael was unabashed.

"So tell us about the new girl," Jude said.

"Katie? She's lovely. Really sweet. Clever, funny . . ." Michael looked dreamy. "I know I've only known her for a fortnight— well, ten days—but she's great. She really is. I think I'm in love."

Sally snorted. "You're always in love, Mikey."

"That's not true," he protested, drinking some wine.

"Well, you always *say* you're in love," Jude said, carrying in a tray with three bowls of pasta and distributing them to the eager diners.

Michael wound some spaghetti on his fork, raised it to his mouth, and then paused. "But really, Katie's wonderful," he insisted.

"Yadda yadda yadda," Jude said through a mouthful of pasta. She had to admit that Sally's sauce, which would probably have made any Italian throw up their hands in horror, was actually pretty tasty. She winked at Sally, who rolled her eyes in response.

Michael was provoked now. "You two can be so sarcastic

sometimes," he said crossly, a strand of spaghetti dangling from his mouth. "Wait till you meet Katie. You'll see. I think she could be the one."

"Yeah," Jude said. "The one after the one before."

Michael started to protest.

"Shut up, Mikey," Sally said, reaching for the remote. "I'm bored with your soap opera. Let's watch a proper one."

They settled back with their pasta bowls, lulled into contentment by the familiar theme tune of the four-times-weekly soap. With Michael's arrival, they were complete. Jude looked from Sally to Michael with utter satisfaction. They were their own little family, the three of them against the world. This was the way it should always be.

And suddenly she felt a violent antagonism toward the hapless Katie. If it weren't for her, if it weren't for all Michael's identikit girls, no outside influences would break up this cosiness. Jude contemplated Sally, who was twirling up some spaghetti on her fork, her eyes glued to the latest developments onscreen. Sally was the only person Jude had ever met who could eat spaghetti while watching television and never get one tiny spatter of tomato sauce on her nice white dressing-gown. Sally was pristine; her flat was as pretty and perfect as herself. Sally hated mess, both literal and emotional. And because of that, Sally would never admit that she still cared about Michael—not just as a friend, or as a brother, but romantically.

To Jude, it was obvious. If Sally had really been over Michael she would be able to admit that she still, in the jargon of pop psychologists, had feelings for him. Everyone had feelings for exes they had loved, even if the break-up had happened a decade ago. There was always some small part of you that nursed nostalgia, that softened at the mention of the ex's name. And if you were honest with yourself, you acknowledged it, because that indicated more clearly than anything else that you had—again in the jargon—moved on and put things in perspective. But if you kept denying those feelings, if you made a best friend out of your ex and denied that you had a vestige of romantic love left for him, then you were doomed never to get over him. It was nine years since Sally had broken up with Michael, and since then all she had had were a few fleeting affairs. She was as tied to him as if she was wearing his ring.

Over the years, Jude had tried to set Sally up with a series of eligible men who, at one sight of Sally's manifold perfections, had been champing at the bit to date her. Sally hadn't sent them packing; much, much worse for herself—and them—she had barely even seemed to notice their existence. So Jude was going to have to think outside the box. Just finding someone new for Sally wouldn't achieve anything.

Jude looked again from Sally to Michael, who were gasping in unison at the latest atrocity of the evil matriarch. They were perfect for each other. And they would never get back together if someone didn't give them a helping hand. Michael would keep dating mini-Sallys in relationships with the lifespan of a dragonfly, and Sally would float along unable to look at any other men seriously because she still had Michael's image imprinted on her retinas. And yet they were clearly meant to be together.

Someone needed to give them both a good sharp kick in their bottoms.

Chapter
Two

*U*pon meeting Sally, and naturally perceiving her as a rival, Michael's new girlfriends behaved in one of two ways. Either they tried to win her over with effusive friendliness, attempting to get her on their side, or, thinking that the success of their relationship with Michael depended on removing Sally from the picture, they were actively hostile. Neither approach made any difference to the eventual outcome, of course, but the girls who picked the first option did tend to last a little longer. There was nothing Michael disliked so much as antagonism, overt or covert. Despite the complicated nature of his romantic arrangements, he would have been the first to stress—ingenuously—how much he liked a quiet life.

It took Sally only a few seconds to place Katie in the effusively friendly category. She was a burbler. Practically as soon as Sally had entered the wine bar, Katie launched into a stream of questions and compliments designed to show how well she had absorbed what she had already learned about Sally from Michael, and how unthreatened she was by being introduced to an ex-girlfriend of Michael's with whom he was on terms of the closest friendship. Michael, who tended to take people at face value, beamed affectionately at Katie as she chattered away at Sally. Every so often he cast a proud look at Sally that said, as clearly as if he had written it on a blackboard: Isn't she fun! Isn't she friendly! Look what an effort she's making! It reminded Sally of a fond parent watching a child show off its latest skill. Maybe, for a finale, Katie would recite some times tables and do long division in her head.

"So you live just opposite Michael in that tower block! And your friend Jude lives next door to you! That's so cool! I'd love to live next door to my best friend!" Katie gushed. "It must have taken you ages to find two flats next door to each other!"

"Well, that's not quite how it happened," Sally corrected, when finally she could get a word in edgewise. "I bought my flat about five years ago and went round introducing myself to all the neighbors on my floor. Jude was the only one who seemed at all nice, so I invited her in for a cup of tea—"

"And you became best friends! That's so cool!"

"Actually, she *made* us become best friends," Jude corrected. "She willed it into happening."

Sally swung round in her chair to see Jude standing behind her, wearing a sheepish expression. Sally attributed this to Jude's being late, and having stuck her, Sally, alone with Michael and BurbleGirl for at least half an hour. Then she saw Scott next to Jude and realized in a flash both why Jude had been late and why she was looking embarrassed. Scott had not been part of the plans for this evening, the customary meet-and-greet session for Michael's new girlfriend. Scott hadn't even been mentioned for days. Sally had begun to think that he might be permanently off the menu. But here he was. She sighed. What with Katie's verbal incontinence and Scott's—well, verbal constipation, to use the same metaphor—the evening was bound to be jerky.

"She sat me down on her new sofa," Jude was continuing, taking off her coat, "and said something like: 'This is great! You know, we should become best friends, and then we can pop in and out of each other's flats the whole time, like they do in TV sitcoms. I always think, God, that's so unreal, nobody actually *is* best friends with their next-door neighbor . . . but it would be so much fun if we could actually do it, wouldn't it?' "

She mimicked Sally's voice and mannerisms so well that everyone but Scott burst out laughing.

"And *I* thought she was mad," Jude continued, smiling at Sally. "I mean, what if we didn't get on? And then we'd be trapped for the rest of our lives, passing in the corridor, or going down in the lift, with nothing to say to each other, and feeling stupid because we didn't turn out to be best friends after all. Or what if we had a massive fight?"

"But actually it turned out just like I said," Sally said complacently.

"She had so much confidence I couldn't resist her," Jude agreed. "And then after a year or so, she said: 'We need something else. Two girls in a sitcom always have some annoying but, you know, comically eccentric neighbor.'"

"And you said: 'Or a gay best friend, or the hunk down the hall they're both madly in lust with,' " Sally chimed in.

"But instead we got landed with Michael," Jude said lugubriously.

"Yeah, talk about drawing the short straw." Sally pulled a face at Michael.

"Yes, how did that happen?" Katie asked, turning to Michael. Despite her best efforts, her voice was a little over-bright. Of course what she really wanted to ask was, Why the hell did you deliberately choose to move in opposite your ex-girlfriend? But this was the closest she could get without sounding shrewish.

"I'd been looking for a flat to buy for a while," Michael explained. "I'd been living in my mother's basement flat ever since leaving college, and it seemed about time I got a place of my own."

"So when I saw a FOR SALE sign across the street I rang Mikey at once," Sally continued.

"Shame it wasn't the same building," Jude said. "Michael could have come over in his pajamas to watch the telly, instead of having to get dressed." She looked at Scott. "He's got the downstairs flat in one of those terraced houses just across the road from us. You know, along from the bus stop."

Scott nodded politely and seemed about to say something, but Michael cut in.

"But this way I know if the girls are in, because I can see if their lights are on," he said contentedly.

"And he always manages to drop round when we're cooking dinner," Jude said, again mainly to Scott.

Sally, who could see what an effort Jude was making to get Scott chatting to the rest of them, waited curiously to see how he would respond. Some jokey comment about not cooking his own meals either, if he lived opposite two girls? Some compliment to Sally and Jude, along the lines of how lucky Michael was to be in such proximity to them? Scott was good-looking,

Sally had to admit, despite his air of detachment. And despite his goatee, which, as a look, she had never been fond of. Wouldn't kissing someone with hair all round his mouth be a bit like—well, going down on a woman? She made a mental note to ask Jude. Still, he was definitely handsome, with those clear gray eyes and his strong bone structure. And she liked the way his tousled, longish hair was pushed back behind his ears. He dressed more trendily than Sally liked in a man; she preferred Mikey's scruffiness, finding it somehow reassuring. But Scott's snugly cut black sweater and gray trousers suited him. Even the goatee worked aesthetically, despite her fanny-snogging reservations. She leaned forward to hear what contribution he was going to make to the conversation.

"Do we need to go up to the bar to get a drink?" he asked.

"No, there's waiters," Jude said, looking around.

Michael, who was facing toward the center of the room, raised a hand and caught a waitress's eye. The wine bar was busy that evening, but the waitress was by their table almost immediately. Accustomed as she was to this, Sally couldn't help smiling; it was just part of the Michael magic with women. Michael was one of those rare men who adored the company of women, and they sensed that instinctively. Scott, unfortunately, lacked Michael's 200-watt brand of charm. He was visibly taken aback when the waitress informed him in a strong Antipodean accent that the wine bar only had bottled beer, and that only Australian to boot.

"They just have Australian and New Zealand wines, too," Michael explained.

Scott, in other circumstances—i.e., when he wasn't

restrained by the presence of several women, one of whom he was dating—would all too clearly have asked Michael why the fuck that was supposed to be any consolation.

"Scott drinks bitter, mostly," Jude explained, looking concerned.

"I do drink wine as well," Scott said—a little defensively, Sally thought. "I just fancied a pint, that's all. First drink of the evening and all that."

He picked a bottled beer, shrugging a touch too visibly as Michael ordered another bottle of New Zealand Sauvignon Blanc.

"I'm sorry," Jude said to Scott.

"No problem." He smiled at her. "You weren't to know."

"Do you want to try some wine, Scott?" Michael suggested, offering his own glass. Scott bristled, and Sally resisted an impulse to sink her face into her hands. She knew Michael hadn't meant to be patronizing, but that was how it had clearly come across to Scott.

"I've drunk Sauvignon Blanc before, thanks," Scott said coldly. "I'm not a big white wine fan."

"Oh well, more for us!" Sally said over-cheerfully.

Katie, looking from Sally to Michael, gave a sycophantic laugh. Michael smiled at her fondly, but the laugh itself fell, embarrassingly, into a void of silence, which was broken only by the reappearance of the waitress with the second bottle of wine. They all—with the exception of Scott—fell upon it as desperately as alcoholic down-and-outs presented with a bottle of nail-varnish remover.

It was clear that the evening was turning into a disaster. Still,

Sally hoped that alcohol would lubricate the rough edges, slowly melding the mismatched collection of people into a convivial unit. At present they were more like magnets in one of those experiments you do at primary school to show attracting and opposing poles.

After their rocky start, Michael and Scott's relations had, if anything, worsened. Certainly they weren't indulging in any of the laddish, hearty boys-against-girls banter that might have been expected in a situation like this. If Michael had been a radically different person, he would have set Scott at his ease by doing a little male bonding. But poor Michael's idea of bonding was offering Scott Sauvignon Blanc—as successful a ploy as if, while he and Scott were showering together in a male prison, Michael had made a joke about dropping the soap. And Scott appeared, in Sally's opinion, to have taken against Michael so strongly that he would barely look at him, much less respond to anything he said.

Which worried Sally. As Jude's boyfriend, Scott was obliged by the strictest codes of social conduct to make some effort to get on with her friends—unless they were racists, fox-hunters, humorless social workers or Billy Joel fans, of course. But Scott just sat back, drank his beer, and took in the awkward conversation without seeming to feel any need to contribute to it. Besides, she couldn't see any signs that Jude's affection was being returned. Scott was so composed; he kept himself to himself, hardly touching Jude. Look at Michael and Katie: that was Sally's idea of a happy couple in the first throes of passion. They were squashed up next to each other in a trestle seat, and despite the fact that their bodies were already pressing against each other they were unable to keep their hands to themselves. If they weren't staring into each other's eyes, or touching each other's arms for no good reason apart from the need for more physical contact, they were holding hands under the table and giggling like schoolchildren. Well, Katie was giggling. Michael simply wore a goofy smirk and beamed at everything she said.

"So, Jude says you're really busy at work, Scott?" Sally tried. It was scarcely a sparkling opening gambit, but at least she was making an effort.

"Yeah, that's right." Scott drank some beer.

"It sounds interesting," Sally pursued gamely.

"Not really," Scott said, putting down his glass and wiping a trace of beer from his goatee. "I'm just taking loads of stock shots. It brings in the money, but it's not what I really want to do."

"Oh, right. And what do you really want to do?"

Bollocks, Sally thought. I sound like a sixth-form career advisor. Why am I asking these stupid questions? Because Michael and Katie are off in their own world, she answered herself, and Scott and Jude are just sitting there like lemons.

"Travel photography," Scott said laconically. "I've done some already, but it's hard to break into."

"Scott's really good," Jude broke in. "You should see some of his work."

Sally nodded politely. She didn't think Scott had a good effect on Jude. Where was all her sarcasm, her liveliness? Admittedly, Sally had only seen her with Scott on a couple of occasions, but both times Jude seemed subdued, as if she felt she couldn't be fully herself in front of Scott.

"Oh, I love photography," Katie broke in. "I've got lots of books. Fashion photography, mostly. Penn, Horst, a few others. I know it's all a bit mainstream, but I really love all that forties glamor stuff."

You could do with a bit of it yourself, Sally reflected. Katie was a very pretty girl, but the baggy striped sweater and shapeless jeans she wore didn't do her any favors. No makeup, and what was that haircut doing? Katie's thick dark hair looked as if it had been cut short inexpertly and then allowed to grow out in patches. Bits of it stuck straight up to the ceiling, giving her a comic clown look. Actually, that sweater was clownish too. Give her three juggling balls and some big shoes, paint her nose red, and she'd fit right into any entertainment that required her to roll around in sawdust and get drenched by buckets of water.

Sally sighed. God, she was being a bitch. Her punishment would be to go through her photograph albums that night and find all the ones of her at Katie's age, twenty-four, thinking she looked deeply cool, when in fact, if you were looking for a circus comparison, she'd been more of a sideshow freak. DMs, black tights with carefully cultivated holes, gigantic oversized black sweaters. Compared to that, Katie looked positively chic.

"I'm off to find the ladies," Sally said, rising to her feet. She didn't actually need to wee that badly, but she was feeling exhausted by the pressure of keeping the evening afloat. Perhaps if she removed herself for a few minutes, they would have found something to talk about by the time she returned.

With wistful envy, Katie watched Sally cross the crowded room. Sally was so gorgeous, and so well-dressed; not in an overdone way, but as if she had just pulled on a simple little frock and pretty cardigan and come out without thinking too much about it. Katie loved fashion photography so much because she was so conscious of being a scruffball herself. The women in a Penn or Horst photograph were so unfeasibly beautiful, so perfectly made up and styled, that they seemed infinitely removed from anything Katie could aspire to, and therefore not a reproach to her. They were just a fabulous, impossible ideal. Someone like Sally, on the other hand, made Katie so insecure she wanted to go into the toilet, beat her head against the wall, and then flush it down the loo. Katie noticed two men turn their heads to look at Sally, and keep looking. They were clearly smitten, but Sally didn't even seem to notice. God, what must it be like to draw so much attention that you could afford to be oblivious to it?

"I'm talking too much," Katie said in an undertone to Michael. "Aren't I? I just want them to like me—well, Sally, particularly, I know how important she is to you . . ."

"You're lovely," Michael said warmly, pressing her hand under the table. "Just be yourself. Don't worry so much."

"Really?" Katie's eyes brightened.

"That's what I first noticed about you," Michael said. "You were so bubbly and fresh and enthusiastic. I couldn't take my eyes off you."

Beaming, Katie planted a kiss on his lips. She caught Jude's eye as she pulled away, and blushed. Michael might call her bubbly and enthusiastic, but being impetuous could make her feel like a stupid, gushing teenager.

Actually, Jude was envying Michael and Katie their easy rapport with each other, the way they were comfortable being physical in public. Scott might take her hand when they were alone together, walking down a street, or, more likely, crook his arm so that she could slip hers through. But she couldn't imagine him reaching over to kiss her in front of her friends. This was the first time Michael and Katie had been out with his friends as a couple, and already they were kissing and hugging. Much as she might tease Michael for throwing himself into relationships, she would love to be swept off her feet the way he had fallen for Katie.

She glanced over at Scott. He was drinking some beer, calm and collected as always. Jude had the feeling that, if Michael and Katie had thrown each other onto the table, ripped their clothes off and started shagging, Scott would scarcely raise an eyebrow. Apart from moving his beer bottle back to stop it from being knocked over. Abruptly, Jude stood up and, muttering something, pushed her chair back and headed for the women's toilet.

Sally was washing her hands. She looked up inquisitively. Jude, answering the unspoken question, blurted out: "He just rang up a couple of hours ago and asked what was I doing tonight."

"Didn't he give you any notice?" Sally said, trying not to sound disapproving and failing dismally.

"He's been really busy at work . . ." Jude didn't answer the question directly.

Sally pulled some paper out of the dispenser. Drying her hands, she said as mildly as she could, "I dunno, Jude, what do you want me to say? You shouldn't let him mess you round like this. I mean, what would you say if you were me?"

"Exactly what you're telling me," Jude admitted, writhing. She fiddled with a strand of blond hair, staring at herself in the mirror, anything not to meet Sally's eyes.

"I'm not saying you should play games or anything, you know that," Sally went on, balling up the paper and throwing it into the dustbin. "It just seems like he's having his cake and eating it. Being busy when he wants, and then expecting you to be available whenever he gets the urge to ring you."

"I know," Jude said. "But he's really trying to get his freelance career off the ground . . . I want to be understanding about that."

"I just think men need to come after you a bit," Sally said, fishing a lipstick out of her pretty little bag and reapplying it carefully. Her lips were stretched back over her teeth and her voice consequently was distorted, as if she had taken her dentures out, but her big brown eyes were focused as they met Jude's in the mirror. "If you jump to attention whenever they call you, they take you for granted."

"I know," Jude said again hopelessly. Of course this was what Sally would say, what any good friend would say. But she had really wanted to see Scott. It had been nearly a week now, and she had been so happy to hear his voice. She would have been incapable of telling him she was busy that evening.

"Don't worry about it too much," Sally said consolingly.

Secretly, she didn't think Jude and Scott would last long. Or she hoped they wouldn't. She thought Jude could do a lot better than Scott. Jude, despite her insecurity about her size, was very attractive; she tended to focus on the fact that she wasn't petite, instead of realizing that she was that dream of many, many men, a tall blonde with nice tits. OK, her legs weren't wonderful, but nobody was flawless, and women always noticed their imperfections rather than their strong points. Sally's bottom, for instance, was as pitted with cellulite as a matched pair of oranges, and she was paranoid about that, instead of reminding herself how nice the rest of her was.

"Aren't you going to wee?" Sally said, noticing that Jude was preparing to exit the toilet with her.

"Nah. Michael and Katie were just making me a bit nauseous," Jude said. "I wanted a break, that's all."

"Oh, they won't last long either," Sally said without thinking.

"Either?" Jude picked her up.

"I mean, more than Mikey and the last one," Sally said lightly, and shot back across the bar before Jude could wonder if Sally had meant something else entirely.

They arrived at the table just as the waitress was setting down another bottle of beer for Scott.

"Would you like another Sauvignon Blanc?" she asked.

"No, we're going slowly tonight, thanks," Michael said, giving her a smile that sent her away with a spring in her step.

"Mikey and the ladies drinking white wine," Sally teased him, picking up her glass.

"I'm just a big girlie girl," Michael said complacently.

Jude snuffled with laughter. Being well over six foot, with a bouncerlike shaved head and the build of a rugby player gone to seed, Michael could afford to make that sort of comment. Nothing less girlie than Michael, with his extra-large sweater straining over his belly, could be imagined. Michael really did carry his weight well, she had to admit. But that was his charisma, too. You didn't notice his physical flaws when he was busy charming you.

"In fact," he was adding, "I think I'm probably a woman trapped in a man's body."

Everyone burst out laughing, even Scott this time.

"No, you know what I mean," Michael insisted. "I like all the things that girls do. Well, nearly. And I love hanging out with women. I've never had male friends, not really. I like having all my girls around me."

He wrapped one big arm around Katie and beamed over her head at Sally and Jude.

"Of course, I would be a lesbian," he said definitely. "I wouldn't want to have sex with men. Nasty hairy *beasts,*" he added, putting on a prim Victorian spinster's voice, "so *rough,* pulling you about like a side of meat . . ."

"Wouldn't you miss having a dick, though?" Scott asked unexpectedly.

The girls stopped laughing and turned to look at Michael. They couldn't help feeling that Scott had raised an important point.

Michael looked very pissed off at having his flight of fancy brought down to earth.

"I've never really thought about it," he snapped.

"Well, think about it now," Jude chipped in, wanting to back Scott up. "Wouldn't you miss it?"

"But I would have *breasts,*" Michael said triumphantly. "I could play with them all day. I don't know how women get any work done."

"Depends how big they are," tiny little flat-chested Katie sighed.

Michael whispered something in her ear that made her laugh and blush.

"I still think you'd miss having a dick," Scott said.

"Maybe," Michael said curtly.

Sally had to repress a snort of amusement. It was ridiculous what men could find to argue about. Meeting Jude's eyes, which were brimming with laughter, she saw that they were both thinking the same thing.

"I'd miss having a willy, if I'd had one and it was taken away," Sally said, enjoying the conversation too much to let it go. At least they were all talking about the same thing, even if there were undercurrents of hostility rippling just beneath the surface.

"Me too," Jude volunteered. "I'd play with it all day long. I don't know how men get any work done."

"Depends how big it is," Sally said, wiggling her finger, and she and Jude broke into fits of laughter. Sally had had a one-night stand, years ago, with an unfortunate man whose willy was no bigger than a chipolata sausage, and now she only had to crook her little finger slightly to send both herself and Jude into hysterics.

"In-jokes are always the funniest," Scott said, smiling at Jude.

"Well, even if Michael doesn't care, *I'd* miss him not having a willy!" Katie said. "*You* know what I mean!" And she winked at Sally.

An awful quiet fell over the group. Katie had killed the conversation stone dead. Sally was deeply taken aback that Katie would play the girlie solidarity card on their first meeting by referring to the fact that they had both had sex with Michael. Even if Katie had said it a year into her relationship with Michael, Sally would have found it odd, but only an hour after they'd met? It was so weird that she had no idea how to respond.

Jude's heart bled for Katie. She could see that Katie was a bit tipsy, and, trying desperately to fit in with Michael's friends, had made a comment that just didn't work. Even Michael looked taken aback. He ran his hand over his shiny shaved scalp, automatically feeling the slight ridge that ran along the center, a gesture that was a comfort reflex for him.

"I should probably be getting back," Scott said, breaking into the uncomfortable silence. "I've got to be up early for work tomorrow."

I? Jude and Sally thought together. Jude couldn't believe that Scott had rung her up only to spend a couple of hours drinking with her and her friends; or had the evening been such a disaster that he just wanted to go home and forget all about her?

"You coming?" he said rather awkwardly to Jude.

"Uh—yeah, yeah, sure," she said, caught off guard and trying not to sound as relieved as she felt. Apart from hoping that Scott wanted to stay the night with her, she had really been looking forward to having sex. That was the trouble with starting to date someone; if you weren't having it for a while, you got used to its absence, and compensated with other things. But as soon as all those hormones got shaken and stirred again, sex was all you could think about. Frankly, Jude had been feeling like a big throbbing moist vagina on legs ever since she and

Scott had had sex for the first time. Didn't men feel that way? Didn't they feel like enormous walking penises? If it had been up to her she would have called in sick for three days after the first time she and Scott had shagged, and spent them all in bed with him. But he had so much self-control; he would never take time off work for her.

"Are you guys staying on?" she said, getting up. Scott held her coat up behind her so she could put her arms in the sleeves. He had some very nice gentlemanly touches.

"No, I don't think so," Sally said a little too fast. She really didn't want to be stuck with Michael and Katie without Jude to lend her moral support.

"Well, we can walk back together, then," Michael said, standing up too. "If you two were going back to Jude's, we'd all practically be going to the same place," he added wistfully. "That's always so nice and cozy."

As it was, Sally had to walk back with Michael and Katie, feeling like a gooseberry; they were arm in arm and scuffling playfully with all the childlike enthusiasm of new lovers. Oh well, Katie would be gone soon enough. Sally didn't see her lasting any length of time. She was much too young for Michael, too naive, too immature. But then, Michael did seem to be dating girls who were increasingly younger. No—the girls were staying more or less the same age. It was Michael who was getting older. Sally wished he could pull himself together a bit, at least enough to find someone closer to his own age.

"Good night," she said, hugging Michael at the entranceway to her block of flats. "Night, Katie."

She gave Katie a nice farewell smile, and Katie lunged forward enthusiastically to kiss her goodnight instead. God, Sally thought, flinching back, she's like a puppy. I wonder she doesn't lick my cheeks and pant all over me.

"See you Sunday," Michael said, kissing the top of her head.

"Oh, right, of course. See you Sunday."

"What's Sunday?" Sally heard Katie ask as she reached for her keys.

Unlocking the main door, Sally grimaced. That wasn't going to be an easy one to answer, though Michael would skate over it. For years, Sally and Michael had been having Sunday lunch with Michael's mother, Stephanie. The two women had always got on very well, and after Sally and Michael broke up, they had kept in touch. Then, Sally and Michael had started to hang out together as friends, almost unable to keep away from each other; gradually he had started taking her round to Stephanie's again, and it had ended up in this lunch ritual with which, though it might seem odd to an outsider, everyone involved was completely happy. Michael was practically Sally's brother by now, and Stephanie a sort of stepmother.

But of course Michael's girlfriends had never seen it that way. No matter how he tried to tell them that it was just a "family thing," they always sulked and complained. Sally couldn't blame them; she'd have felt the same if she had been in their situation.

My own flat, Sally thought as she closed the door behind her. My own lovely flat. Calm and peaceful and exactly the way I want it. She pictured Michael, doubtless arguing with Katie about the Sunday lunch situation at this very moment, and Jude, who she couldn't help thinking was letting herself be pushed back and forth by a guy with a goatee—good-looking, admittedly, but without much to say for himself. She, Sally, might not be having sex tonight, but she had her whole big bed to herself, with no man complaining if she wanted to read some stupid gossip magazine before turning out the light, or leaving his enormous smelly shoes scattered over the floor for her to trip over if she needed the loo in the middle of the night—or, come to think of it, leaving the toilet seat up so her bottom fell into the loo if she didn't notice in time. Sally got undressed, flossed and brushed, turned out all the lights except for one small bedside lamp, which cast a golden glow over her peach duvet, and curled up happily in bed with a cup of diet instant chocolate (she should have brushed her teeth after the chocolate, of course, not before, but she knew she'd be too sleepy to get out of bed) and the latest issue of the *National Enquirer,* her particular guilty pleasure:

TRAGIC HEARTBREAK OF OSCAR-WINNING STAR, the cover blared. HUSBAND HITS ON LAP DANCER IN VEGAS!

Breathing a deep sigh of satisfaction, Sally turned the page to read all about it. But just before she settled into the magazine, she looked up at her bedroom window. Her curtains, as always, weren't completely closed; there was just enough of a chink to see if Michael's bedroom light was on, if you knew through long practice exactly what angle to look at. And Sally did. It was a nighttime ritual of hers. There was a small flickering glow in his window, probably a candle by the bed. It wasn't the same, of course, when he had a girlfriend in there with him. Still, there was always a comfort somehow in checking that Michael was safely there, just across the street.

Chapter
Three

"*D*id you and Michael lock horns a bit tonight?" Jude asked Scott as they drove back to his flat.

By the faint light of the dashboard and the sodium of the street lamps, she saw Scott grin. Jude always felt a flush of satisfaction when she was the one to make him smile; he was so much more handsome then, losing that air of gravity that made Sally and Michael think he was a dull stick.

"Nah, not really," he said, still grinning. "He just wound me up a bit, I suppose."

"Did he say anything to you?" Jude bristled at the thought of Michael being rude to Scott.

"No, no. That's sort of the point. He didn't say anything. He wasn't joking when he said he didn't like blokes that much."

"That's why we get on with him so well," Jude said. "It's so easy to talk to Michael, you can say anything to him."

Scott shrugged. "Fair enough."

He said no more. Scott was quite content to have an easy silence fall between them, which always made Jude a little nervous. She was so used to hanging out with Sally and Michael, an endless stream of banter and teasing and casual speculation running between them all. Silence usually meant that one of them had something depressing on their minds; it was never a good sign.

She looked at Scott's hands on the steering wheel and was overcome with a rush of lust. With other boyfriends, she would have put her hand on their thigh, run it slowly along and upward, stroking gently as she went, then gradually reached between their legs . . . but with Scott, she was nervous that he would push her hand away. He was the least impulsive person she had ever known. When she first met him, Jude had been very attracted to his air of self-sufficiency, tempered as it had been with the fact that he had sought her out at that awful party, come over and talked to her all evening, and rung her the very next day. You didn't mind someone shutting out the world as long as they were happy to take you inside with them. Still, she found it hard not to know what he was thinking most of the time.

Even the way he had asked her out had been considered, conveying the message that he had taken things in clearly planned-out stages: attraction, followed by several hours' getting to know her, a pause for reflection, and then the request for her phone number. It wasn't just someone lunging drunkenly onto you trying to shove their tongue in your ear. Right from the start she had had the impression that Scott wouldn't do anything he hadn't thought over carefully in advance.

His flat was more evidence of that. It wasn't clinically tidy, in a scary, anally retentive, I-only-have-sex-with-corpses-that-I've-sterilized-first-in-bleach kind of way, but everything definitely had its place. At least he had a nice big sofa. And all the wires protruding from the game consoles in front of the giant TV made the place look, if not homey, exactly, then a bit more lived-in.

"Do you want a drink?" Scott asked.

"Yeah, that'd be lovely."

"I think I've got some red wine . . ."

He came through from the kitchen with a bottle of beer for himself and a glass of wine for Jude. She was sitting on the sofa, but carefully at one end. Though she and Scott had been seeing each other for a month or so, this was only the third time together having sex; Scott had been working so hard that the dating had been strung out, and they were still in that awful clumsy early stage where they were feeling their way, not wanting to take whatever was growing between them for granted. Really, what Jude would have liked to do was throw herself on Scott the instant they walked in the door, but his composure blocked her. If he'd touched her at any time, in the car, or walking to the flat, she would have kissed him immediately; but now she felt frozen, and clutched her glass of red wine as if it were some sort of lucky talisman.

"I didn't much take to Katie," she said, just to fill the silence.

"Well, she is a lot younger," Scott said fairly.

"Yes, and it's always an uncomfortable situation, meeting your boyfriend's friends for the first time."

"Come to think of it, didn't you say they only met a couple of weeks ago?" Scott said. "So she can't *really* be his girlfriend, then. I mean, they'll barely know each other still."

Well, so much for you and me, Jude thought. Perversely, now that Scott had said that, she wanted him to throw himself at her feet and beg her on his knees to be his girlfriend. It was awful how a touch of rejection could make you yearn for whoever was rejecting you.

A silence fell. Jude stared at the surface of her wine as if it would reveal the winning lottery numbers for this week if she just concentrated hard enough. Scott drank some beer, put the bottle down, looked at his knees, picked the bottle up again, examined its label with seeming fascination, and finally said uncomfortably, "Do you want to stay?"

"What?"

"I mean, do you want to stay here tonight?"

Was that a trick question? Jude looked over at him suspiciously, but he just seemed nervous. *Men,* she thought, sighing. What the fuck did he think she was here for? A free glass of wine and lots of embarrassing pauses? If he had been over at her flat, she wouldn't have dreamed of asking him if he wanted to stay; a man who had previously had sex with her, visiting her flat at eleven-thirty, might as well have I WANT TO GET LAID written on his forehead in marker pen. Why did men assume that women were any different? She plucked up her courage and said, fauxcasually, "Only if you were planning to have sex with me."

"Um, well, I think that could be arranged," Scott mumbled.

"OK, then."

"OK what?"

"OK, then, I will stay," she said. "Shall I spell it out for you?"

"No," Scott said, putting down his beer bottle. "I think I've got the message. Why don't you come over here? You're miles away."

His eyes were bright, but he didn't hold out his hand, or move over toward her: he waited for her to shift herself awkwardly along the sofa to him, and by the time she reached him it felt as long as a catwalk. The least he could do, she thought, was to pull her straight into his arms, after she had made an idiot of herself dragging her bum along the sofa. But he didn't, he just sat there smiling at her.

Fleetingly she wondered whether this was all worth the embarrassment, the awkwardness. Maybe she should just have gone home and curled up with the latest novel that was absorbing her, a packet of chocolate biscuits and a glass of milk to dunk them into, her vibrator waiting in reserve as a bedtime treat. Kept everything on her own terms, without all this messy confused collision of egos and desires.

Too late now, of course. Scott, finally, was kissing her, his hands running up and down her arms, pushing back the sleeves of her sweater. He had told her before how sexy he found the fact that, like her shins, her arms were lightly covered in fair hairs that bleached white in the sun. Jude found it hard to believe him; it was hard for her not to wince away when she felt him caressing her arms. She wanted to be like Sally, who was almost as smooth and hairless as a baby. Jude always felt like a gorilla by comparison. An albino gorilla. She had a pouf of hair at her crotch, springy and thick as a Brillo pad. Scott particularly loved this. Jude thought he was a perverted lunatic.

But as soon as his tongue slid into her mouth, as soon as she smelled his skin, she couldn't think about much else except taking all her clothes off and pounding herself onto him. So that was what she did. He almost made her come this time. He was very attentive, and it was good enough to make Jude writhe and thrash around and yell "God, yes!" a lot. She wouldn't fake it, but she wouldn't disabuse him if he thought her excitement meant he'd got her there.

Jude wasn't too worried about this failure. She had practically never been with anyone who made her come the first few times they had sex; it usually took a while, getting to know a new body, new fingers, a new mouth, gradually letting go into them, feeling yourself melt gradually into orgasm. She was OK with waiting.

As she fell asleep, it wasn't that she hadn't come that nagged at her; no, it was having to put her sweaty, creased clothes on the next day and rush home early to shower and change. This was one of the big annoyances of starting to see someone. You couldn't store things at his place, or bring round a bag with makeup and work clothes; it looked too domestic. No, you had to turn up at his with nothing but what you stood up in, since the whole atmosphere would be destroyed if you didn't seem spontaneous. And then, lax and feeble from a night of sex, you had to scrabble the next morning to get back home, change, and make it into work reasonably on time while checking yourself for suspicious bruises and bite marks. Next time, she determined, Scott could sleep over at hers.

She made a mental note to wash the sheets. Scott's standards of hygiene were much higher than her own.

Chapter
Four

"What about this?" Sally picked a silk scarf off the display table and held it up for Jude to see. It was peacock blue, with swirls of aquamarine and pale green. "It's sort of Pucci-ish, seventies psychedelic, really pretty . . ."

Jude eyed it doubtfully. "I'm not sure."

"Oh, come on! Look!"

Sally tied the scarf round her head. The rich blue set off her pale golden skin wonderfully. Sally's skin was actually the color that most people called olive, but this had never made any sense to Jude, since Sally was neither black, khaki, or virulent green.

"Or she could put it through her jeans, instead of a belt . . . or roll it up and tie it round her neck like a bandana . . ."

"Sal, this is *Katie* we're talking about," Jude pointed out. "She's not like you."

"She doesn't have to be able to write a book called *Twenty Ways With Your Fabulous Pucci* to know what to do with a *scarf*," Sally said.

Jude just looked at her.

"I could show her," Sally said, a trace of sulkiness creeping into her voice.

Jude still didn't say anything.

"I could do her pretty little drawings showing her which way to twist it," Sally said, beginning now to see the funny side. "I could video myself wearing it in lots of different ways. I could video *you* being shown by me how to wear it in lots of different ways. I could—"

"Effortlessly make her feel like a complete style failure," Jude finished.

"I expect you're right," Sally sighed. "I just thought, Katie does do that whole tomboy thing—for want of a better way to put it," she added a little bitchily, since Sally found it impossible not to comment if someone had poor fashion sense, "and, you know, the bandana thing might go with that . . ."

She tailed off, looking at Jude. "No," she said finally. "OK. You're right. God, this is so *difficult*. And that scarf really would go with her skin and hair."

"It looked wonderful on you," the stallholder said sycophantically.

"Well, we have the same coloring," Sally said, fingering the silk. "How much is it?"

"This is supposed to be a buy-a-birthday-present-for-Katie expedition," Jude said as they strolled away from the stall. They were moving slowly. Sally couldn't walk faster than an amble while removing her belt and threading the scarf through the waist loops of her jeans. "So far we've got three things, which would be doing really well if they weren't all for you."

"It's *Portobello Market on a Saturday,*" Sally said haughtily, fighting back. "What did you expect?"

"No, fine, I'm just pointing out that the Sally-to-Katie ratio is a little unbalanced right now. That's all."

"If you'd buy a couple of things for yourself, you'd loosen up a bit," Sally sniffed. "I don't understand how you can wander through here and not pick anything up. You have a heart of stone, Jude Baxter."

It was all very well for Sally; she was petite and pretty, with the kind of face and body that lent themselves perfectly to being accessorized in a myriad different ways. If Jude had tried to belt her jeans with that scarf, she was pretty sure she would barely have got the ends to meet. In her teens she had experimented with makeup and jewelery and frilly skirts, and finally given up in despair, feeling almost like a man in drag. She hardly wore makeup now, just some mascara and lip gloss—plus concealer when necessary—and though technically this should have conveyed a sense of superiority, as if she felt herself to be more confident than the girls who couldn't leave the house without curling their eyelashes and lining their lips, in practice that was not the case. She thought Sally looked exquisite all made up, like a perfect little doll with shiny, sticky red lips and dark smudgy eyes.

Sally looked at her narrowly and drew her own conclusions. Sally knew Jude pretty well.

"So you don't think we should get her anything to wear?" she asked.

"Well, if we find the right thing . . ."

"What?" Sally said hopelessly. "Yet another stripy sweater?

She's got hundreds already! It's been what, two months since we met her, and I've never seen her in anything else! Have you?"

"Spring's here," Jude pointed out. "We could buy her some stripy T-shirts."

Sally giggled. "I do love it being warm," she said, looking down at her pretty little mules and pink-painted toenails. "I love bringing out all my sandals and being able to roll up my jeans without getting frostbite on my ankles."

"Make the most of it," Jude said dourly. "It's supposed to pour next week."

"Fuck. Why don't we just go and live in Miami? What are we all doing in this stupid damp country anyway? Oh, look."

She wove her way through the thick mass of people to a stall selling turquoise and silver jewelry. Wiggling to the front, she became absorbed in utter concentration for a few minutes. Jude knew better than to disturb her. It would have been like asking a priest halfway through Communion what time it was. Finally Sally emerged from her trance and reached for a small pair of hoop earrings, crusted with turquoises along the slender twin curves. She handed them to Jude.

"Go on," she said.

"Go on what? If you want my opinion, which you usually don't, I don't think they'd suit Katie at all."

"Not Katie, you big moron. *You.*"

"I really don't think so."

Sally almost stamped her foot with impatience. "Will you just *look,*" she said crossly, picking up a hand mirror and giving it to Jude.

Gingerly, Jude held up one of the earrings to her lobe, the

mirror in the other hand. Her reluctance was motivated solely by her anticipated terror of the image that would be reflected. Expecting a large, mannish-looking girl whose ridiculously pretty earring only made her look even more so, she was taken aback by what she saw. The hoop was discreet—not like the ones Sally was currently wearing, which hung almost to her shoulders—and the turquoise not only contrasted prettily with Jude's blond bob, but brought out the green in her hazel eyes.

"It's not bad," she admitted.

Sally rolled her eyes, but managed not to say, "Told you so."

Jude tilted her head, letting her hair fall over the earring, watching the turquoise gleam blue-green through the short blond strands, momentarily enchanted by her own image. She looked almost pretty. Sally was a magician.

"That looks nice," said a man standing next to her.

She turned in surprise. Men she didn't know rarely spoke to her; she wasn't Sally, who was always getting whistled at or complimented or asked if she came here often and wanted a drink.

"Paul!" she said, recognizing him. Well, that explained his having talked to her. "Hi! Sally, this is Paul Duffy, who works in my office."

"Jude manages all of us," Paul said, smiling at Sally. "She doesn't let us get away with anything. Which is exactly what we need."

Paul had put that very nicely. Actually, Jude was simply a glorified secretary. Now that computers were so commonplace, and the younger generation of men so accustomed to using them, secretaries were a dying breed. You were called a Personal Assistant, if you only had one boss to answer to, or an Office

Manager, if, as in Jude's case, you had plenty. The title might be more imposing, but the pay, naturally, wasn't equally dignified. Jude didn't much like her job, but she couldn't think of anything else she'd rather do instead. And the atmosphere was pleasant enough.

"You're an architect?" Sally asked Paul politely.

"Pretty low down on the rungs for now," Paul said modestly. "But yes, I am. So you're a friend of Jude's?"

"We're best friends and we live next door to each other. It's like a sitcom," Sally said, smiling. No matter how many times she said that, it always amused her.

"I haven't seen you round the office," Paul said. "I mean," he corrected himself, blushing slightly, "I haven't seen you coming by to meet Jude, or anything . . ."

He tailed off, clearly realizing that this sounded idiotic. There was no reason why he should ever have seen Sally. But, however clumsily, he had conveyed what he wanted to: that he regretted not having met her before now. Jude grinned. This wasn't news to her. She had spotted it as soon as she turned, recognizing Paul, and seen that his eyes were sliding down and to one side of her, where Sally stood, looking so pretty with her hair caught in two stubby plaits and her sunglasses propped stylishly on top of her head.

"Are you two out for some shopping?" he asked.

"No," Jude said naughtily. This was mean. It was so obvious that they were. Paul reddened again and Sally took pity on him.

"What we're *really* supposed to be doing," she explained, "is buying a birthday present for someone. But what we're *actually* doing is spending too much money on ourselves. Well, mostly me, I'm sorry to say. I'm trying to talk Jude into getting something so we can even up the score a bit and feel guilty together."

"Those earrings are very nice," Paul said, in the gruff, awkward tone that straight men use to compliment women on items of clothing.

"I'll think about it," Jude said, putting them down, to the great disappointment of the stallholder, who had thought a sale was definitely in the offing.

"She's always like that," Sally said confidentially to Paul. "She takes *ages* to decide on things. It drives me mad. Is she like that at work?"

"Not at all," Paul said, smiling at Jude. "The opposite. She knows exactly how everything works and what everyone ought to be doing. We'd be lost without her."

"You wouldn't have any biscuits without me," Jude corrected sternly. "The men expect the biscuits to arrive by some miraculous osmosis," she explained to Sally, "and the women refuse to buy any. Apart from Sarah," she added more for Paul's benefit, "who only buys Ginger Nuts because she hates ginger so she knows she's safe from eating them."

"Is *that* why there's always a packet of Ginger Nuts in the tin?"

Jude nodded solemnly.

"Another office mystery solved," he said happily. "I told you, Jude knows everything."

A silence fell on the group. They were at that awkward moment where Jude and Sally ought to wander off in search of the elusive present for Katie, and Paul should make his goodbyes-and-see-you-Monday-morning. But it was clear that Paul wanted to go on talking to them, or at least to Sally.

Jude made a swift decision. Paul was very nice, surprisingly so. Or maybe it wasn't a surprise, it was just that Jude didn't hang out much with people from work. She had a chip on her shoulder about being only the office manager, while the rest of them were all highly educated architects or designers with degrees coming out of their ears and, doubtless, posher backgrounds than her own. She didn't mind Sally and Michael being posh, hardly noticed it anymore. But Sally and Michael had overridden her usual class-consciousness from the first, trampled over it without even seeming to realize that it was there, or that there was any difference in their backgrounds. It was one of the many reasons she loved them so much.

She pulled her thoughts back to Paul. He *was* nice, and he was clearly keen on Sally. Looking from one to the other, Jude began to hatch a cunning plan.

"Are you busy, Paul?" she said. "Or do you want to walk along with us for a bit?"

Paul's eyes brightened. "Um, yeah, absolutely," he said. "I only popped out to stretch my legs and get a coffee anyway."

Lives round the Notting Hill area, Jude noted. *Very* eligible.

"You didn't tell me there was someone at work you liked!" Sally said enthusiastically.

Jude stared at her blankly, the cup of frappuccino suspended halfway to her lips.

"What are you *talking* about?" she said.

Sally gestured impatiently inside the café, where Paul had

just gone to find the toilet. Actually, he hadn't quite put it that way; he had said, "Will you excuse me for a moment?" Paul was definitely well brought up.

"You mean *Paul?*" Jude said in utter disbelief.

"Of course! He seems very nice. I can't believe you haven't mentioned him before."

"Sal." Jude put down her stuffed croissant. "Two essential points here: a, I am still seeing Scott—"

"Well, I know, but—" It had been two months since that night in the wine bar, and Sally had not warmed to Scott in the interim. She still felt he wasn't seeing Jude enough.

"And b, which I can't *believe* you didn't spot for yourself, Paul couldn't give a monkey's about *me.*"

"What?"

"Sal, Paul Likes You, Not Me. Shall I write it down on a napkin for you, with diagrams?"

Sally considered this theory. "Are you *sure?*" she said doubtfully.

"Yes, you idiot!"

"But you asked him to come to Katie's birthday party tonight! I thought that was for you!"

"Oh, Sal, you can be such a *prat . . .*" Jude sighed.

Paul had accepted with alacrity. Not being as much of an idiot as Sally, he could tell perfectly well that Jude hadn't issued the invitation because she wanted to bump bodies with him. Whatever plans he might have had for his Saturday evening had been thrown to the winds without a backward glance. The thought of being at a party with Sally had perked him up faster than a nipple in sudden contact with an ice cube.

"And he's talking just as much to you as to me," Sally pointed out.

"Yeah, but it's not me he's staring at with moony eyes."

It was a constant source of amazement to Jude that Sally was so deluded when it came to men. She simply couldn't tell when they were pursuing her. Jude had seen many, over the years, give up in despair, and she was determined that this time things would be different. Not that she was doing something as basic as setting Sally up with Paul; oh no. Sally's situation was much too complicated to be resolved by such a simple solution. Jude wasn't casting Paul as anything but a decoy, a stalking horse.

A very good-looking stalking horse. That was essential. A man as handsome as Paul could make any ex-boyfriend jealous. Jude hadn't noticed his good looks that much in the office, partly because she didn't go much for men in suits, and partly because Paul was so fair-skinned, which wasn't her type. But, observing him now as he wove his way through the series of small iron tables clustered tightly outside the café, she noticed that he had a very nice body—good muscular forearms, dotted with gold-tipped hairs, and a narrow waist. And he seemed like the kind of blond who would go golden in the sun, rather than lobster-pink.

"So," he said, pulling up his chair and reaching for his coffee, "are you girls still happy with the present you got?"

"Oh yes, I think so," Jude answered. "They're very Katie. Or if they're not, at least they look as if we've tried."

They had bought Katie a pair of silver earrings in the shape of parrots, set with tiny garnets and aquamarines. Sally had judged that they looked reasonably expensive but were jokey enough to go with the kind of thing that Katie wore.

Looking at them now, a horrible thought dawned on Jude.

"Sal," she said, trying not to laugh. "Do you know what we did? I just realized why we went for parrots. The *stripes.*"

Sally stared at her for a moment and then burst out laughing. "Oh my God," she managed to say between giggles.

"What is it?" Paul asked.

Jude explained to him about Katie's penchant for wearing stripes.

"We must have thought 'pirate,' subconsciously," she explained. "So when we were choosing from all those birds—"

"You picked out two parrots for her shoulders!" Paul finished, grinning.

Jude picked up one of the parrots. "You like your pretty shoes, Dorothy?" she squawked. "Pieces of eight! Pieces of eight!"

Sally laughed even harder. Paul looked at her and their eyes met; it was one of those shared moments of amusement that, at least temporarily, bond people together faster than hours of conversation. Paul could barely take his eyes off Sally. Jude observed it with great satisfaction. Operation Stalking Horse was well under way.

Chapter
Five

"*T*his is so pretty!"

The exclamation burst from Sally quite spontaneously, and Katie, who had opened the door to them, beamed with pride.

"I spent all day getting the place ready," she confided.

"We would have come over and helped," Sally said. "Mikey told you that we offered, didn't he?"

A faint shadow creased between Katie's straight dark eyebrows. Sally couldn't help noticing that they needed plucking; they looked like twin millipedes stretching out their legs after a long walk. She itched to pop back across the street and grab her tweezers.

"Yes, he did," Katie said, after a heavy pause. "But we wanted to do it on our own."

"Oh, but it's a shame to have to do all the work for your own birthday party!" Sally protested. "We could at least have taken over while you got ready."

Jude winced. Sally was saying all the wrong things. Jude had seen this situation, with variations, repeated many times before: Michael's new girlfriend trying to establish her own territory, plant her flag in Michael's conquered body, as it were, while Michael and

Sally remained sublimely indifferent to her efforts. And then there was Sally's faux pas about Katie needing time to get ready. Katie had clearly just pulled on a slightly more party-appropriate top than her usual T-shirts—it was made of thermal cotton, but at least it was lace-trimmed and strappy—over the combat trousers she had been wearing all day. Jude watched Katie taking in the difference between her own sartorial efforts and Sally's.

"It does look really gorgeous," Jude said to help out. "I'd barely have recognized it as Michael's grotty old dump."

This was a wild exaggeration, but it brought a smile to Katie's face.

"And the music's great," Sally commented. "Makes a change from Michael's endless jazz."

"I kept telling him you can't play Coltrane or Miles Davis at a party," Katie said. "I just brought over all my hip-hop CDs and loaded up the stereo before he could make a fuss. He doesn't seem to be minding it that much."

Sally rolled her eyes. "You wait, he'll go on about it when he's had a few drinks. He's so set in his ways."

"Drink!" Jude said quickly, before Katie could take offense at Sally knowing Michael better than she did. "That's a good idea. We brought some bubbly."

"And a birthday present," Sally added, handing it to Katie.

"Oh, thank you—you didn't have to."

Katie led the way through to the kitchen, where the girls cracked open their bubbly. Sally had got Jude into drinking champagne—only a supermarket brand, but still champagne—something Jude would never have dreamed of trying before she met Sally. And Sally had a rule: if you were going to bring it to a party, you deserved a glass of it yourself. Katie clinked glasses with them but didn't even sip hers, disappearing immediately afterward, muttering some excuse barely audible over the insistent pounding beat of the music.

"She doesn't like me," Sally said mournfully.

Jude shrugged. "They never do. I don't know what you expect."

Sally drank some champagne. "The place does look lovely, doesn't it?" she said as they strolled into the living room.

Katie had filled every square inch of shelf with tiny flickering candles, and festooned the rooms with strings of electric lights designed to look like miniature red and gold Japanese lanterns. These were the sole sources of illumination; the effect was magical. Small vases filled with thick clusters of red carnations were dotted through the rooms, and Katie had even twined more lantern lights around the banister of the staircase. It was about ten o'clock, and though there were quite a few guests already, the party was only just getting started. People were still sitting around talking, rather than flirting raucously and dancing on the tables.

"Where's Michael?" Jude wondered. Michael was usually the life and soul of any party he attended, let alone his own.

Sally looked puzzled. "I don't know. Maybe he and Katie're having a birthday snog upstairs, or something. He'll be down soon enough. Ooh, look, there's Bill and Siobhan. I haven't seen them in ages."

She waved at Bill and Siobhan. "Want some bubbly?" she called. "God," she said to Jude, "I know practically everyone here. Where are Katie's friends?"

"They'll be along later," Jude predicted. "They're much younger, remember? That lot don't think parties start till midnight."

Jude had got it nearly right. Katie's friends started filtering in after about eleven-thirty. It was easy to tell the difference between Michael's and Katie's social circles, even in the flatteringly dim, rosy-toned lighting. Both sets were, in the main, fashionably dressed, but the over-thirties had adapted the fashions to themselves, and to their comfort, rather than following the worst excesses. Thus Sally's one-shoulder top was black crêpe and elegant, and her hipster trousers showed a discreet flash of thong—blink and you'd miss it—if she bent over. While her twenty-three-year-old equivalent wore a top held precariously over a single shoulder with a piece of dyed string, her trousers cut so low that only her jutting hipbones seemed to be keeping them up. And her thong was worn deliberately high to announce to all the world that yes, she knew it was showing, and no, she didn't care.

"We were never like that ten years ago," Bill said, poker-faced. "We were always cool and our clothes were never stupid."

"*Right,*" Siobhan, his wife, said, dissolving into laughter. "I had a pair of transparent green cheesecloth harem trousers when I was sixteen."

"Oh, look!" Jude said. "It's Paul! Paul!"

She waved at him over the crowd. One of the many advantages of being tall. Sally was in three-inch stiletto heels—the kind you can only wear if you're just tottering across the street to your friend's house and no further—and she was still nowhere near being on a level with Jude.

No one would ever have mistaken Paul for one of Katie's friends. He was clean, freshly shaved, perfumed with aftershave and wearing a T-shirt and trousers that fit him without either being too tight or too baggy. Jude was pleased with herself. Bumping into him might have been an accident, but she had made the most of the opportunity.

"So, did she like the earrings?" he asked Sally as soon as the polite preliminaries had been exchanged.

While Sally was explaining that as far as she knew Katie hadn't opened her presents yet and assuring him that no, Katie wasn't currently wearing a stripy T-shirt, Jude scanned the room for Scott. He had said he would be working late, but that he would drop in if he could. She hoped he would make it. Jude was still feeling ambivalent about him, unsure whether she was fixing on him because he was the current man in her life, or because her feelings toward him really were growing. But every time she saw him she was glad, which must count for something, mustn't it?

She didn't see Scott. But she did spot Michael, coming downstairs and, to her surprise, going out the front door. Squinting through the front window, she could see him outside on the tiny, stubbly, handkerchief-sized square of grass that an estate agent would describe as a front lawn. He was standing there, unmoving, staring at the cars buzzing down the Caledonian Road.

It was a perfect opportunity to start Phase Two of Operation Stalking Horse. Jude left Paul and Sally chatting and made her way outside. She paused for a moment on the doorstep, watching Michael. He was still standing there, immobile, his shoulders hunching forward slightly.

"Michael?" She stepped onto the little patch of grass and took a couple of steps toward him, not wanting to crowd him.

Michael turned his head.

"Oh, Jude, it's you," he said on a long sigh.

"Is everything OK?"

"No. Well, maybe. I don't know. I've just had a bit of a shock."

"Anything I can help with?"

Michael exhaled heavily again. This time it was a cross between a sigh and a laugh. "I wish it was," he said. "I don't know. It's my fault too, of course."

By now Jude was naturally dying of curiosity. She racked her brains to think of a question that would prompt Michael along without being too intrusive.

"Aah," Michael said finally. "I feel like baying at the moon."

Jude looked up at the night sky. It was dark, for London: the pollution meant that you never saw the rich velvet black of a country sky. A crescent moon with a sharp outer curve and blurry inner edges, like a torn-off fingernail, hung white and clear above them. A few faint stars were shining fuzzily through the clouds. It was extraordinary how calming just tilting your head back and looking at the night could be. Even though they were sandwiched on this small spot of open ground between the thumping sexy beat of the music and the cars rushing past, everything seemed to fade, partially dissolve, compared to the still, small, white moon in the dark sky. Jude lost herself for a few contemplative seconds.

She was brought back to earth by Michael saying in a slightly more upbeat voice: "Come on, give me a hug. That'll help if anything will."

Jude wasn't that much shorter than Michael in her heels. And she was strong. Michael seemed to need to be enfolded, and she did her best to get her arms as far around him as she could, squeezing hard. Michael squeezed back with equal pressure, his round firm belly pressing into her like a bolster that had somehow got caught between them. It was oddly comforting. And Michael was so physically confident, so sure of himself, it made the fact that his body was less than perfect seem utterly unimportant.

"Wow," Michael said into her ear. "You're so . . . tall. And strong," he added.

Jude knew he had been going to say "big," and substituted "tall" at the last minute. She was used to it. You could say "big" about a man, and it would always be flattering; but to a woman it never was. Just as you could never say "thin" to a man as a compliment, whereas it would have a woman glowing with pleasure.

Jude thought of all the times she had heard the word "big" used about herself. She knew, honestly, that she wasn't fat. But she had never known what it was like to feel small and dainty. Her feet were like boats compared with Sally's. No man, apart from, perhaps, a heavyweight wrestler, would be able to sweep her off her feet, let alone pick her up, put her against a wall, and have sex with her without her feet touching the ground. All this could not help but make her feel unfeminine. So it was with considerable irony that she said: "No, I expect you're not exactly used to girls my size."

"Do you know what?" Michael said, as if taken by surprise. "You're right. I expect all my girlfriends *are* on the short side."

Jude rolled her eyes. Men could be so blind to their own egregious behavior.

"But there's something very sexy about a woman you can stand eye-to-eye with," Michael said, immediately redeeming himself. "I never realized that before . . ."

He smiled at Jude and she knew he meant it; he wasn't just saying it to make her feel better. Michael was nothing if not genuine.

"Sofie wasn't that short, I suppose, but she was very . . . frail," he continued reflectively. "Delicate. Sofie was very vulnerable-seeming. Well, maybe she *was* shorter than I remember. Katie's so tiny that everyone seems like the Incredible Hulk compared to her . . ."

His voice tailed off and he dropped his arms from around Jude, stepping back.

"Michael? What is it?"

"Oh, nothing. Well—" He took a deep breath. "There is something, but— Look, I'm going to go back inside. Sorry about this, Jude." He patted her arm briefly. "I've just got things on my mind."

Jude stood staring after him for a minute. What on earth was going on with Michael? The only guess she could make was that he and Katie were having a massive fight. Still, Jude had seen Michael in fights with girlfriends before, many, many times, and this was not how he reacted. He was rarely that affected by them. In fact, he would often pop round to Sally's afterward and tell her and Jude all the gory details, with as much relish as if they had happened to a good friend, rather than to himself. She had never seen Michael in such an odd mood in all the years she had known him.

She went slowly back inside. In her absence the party had made that vital alteration that any party needs to undergo around midnight; people were no longer standing around talking in the middle of the living room, they were boogying on down instead. The small room was already hot and sweaty. Jude wove her way through the thrusting pelvises to Sally, who was dancing near the fireplace with Siobhan, a big smile of pure happiness on her face. Sally adored dancing. Jude slipped her glance to the side. Sure enough, there was Paul, drinking a beer with Bill, leaning against the wall, watching Sally and Siobhan. Quite a few of the younger men were dancing, whooping it up and clapping their hands, but once straight men hit the thirty mark they were much less likely to be found on the dance floor. It was as if they felt their age exempted them. Or, more likely, that they had always hated dancing, and now were old enough to realize that you didn't need to gyrate round girls to pull them. Except perhaps literally.

"Great party!" Sally shouted up at Jude. "Katie should be really pleased!"

"Yeah!" Jude yelled back. She hadn't seen Katie anywhere, and Michael, too, seemed to have disappeared to the further reaches of the flat. Still, she wasn't going to tell Sally what had just transpired. She knew that if Sally suspected something was wrong with Michael she would immediately go and try to sort it out, abandoning Paul to his own devices. Damn. She had been so distracted by Michael's odd mood that she hadn't even mentioned Paul to him. She would have to look out for an opportunity later. If he were having a fight with Katie, this might well be the perfect moment. Michael would unquestionably be jealous at seeing Sally being courted by good-looking, eligible Paul. And if he and Katie were going through a rocky patch, that might spur him onto realizing that it was Sally he really wanted, had always wanted. Jude wasn't being over-ambitious; she didn't think she could push Sally and Michael into each other's arms in the space of a few hours. But she could certainly start sowing the seeds.

And some skillful matchmaking might compensate her slightly for her own feelings of abandonment. She had checked her mobile before coming back into the party; Scott hadn't left a message. Oh well, maybe she should just pick up a twenty-two-year-old and take him home, by way of distraction. She looked round the room at the prospects in their shell necklaces and layered shiny T-shirts, their skin still a little pocked here and there as the last traces of adolescent acne faded away. Jude shuddered. Forget even flirting with one of them. She would just have to dance till she was too tired to think about anything but how close her bed was.

Several funky seventies hits and quite a lot of sexy hip-hop later, Jude was grinding away, as happy as someone could be whose boyfriend hadn't shown up, when the music came to an abrupt halt. The dancers, thinking it was complaining neighbors or a stereo malfunction, gave a great groan of protest that rose to the ceiling.

Then, from the kitchen, a few voices started singing:

Happy birthday to you . . .

and Tash, Katie's best friend, entered the living room, carrying a large cake thickly flickering with candles. Other friends were pushing Katie forward. She looked dazed, Jude observed. But anyone who didn't realize that something was wrong would just attribute it to surprise and too much alcohol.

Happy birthday, dear Ka-a-tie . . .

Happy birthday to you!

The room erupted into cheers. Katie bent over and blew out the candles. Everyone clapped. Tash withdrew, moving carefully to avoid tripping: her jeans were cut so long and wide at the bottom that they concealed her trainers completely. Michael appeared, coming downstairs and making his way through the dense cluster of people to stand behind Katie, his big hands pressing her shoulders. She looked up and said something to him. He bent down to whisper an answer in her ear. She reached up and covered his hand with one of hers. Her face looked pale and drawn, but she was trying to smile. It was clearer than ever to Jude that whatever problem Michael had was related to Katie. Towering behind her small slender body, he looked like a very gloomy giant.

"Katie! First piece! And Michael!"

Tash returned, handing them each a paper plate with a slice of cake on it. "Peanut butter and chocolate, your favorite!" she announced happily.

"Thanks, Tash," Katie said, smiling. She picked up the plastic fork and cut herself a piece of cake. Michael had already eaten half his slice in one bite. Feeding Michael was like being a stoker shoveling endless scoops of coal into a steam engine. As long as the train was moving, you had to keep feeding the fire.

Katie, chewing, said through her mouthful: "Mmn, this is *great!*"

Tash, who had been waiting for the verdict, swished happily back to the kitchen to cut more slices. Katie forked up another piece, started chewing it, and then clapped her hand to her mouth. The fork went flying. She shoved her plate at Michael and made a dash for the staircase, flying up it as if her feet were barely touching the treads.

Tash, luckily, hadn't seen this debacle, and most other people were too occupied either in dancing again or queuing up in the kitchen for a piece of cake. Sally and Jude exchanged glances.

"What's up with her?" Sally said.

"Dunno."

"Is Michael OK?"

Damn, that was exactly what Jude had wanted to avoid. Sally was already crossing the room to Michael. He stuffed Katie's leftover cake into his mouth and turned in the direction of the stairs, Sally following behind him. Jude, sighing, went after Sally, hoping to detach her as soon as possible. The more Sally behaved like Michael's concerned younger sister, the less likely it was that he would ever see her as the woman of his life.

"Mikey?" Sally called. She bounded up the stairs after him and caught him at the top. "What's wrong? Is Katie OK?"

The top floor of the flat was small, consisting of Michael's bedroom, a tiny box room and the bathroom at the end of a stubby corridor barely longer than it was wide. From the top of the stairs, even with the music and laughter below, the sounds of Katie throwing up were unmistakable. Michael's face was sagging so visibly that Jude had a sudden flash of what he would look like as an old man.

"Has she got food poisoning?" Sally said. "I've still got some of those antiemetics, remember? I could pop over and get them for her . . ."

Michael shook his head. He looked around, but they were the only people in the corridor. Through the open door of his room Jude could see a couple writhing around on Michael's bed, on top of all the coats, but since one of them had what looked like the other's entire right ear in her mouth and they were both making loud, moaning, constipated-sheep noises, the risk of them eavesdropping was clearly minimal.

"You might as well know sooner or later," Michael said unhappily. "I was going to tell you anyway, Sal. Katie's pregnant."

Chapter
Six

The first person Jude saw as she descended the stairs was Scott. Despite being disoriented by the news she had just heard, her heart leapt. For a moment, taken aback at her pleasure in seeing him, she wondered whether she had made a mistake, as he had his back to her; but no, that was definitely Scott's leather jacket, Scott's tousled hair, and Scott's customary stance, standing slightly removed from everyone else at the edge of the living room. Scanning it, she hoped, for her.

"Hey," she said, tapping him on the shoulder, deliberately sounding cool to conceal her happiness.

"Hey!" He swung round. "Whew, I was worried you'd gone already! I'm sorry I was so late. My computer crashed. I had to spend a couple of hours getting everything back and running."

He kissed her, a sweet lingering contact of lip to lip, then pulled back a little.

"Are you having a good time?" he asked, surveying her. "You look a bit . . . funny."

"Something very weird just happened," Jude said. She knew "weird" was scarcely the most appropriate word, but she couldn't think of a better one just then. The dancing was still in full swing. Some hip-hop song was on, causing everyone to back their bottoms into each other and whoop a lot, circling their arms in the air as if they were cranking up an engine.

"What is it?" Scott said. "Are you OK?"

"Cake?"

Jude swiveled slightly to see a girl with a big smile on her face, pushing two paper plates at them. Jude couldn't help feeling ambivalent about the cake, having just spent the past ten minutes hearing Katie reprocess her own piece into liquid vomit, but it was easier to take the plate than explain why she didn't want to.

"Great," Scott said, naturally having no such reservations. "This is birthday cake, right?"

"Peanut butter and chocolate," Jude said.

"Yum." He dug in happily.

"Not if you're the birthday girl," Jude said dryly.

"What?" He looked at her more narrowly. "Look, what's wrong?"

Jude looked down the corridor and through into the kitchen. The living room was a no-go area, being full of dancing bodies, and the rest of the ground floor was lined with people with flushed faces shouting happily at each other and stubbing cigarettes out in platefuls of discarded cake. No privacy there. And upstairs was out too. Katie was in Michael's bedroom, the two lovers having been expelled from their Eden on top of the coats in a scene that had been embarrassing for everyone; by the time Katie had finished voiding her stomach and needed to lie down, the male had had a part of the female in his mouth which was considerably more intimate than an ear.

"Why don't we get a drink and go outside for a bit," she suggested, unable to face the party.

"Whatever you want," Scott said amiably. "I just came to see you."

It was cold outside, and Jude hadn't brought a jacket. Scott saw her shivering, and took his off to put around her shoulders. It smelled of new leather and—the collar lining, slightly—of Scott. Why was it so comforting to wear an item of your boyfriend's clothing? Jude wondered, hugging the jacket around her. Old shirts or T-shirts, jackets that were oversized on you, no matter how tall or big-boned you were . . . maybe that was why. It made you feel like someone who cared about you had his arms around you, his scent infusing his clothing like essence of him.

Michael had put a small bench in the front garden. Nailed to the ground, of course, and not too smart, in case it invited graffiti. This was the Caledonian Road, after all. But it was just the right size for two people who didn't mind sitting close to each other.

"This cake is really good," Scott commented, finishing the last forkful.

"Here," Jude said, "have mine."

She drank down half of her vodka tonic instead, and had a coughing fit. She hadn't realized quite how strong she'd made it. It tasted like neat Smirnoff to which the tonic bottle had just been shown in passing. Still, it was certainly warming her up.

"You never say no to cake," Scott said, taking her plate. "Something really must be wrong."

"Oh, I'm still a greedy cow," Jude said wryly. "But I just

heard Katie throwing up hers, and it put me right off it for the moment." She explained briefly what had happened upstairs.

Scott listened until she'd finished, without interpolating comments or questions; he was good at that.

"So what happens now?" he asked, stacking the plates and forks and putting them down at his feet.

"I don't know," Jude said. "I just don't know. It's such a mess." She sighed. "I feel so sorry for everyone. Michael said it was a complete accident, and I'm sure that's true. I can't see Katie trying to get pregnant deliberately. She's so young, and she and Michael have only been together for a couple of months. And she just doesn't seem that kind of person. You know, she seems quite independent, she's got a good job . . ." Her voice trailed off.

After a while she added, "And Sally was really shocked by it, I could see. It must be incredibly weird for her."

"I thought they broke up years ago," Scott said, surprised.

"Yeah, but they're so close. They're like brother and sister."

"Well, if they really are like brother and sister, it shouldn't be *that* weird for her, should it?"

The common sense of this was deeply annoying. Jude shrugged irritably, as if trying to push Scott off her shoulders.

"You don't understand," she said.

"Well, then, help me to understand," Scott said, annoyance creeping into his voice to mirror Jude's. "Either they're going out, or they're not. And if they're not, but they're still managing to be friends, good for them—but Sally shouldn't be freaked out if Michael has a new girlfriend who accidentally gets pregnant."

This was all completely logical. Jude could see that. But she felt that Scott was being deliberately obtuse, rather than entering into her feelings and trying to see things through her eyes, which was surely what a boyfriend should do.

"They're really close," she said again. "It's like a family thing. Michael's mum practically adopted Sally. And we never thought for a moment that Michael would stay with Katie. They were having lots of fun, but in the end they don't really have anything in common." She gestured behind them, toward the house. "Look at her friends and his friends. They don't have a word to say to each other, beyond 'More cake?' 'Oh thanks, lovely.' And now this has happened . . . God, what an awful mess. Michael looked poleaxed."

She ducked her head and rubbed her face with her hands, massaging her eyebrows, trying to calm herself down.

"Don't you think you're getting a bit too caught up in all this?" Scott suggested.

"No, I don't," Jude snapped. Scott was saying all the wrong things. "It's important! One of my best friends has got his girlfriend pregnant!"

"Yeah, I'm not saying *that's* not important. It's all this Sally and Michael stuff, it just doesn't seem that any good's going to come of this situation, and I don't think you should get too involved in it—"

"Look, I know them and you don't, OK?" Jude said angrily. "On the few occasions you've met them you didn't seem that interested in getting to know them, either."

She drank some more vodka. By now she was wondering if she'd remembered to put any tonic in it at all. Had she just absentmindedly tilted the bottle over her glass without unscrewing the top?

"I thought we'd established that Michael doesn't like me much," Scott said mildly.

Jude ground her teeth in frustration.

"Look," he said. "Why don't we get off this freezing bench, go back to yours, have a drink or a cup of tea or something, and get things in perspective a bit, OK?"

He might as well have produced a red handkerchief from his pocket and waved it tauntingly in front of her face. Jude lowered her horns and charged.

"How *dare* you say I haven't got things in perspective!" she said furiously. "This is a really awful situation! I've got a right to be upset and confused by it! And you're just talking as if I'm some hippy-dippy moron!"

"Jude, I'm not—"

"Yes you are! Sally and Michael are my best friends, Sally's upstairs right now cleaning Michael's girlfriend's peanut butter and chocolate puke off his toilet"—Scott, with two slices of cake inside him, turned a little green at this—"and all you can do is tell me I'm making too much of a fuss! God! What would you consider serious? How would you have felt if I'd told you that your computer crashing wasn't that serious and you needed to get things in perspective?"

Scott made a fatal mistake.

"But that's different. I've already fixed that," he pointed out. "I didn't come to you with a problem and expect you to sort it out."

It was a typically male response, which Jude would have known if she hadn't been a little drunk and more than a little incensed. Every sensible woman knows that the average hetero-sexual male would rather gouge out his eye than let his girl-friend see him emotionally upset—or fail to offer a nice clean concrete solution to her problems.

Scott realized a few seconds later what he had done. "I didn't mean you wanted me to sort it out," he said quickly, "only that—"

"Well, I'm sorry I'm not as together as you are, OK?" Jude said, rising from the bench majestically. Standing up was harder than she had expected. Her head was swimming. Synchronized swimming: lots of somersaults and flutter-kicks. "I'm sorry I can't magically make all my problems disappear like you can," she continued. "Not that this *is* my problem, it's Michael's and Katie's, but—well, any of *my* problems."

Jude felt that, rhetorically, this could have sounded better. But it was the best she could do right now. She took off Scott's jacket and threw it at him. He grabbed at it to avoid it falling on the cake plates. Suddenly, she felt very tired.

"I *am* going home," she announced. The party held no fur-ther attractions for her, and if she went back upstairs she would feel like a third wheel to Sally and Michael. Or maybe a fourth wheel, if you added Katie to the equation. But that couldn't be right. Surely you'd *want* a fourth wheel. It would make you into a car. This was all very confusing. Home was seeming more attractive by the moment.

"But by myself," she added firmly. "I shall take my boring problemsh home with me sho *you* don't have to sholve them!"

She turned on her heel with what she thought was great dig-nity and stalked off down the garden path. She had some problems with the latch of the gate, but finally, after much cursing and shoving, it opened.

"Jude?" Scott was just behind her. "Jude, look, I didn't mean to—"

"Just go away!" she shouted. "You don't undershtand! You're completely—un-undershtanding!"

And she stormed across the road. A few cars honked her, but she made it across without causing a multiple pile-up or twisting her ankle.

"Fine!" Scott shouted as she went, roused to uncharacteristic fury himself by this rejection. "I don't know why I even bloody *tried* to understand!"

Jude was righteously angry. And it was definitely, in her opinion, with righteous anger rather than advanced intoxication that she slammed her front door, stripped off her clothes, threw them in all directions and fell heavily onto her bed. Through the vodka haze, she remembered something Scott had said to her, the first time they went out: that he was working so hard that he really didn't have time for anything else, let alone a girlfriend. She had ignored it at the time, unsure as to whether she wanted a boyfriend either, and thinking, too, that it was just one of those things that men said in the early stages as a prophylactic against the woman waking up the next morning expecting an engagement ring. But it had nagged at her ever since, and now it returned to her mind as if it were written in letters of fire three feet high. No time for anything else, she thought. No time to listen to anything that's going on in my life for more than five minutes, all he wanted to do was come back to mine and get his end away . . .

Her last conscious word was *"Bashtard,"* muttered angrily into her pillow.

When she woke up later with a pounding head, the anger had all evaporated, of course, to be replaced by pain and self-pity and the urgent need to wee. But the memory of Scott's words remained.

"Smells like a male brothel in here," Michael observed.

Sally and Michael were sitting in the bathroom. Michael was on the toilet and Sally on the edge of the tub. Katie, over-wrought and exhausted, had fallen asleep in Michael's bed, and the vomit on the bathroom floor was now a distant memory, thanks to Sally's vigorous application of cleaning fluids.

"You didn't have any air freshener," Sally explained. "I sprayed some of your Indecence around instead."

"My indecence?" Michael said blankly.

"Your aftershave."

"Oh, yeah. I hardly ever use that. Lizzie gave me that. Or maybe it was Marie."

He lapsed into reminiscence for a moment, as he always did when naming his ex-girlfriends.

"What are you going to do?" Sally said.

"Oh God, I just don't know." Michael ran a hand over his shiny scalp, a gesture he always made when perplexed. "It's like you're asking me what I should do about the Third World debt, or institutionalized racism in the police force. It feels too big a problem for me even to get a grip on."

"Is Katie—um, *sure?*" Sally asked.

"She did two tests. But she knew anyway. She just woke up

one morning and puked and was sure she was pregnant. She said she felt completely different."

"How did it happen?"

It was a tribute to the friendship that Michael and Sally had established that they had never had any problems or awkwardness talking about their sex lives to each other, post break-up.

"She got food poisoning," Michael said gloomily. "She was on the loo for hours. We went to a French restaurant for lunch last month, and she must have had a bad mussel. Of course she didn't think of it at the time—you don't, when the world's falling out of your bottom—but she's on the pill, and obviously it got washed out with everything else." He laughed, with no humor behind it. "I remember trying to cheer her up by telling her that she should just look at it as a good purge. Cleaning out the system. Well, it certainly did that."

"You weren't using condoms?" Sally asked.

Michael shook his head.

"Mikey."

"I hate them," Michael said, sounding exactly like a little boy refusing to eat his greens. "You know I hate them."

It was the kind of story that sent cold shivers down Sally's spine; there but for the grace of God go I. How easy it was for one tiny accident, one bad mussel, to change the whole course of your life. She couldn't help thinking, too, that Katie must be pretty fertile to have got pregnant like that, from one missed pill. Sally, who had never had an accidental pregnancy, found herself guiltily half-envying Katie for this proof of fecundity. At least Katie knew she could, if she wanted to. Lately Sally had been reading those articles in women's magazines that she usually skipped—the ones about IVF and egg donation and fertility falling off drastically after thirty-five—with a kind of horrified anticipation. Was that what she might have to go through? Not that she had a boyfriend, of course, but she had always thought she would have children one day . . .

She recalled her wavering thoughts with an even larger surge of guilt. There was poor twenty-five-year-old Katie next door, puked out and miserable, while she, Sally, was actually, in some sort of twisted way, envying her condition. Sally imagined herself pregnant at that age, and shuddered.

"So, has she been to a clinic yet?" she asked practically.

"No. She only just found out yesterday."

"God, the day before her birthday party. And having to go through with it and pretend to be happy in front of all her friends. How awful. Poor girl."

"Yes," Michael said distractedly, but Sally could tell that he was thinking of how awful it was for him, too. Well, why shouldn't he? she thought loyally. It was his problem almost as much as it was Katie's.

"At least she's found out straight away," Sally pointed out, trying to emphasise the positive. "There's long NHS waiting lists, but she's got plenty of time."

"For what?" Michael said blankly.

Sally wanted to slap him. She loved Michael dearly, but sometimes he could be incredibly obtuse. "For the—"

Somehow she found it difficult to say the word "abortion" in relation to Michael's baby.

"For the—" she started again. "You know, the *termination,*" she finished, finding with great relief the officially approved euphemism.

"Oh *no,*" Michael said, sounding as if it was Sally, in his opinion, who was the obtuse one. "That's the whole thing. Katie wants to keep it."

Sally stared at him till her eyes went out of focus and his features turned into a mushy haze. Her head was spinning. She was speechless.

"Yeah," Michael said eventually, seeing her reaction. "That's what this is all about."

"But you've only been going out for a couple of months!"

"I know. But she's a great girl, she really is. And she just doesn't want to get rid of her baby. Our baby," he added conscientiously.

"How do you feel about it?" Sally couldn't believe that she was managing to construct complete sentences. Her brain felt like liquid goo.

"Well, I'm not getting any younger—"

"You're thirty-five!"

"And I always wanted to have kids—"

"But you hardly know each other!"

"And Katie's really amazing, she's so full of life and fun—I think this might be exactly what I've been waiting for."

Michael actually beamed. His voice had been getting stronger with every phrase.

"Yeah," he said. "I think this might be it. I really do. I mean, I had to settle down some time. Maybe this is God's way of telling me to get on with it."

"You're an atheist," Sally muttered.

"It's pretty cool, actually," Michael said happily. "Thinking that Katie has this life growing inside her that I helped to make—it's incredibly exciting. I hope the poor little sod doesn't get my hair, though," he added thoughtfully. "Or lack of it." He leaned sideways to look at himself in the mirror behind the bath. "Or my nose," he said ruefully. "Or—Christ, let's just hope it takes after Katie . . ."

There was a candle holder on the shelf above the sink, a glass mosaic jar made of shards of mirror soldered together. Staring blindly at it, Sally gradually began to make out slices of her face reflected in it at crazy angles, like funhouse mirrors; eyes and noses and pieces of cheek hanging over each other like a particularly deranged Picasso. Or an Alice in Wonderland puzzle that would never fit together. That was how she felt. As if someone had splintered her into a million pieces, and all the king's horses would never put Sally together again.

Chapter
Seven

*P*regnancy is supposed to be the stage in a woman's life when she looks most beautiful. You bloom; your hair is luxuriant (though you lose a lot after the birth, apparently: locks fall out on your pillow as if you were molting—no wonder there's post-partum depression); your skin is clear and radiant, and you're so pumped full of happy hormones that you sail along on your own personally tailored high.

Katie stared at herself again in desperation. Her cheeks were gaunt. Any more weight loss and she would begin to see the outline of her teeth through them. Her skin, usually a healthy-looking pale yellowy-gold, was as faded as a nicotine stain, and every line of her face was pulled down with exhaustion and mal-nutrition. This was what she'd looked like when she had that bad bout of dysentery in India.

She had lost at least five pounds since the morning sickness had started. How she wished it were truly only morning sick-ness. Katie could keep nothing down at any time of day. Ginger capsules, ginger tea, none of the other herbal anti-emetics had helped. Sometimes the occasional dry cracker lodged itself in her stomach and didn't come straight up again, but that, Katie suspected, was only because her stomach was so worn out from contorting itself into convulsive spasms twenty-three hours out of twenty-four that occasionally it let something pass out of simple exhaustion. She was sure she stank of vomit, and washed herself compulsively. Her breath, she knew, was unspeakable, but she couldn't do anything about that. Gargling with mouth-wash was impossible. Even the smell of mint sent her heaving over the nearest receptacle.

She had called in sick at work, saying she had terrible stom-ach flu, and she sounded so awful that everyone had begged her fervently not to come back till she was fully recovered. No problems there, she thought dryly; even when she did return she would look so wasted that nobody could possibly suspect her of malingering. She knew she should tell them that she was pregnant, but not yet. Not until she was three months gone and the baby was safe. The books said that all this throwing up was a good sign; her body was protecting a healthy fetus from any-thing that might distress it. Meanwhile the fetus was happily sucking any nutrition it needed from Katie's already exhausted body. She poked gloomily at her teeth. If she didn't manage to get some calcium inside her soon, they would crumble away from the inside as her baby vampire leeched away at her.

What could she wear that was smart enough? She rifled once again through her small store of clothes. Katie had always been on the move. Up till now. She was a traveler, a backpacker, the kind of person who could live out of a small canvas bag for months on end. For the past couple of years she had been in almost perpetual motion: she'd been to every single continent but Antarctica, she'd thrown herself happily into every adventure going, and yet the prospect of having lunch with Michael's mother was more terrifying than bungee jumping and camel racing combined. If such a thing were possible.

Everything Michael said about his mother made her increasingly nervous. And the things Michael told her that were designed to put her at ease were the ones that particularly sent her stomach roiling. How had she found herself in this situation? She pulled out her only dress, the one she wore to smarter job interviews. It was black and made of a crinkled crêpe material, which was advertised as being ideal for traveling: roll it up, stuff it in the corner of a backpack and just unwind it when you need it. Presto, good as new. So far it had always worked. But staring at it now, she knew it wasn't right. The trouble was, she had no idea what would be.

For the first time in her life Sally found herself wishing that Hampstead were much further away from the Caledonian Road. Next to the Docklands, perhaps. Or Ipswich. She would have welcomed the chance to spend a long time in the car, her brain at least partially engaged by the automatic procedures of driving, letting herself assimilate slowly what she was going to encounter at her destination. For the first time ever in Sally's experience—not counting herself, of course—Michael was introducing a new girlfriend to his mother. Worse: Katie wasn't just a new girlfriend, she was the prospective mother of the first Gwynne grandchild.

Neither Mrs. Gwynne nor Michael would have dreamed of excluding Sally from this Sunday lunch. Sally was part of the family by now. Besides, keeping Sally away would have made it

seem as if she were somehow Katie's rival, or had been sup-
planted by Katie, and Michael's mother was much too sophisticated to create that kind of impression.

It was for precisely those reasons that Sally wouldn't have
dreamed of refusing. She had drawn the line, however, at going
there in the same car with the two of them. Michael and she
had always driven there together before, and he had rung her
several times that morning, leaving messages asking her if she
wanted a lift, but she hadn't picked up, hiding out till, standing
by the side of her living-room window, she saw his car pull
away. She wondered how many hundreds of times in the future
she would stand by that window, watching Michael carefully
escorting a heavily pregnant Katie, and then pushing a baby
stroller . . . Sally had a sudden vivid picture of Michael with a
baby carrier strapped to his chest, beaming down at the infant,
Katie's diminutive hand in his. She wondered if Michael would
ask her to babysit. The idea almost made her clap her hand to
her mouth and pull the car over to the curb so that she could
vomit like the happy mother-to-be.

Sally's head hadn't stopped spinning since Michael had told
her about Katie's pregnancy. The night of the party, she had
been incapable of dragging herself away from Michael; even
though talking over the situation with him had shattered her,
being without him would have been even worse, as if it were
only Michael's presence that was stopping the pieces flying away
in all directions. A friend of hers, years ago, had turned up on
her doorstep, having done some acid: Jake had literally needed
to hold onto Sally for the next five hours, breaking down into
spasms of terror at the thought of not being in physical contact

with someone. In the bathroom with Michael, Sally had understood for the first time what Jake had been going through, and felt a retrospective guilt for his distress when she had insisted that he would have to wait outside the door while she went to the toilet . . .

Sally would have stayed with Michael all night if he had let her. Only her pride prevented her from clutching his arm as convulsively as Jake had done with her. It had been Michael, finally, who said wearily that he needed to see how Katie was doing, put a glass of water for her on the bedside table, as she must be dehydrated, and Sally had realized, really for the first time, that she was on her own. She went downstairs searching for Jude, but Paul, who intercepted her immediately, informed her that Jude had left with a tall man with a goatee. Paul thought Sally had a migraine and insisted on walking her home, opening the gate for her, checking the traffic as they crossed the road and generally behaving like the perfect white knight. She noticed all this, but as if from a million miles away, as if the Sally walking next to Paul were in a trance, and the real Sally were floating free above them, watching her walk and talk and even smile while all she wanted to do was scream and cry and hit things till her knuckles bled.

As soon as the downstairs door shut behind her, she started crying: in the lift, down her corridor, into her flat, sobbing so hard she could barely open her eyes. Most unusually for Sally, who was fastidious about her appearance, she didn't brush her teeth or cleanse her face or take off her makeup that night. She couldn't bear the prospect of looking at herself in the bathroom mirror. Whatever she saw, no matter how pretty and well cared for, would be the face of a loser. A failure. She wasn't even pretty right then, with her skin blotchy and her eyes so pink and swollen.

Sally had cried herself to sleep harder than she ever had in her life, harder even than when Michael had broken up with her nine years ago. In the morning there were mascara and eyeliner stains smeared all over her lovely peach pillowcases. And every night this week had been the same. The only difference was that she had taken her makeup off first.

Sally bit her lip hard and took a series of deep breaths. Paused at a traffic light, she pulled down the sun-visor mirror and took a good look at herself. She was as neat and groomed as ever, her eyes clear (thanks to judicious use of eye drops), her lipstick a pretty pink. She had taken even greater pains with her appearance than she did normally. The only thing that would get her through this lunch—without breaking down into hysterics or slamming Katie's face repeatedly into her plate—was pride and, thank God, she had plenty of that. Suddenly she wished Jude were with her. Michael would have been happy to invite her too, and Jude's presence would have made this occasion a little less special, a little less Princess-Katie-Meets-Her-New-Mummy. It would have stolen some of Katie's thunder. Sally kicked herself for not having thought of it before.

"Teaching English as a foreign language?" Stephanie Gwynne inquired, sounding as if this information was new and interesting to her, though Katie was sure that she must have already heard it from Michael. "That must be fascinating. You must be terribly good at grammar."

"Oh. No. Not as much as you'd think. I mean, yes and no," Katie stammered. She was certainly not going to claim good grammar skills. She'd never needed much grammar for English lessons anyway, not at the level she taught. She crossed her fingers and prayed Mrs. Gwynne wouldn't try to engage her in a conversation about proper uses of the subjunctive.

Katie was so intimidated by Mrs. Gwynne that she could barely speak. And the *house*. It wasn't designer chic, all white sofas and dense clusters of roses in silver vases and a single perfect rug on polished floorboards; that would have been much less scary, as it would have indicated that Mrs. Gwynne was a slavish follower of fashion, and thus weak-willed. No, it was much worse than that. This house, set in a quiet Hampstead back street, was the work of a lifetime. The paintings and the furniture and the carpets and the little *objets d'art* had clearly accumulated over decades, each one rich with memories and associations. There was no overarching, unifying style, just the embodiment of Mrs. Gwynne's taste in all its varied manifestations. And because it wasn't perfectly maintained, it was cozy. The upholstery on Katie's armchair was fading at the edges, the old brocade a little ragged around the arm studs, the cushion and springs beginning, gently, to sag. It felt as if generations of Gwynnes had settled happily into that armchair, wearing it down over decades till it became a sort of family heirloom, priceless with sentimental association.

Through the French windows Katie could see the garden, which was equally beautiful, with that same slightly shabby, lived-in quality: overgrown trees, grass not perfectly mown, a riot of pale golden daffodils and violet crocuses spreading beneath the gently crumbling high stone wall that bordered the garden. It was the kind of garden that made you immediately want to wander out onto the thick lawn with a book and fall asleep beneath a tree.

"Actually, I'm doing teacher training now," Katie said, dragging herself back to the conversation. "I've been traveling a lot over the last few years, I thought it would be nice to stay put in England for a while."

"Oh, that must make a nice change, teaching people who can actually speak your language," Mrs. Gwynne said sympathetically.

"Well, yeah," Katie agreed. "But I really prefer teaching foreigners. I like the challenge."

"Katie's so young and enthusiastic," Michael said, smiling at her affectionately. "She's got so much energy."

"Well, that'll be good for when the baby comes," Mrs. Gwynne said approvingly. "I was in my thirties when I had Michael," she told Katie, "which was considered *very* late for a first baby, and all my friends who'd started having babies younger said the later ones were much more tiring. Your body just doesn't bounce back the way it did once. Of course, it's tiring anyway . . ." She sighed. "Well, you'll have Michael to help out. That's the good thing with him being freelance."

"Yes," Katie said rather doubtfully. Much as she adored Michael, she wasn't sure how much practical help he would be.

"Oh, I know he's not wonderful about the house," Mrs. Gwynne said, smiling at her. "You'll have to keep him up to the mark."

"Right," Katie said, even less convinced by this. She smiled back at Mrs. Gwynne, however. She couldn't think of her as Stephanie, though that had been the first thing Mrs. Gwynne had said to her: "Do, please, call me Stephanie. 'Mrs. Gwynne' sounds so horribly formal." Which of course had been much more intimidating than if she had said nothing on the subject at all.

"What's for lunch, Mum?" Michael asked. "The usual?"

"Yes, of course. Alessandra's lasagne."

"Yum," Michael said, relaxing comfortably into the sofa. "My favorite."

Mrs. Gwynne smiled confidentially at Katie.

"I'm a terrible cook," she said. "Well, actually, to be honest, I never really tried. I've always had more interesting things to do. Poor Michael was awfully neglected as a child, I'm afraid. Not many home-cooked meals, unless one of his nannies was any good in the kitchen. I live off deli snacks, frankly, unless I'm out to dinner. Olives, stuffed vine leaves, cheese . . . I eat lightly as a rule. But for Sunday lunch I get my cleaning lady to cook something I can heat up. She's very good. And it seems more appropriate for a Sunday lunch, doesn't it?"

This seemed to expect a "yes"; but Katie felt somehow that a "yes" would make her seem too intimidated, as if she would spinelessly agree with anything Mrs. Gwynne said. She returned Mrs. Gwynne's smile instead, which appeared to be an acceptable response.

When mentioning the more interesting things she had to do, Mrs. Gwynne had clearly been referring to her work. She was a painter, specializing in portraits: quite well known, with regular shows in Bond Street. The top floor of the house was her studio.

She had lots of arty friends, and Michael had attended her parties since he was very young. She had painted Michael many times; there was a whole series, some of which she might show Katie later on that afternoon. All these intimidating facts Katie had committed to memory from Michael's anecdotes about his mother. Katie had expected someone considerably more absentminded and arty: straggling gray hair in a bun; paint-stained hands; a nice, lined face with eyes that always wore a slightly absent expression, as if thinking about her next portrait. And a house in a state of homey, artistic disarray, with dust on the mantelpieces and canvases propped everywhere.

That had seemed daunting enough to Katie, who was not remotely creative, who had no interest in galleries or the theater, and dreaded questions designed to elicit her tastes. But now she longed for the absentminded artist of her imagination. The reality TV shows and hip-hop CDs which were her preferred ways to relax wouldn't have gone down that well with the imaginary Mrs. Gwynne, but she shuddered to imagine what the real one must be thinking of her. Though Mrs. Gwynne had the voice and manner of an upper-class matriarch, she wasn't sporting the pearl necklace, crisply streaked bob, and smart little black dress that went with it. Again, that would have made it easier for Katie to dismiss her as a stereotype. Instead, she was wearing jeans—with a silk sweater, but still jeans—and her ashy blond hair was cut short. It was a beautiful color, and very well judged: just like ashes, which dissolved as soon as you stirred them with a poker, the gray melted gently into the pale faded gold, setting off skin which, though still beautiful, was undeniably aging.

"I know you probably won't be able to eat the lasagne, Katie," Mrs. Gwynne was saying sympathetically. "Michael tells me you've been suffering from terrible morning sickness. So I got in lots of different crackers, and there's bread, which I could toast for you. And I bought a big bottle of Diet Coke yesterday and took the top off so it would go flat. A friend of mine's daughter—Laura Stevens, Mikey, remember her? She's having a baby. Anyway, apparently flat Diet Coke has really helped her keep food down. I thought it might be worth a try."

"Thank you very much," Katie said, touched by Mrs. Gwynne's concern.

"Would you like some now?"

"OK," Katie said, deeply embarrassed, "but if you could show me where the bathroom is in case I need to make a dash for it—"

"It's just down the end of the corridor," Mrs. Gwynne said, swiveling to point through the living-room wall to the location of the bathroom. "Michael, why don't you get Katie some Coke? It's on the kitchen counter. Don't put any ice in it, it's meant to be room temperature. That's less irritating to the stomach."

"I know that, Mum," Michael said, rolling his eyes. He heaved himself off the sofa, saying, "Isn't it about time for lunch, anyway?"

Mrs. Gwynne smiled at Katie.

"He was always hungry, even when he was little," she said confidentially. "One of his nannies used to say he was a baby dustbin. At least he never had any food fads. He'd eat anything that wasn't nailed down."

"I'm incapable of being embarrassed by my mother," Michael said cheerfully, heading off to the kitchen.

"We'll eat soon," Mrs. Gwynne said. "I just thought you might like to see if the Coke helps before trying solid food, Katie. Though it's nearly one, and I've got the lasagne in the oven—"

She glanced at her slim silver watch just as the doorbell rang; the two events seeming perfectly timed.

"Oh, there we are. I needn't have worried. Sally's never late. Michael, will you let in Sally while you're up?" she called.

Katie heard the front door opening, and Michael and Sally exchanging their usual fond hug.

"Stephanie!" Sally said, appearing in the doorway. "How are you?"

"Good, good, thanks, dear—oh, don't you look pretty!"

Sally, in a bright pink sweater and cream skirt, had got the whole lunching-with-Michael's-mother ordeal exactly right, Katie thought bitterly. Simple, fun, and, as Mrs. Gwynne had observed, remarkably pretty. Katie's black dress was too formal and proper by comparison. Not to mention that, in her current emaciated state, Katie gave it about as much shape as a wire coathanger. She felt skinny and overdressed by comparison.

"Oh, how nice, you're wearing the earrings Jude and I got you!" Sally said cheerfully, coming over to kiss Katie hello. "I'm so glad you like them!"

Katie put up one hand automatically to touch the parrot earrings. It was a reflex, and as soon as she touched one she realized that she was fighting an impulse to tear them out and grind them underfoot. Sally and Jude's card had got detached from the box in the scrum of the party, and Katie had assumed, seeing the earrings, that they had been given to her by an old friend who knew how much she liked birds. She loved the earrings. Or she had, until she realized their provenance. Somehow, Sally reading her tastes so well seemed almost the worst injury of all—worse almost than Sally turning up here for lunch, on what was supposed to be Katie's official introduction to Michael's mother, and being greeted in a way that clearly showed what a frequent and welcome guest she was. *Bitch*, Katie thought viciously. *I wish I could stick her parrots up her stupid arse.* She pressed her hands over her stomach as if reminding herself of what she had and Sally didn't.

"Shall we go through?" Mrs. Gwynne consulted her watch again. "It's just time to take the lasagne out. Oh, and I have some really good news! Guess who's coming to visit?"

Michael was already in the dining room, pouring red wine for everyone but Katie. "Sorry, sweetie, none for you," he said with an apologetic hug, indicating her glass of Diet Coke.

"Oh, she can have a little wine as soon as her stomach settles down," Mrs. Gwynne said cheerfully. "My mother was told to drink beer all through her pregnancy. Everyone did in those days."

"You'd better avoid it now, though," Michael said doubtfully to Katie. "Don't you think? Even if it didn't come up again, you'd be pissed as a fart on two sips. You haven't had solid food in days."

Katie looked wistfully at the wine. There was nothing she would have loved more than to dilute the violent resentment she felt toward Sally by knocking back a couple of glasses. But she knew Michael was right. The wine would go straight to her head. She imagined herself in a drunken tirade, tearing out Sally's earrings and throwing them on the table, shouting obscenities at her, and giggled at the thought.

"What?" Michael said.

"Oh, nothing," she said demurely. "I was just imagining me getting drunk, that's all."

She smiled at Sally, feeling better. After all, she, Katie, was the one carrying Michael's baby. Sally had had her chance with him and blown it. Katie was the daughter-in-law here, the one about to have Mrs. Gwynne's grandchild. Sally was just a sad old ex who hadn't known how to let go. Katie reproached herself for the pettiness of these thoughts, but she couldn't help them.

Michael dropped a kiss on top of Katie's head and pulled up the chair next to her. Katie reached for his hand and clasped it tightly, holding it on top of the table, so Sally could see. God, Katie realized, she was behaving like a six-year-old who was crowing because she had possession of her sister's favorite teddy bear.

Mrs. Gwynne cut an enormous, dripping piece of rich, meaty-scented lasagne, slid it onto a plate and handed it to Michael.

"Lion's share for Mikey," Sally said, laughing at him. "Sorry, Stephanie, you were saying something about a visitor?"

"Oh yes, my news!" Mrs. Gwynne said, reminded of it. "You'll never guess! She rang me just a few days ago—she wants to come to London to go round some galleries, and thought she might be able to stay here—well, of course I said yes . . ."

She handed Sally a plate of lasagne.

"Sofie!" she finished. "She'll be here at the beginning of next week! Won't that be fun? I told her about you and the baby, Katie, and of course she's very curious to meet you—"

Michael's fork clattered against his plate. He hadn't quite dropped it, but the involuntary chink of metal against china was loud enough to interrupt what his mother was saying.

"Who's Sofie?" Katie said blankly.

The room went eerily quiet. Mrs. Gwynne and Sally, she realized, were staring at her. And then, as if on some unspoken signal, they both turned to look at Michael. He was looking down at his lasagne and didn't meet any of their eyes, not even Katie's. But she noticed immediately that the tips of his ears were bright red.

Chapter *Eight*

"*Y*ou mean she didn't *know?*" Jude said incredulously. "How could she not *know?*"

"They haven't been going out that long," Sally said. "And you don't get the full Sofie myth at first. Michael waits a while before dropping it on you."

"How long did it take with you?"

"Couple of months. Katie was probably just about due for it, and then of course he got distracted by, oh, I dunno, Getting Her Pregnant."

The capitals on Sally's last three words came as clearly down the phone line as if Sally had been there in person, writing them on a blackboard.

"God, I wonder what he's told her," Sally continued. "Now, I mean. Post-lunch-embarrassing-moment."

"The usual, probably," Jude suggested. "I mean, doesn't he do that with everyone? Lizzie and Wendy told you he said exactly the same thing to them as he did to you."

"Oh yeah. He tells everyone the same Sofie story. First love, eighteen years old, blah blah blah, heart thoroughly broken, didn't think he could ever trust a woman again, more blah blah

blah, big flashing warning sign and alarm sirens going whoop whoop whoop, melting gaze, heavy metal doors slamming down all around you as the trap closes, your heart bleeds for him and you resolve to Be The One Who Will Never Let Him Down . . . and it's only afterward that you realize no matter how much he said he loved you, he never talked about the future, let alone telling you he *wanted* you to Be The One, etc., etc., but by that time *your* heart's thoroughly broken and the mention of Sofie's name brings you out in hives, blah blah fucking blah."

"Oh *Sal,*" Jude said in sympathy before she could stop herself. She too had heard this before, from Sally, and more than once; but there was something about Sally's dispassionate summary that caught at her heartstrings now. Knowing how much Sally would hate her pity, even involuntary, Jude managed to follow up almost instantly with a: "Poor little Katie. To think she's got all that to go through."

To her great relief, Sally focused instantly on that.

"I *know,*" she said. "But I was wondering if he might have diluted it down for Katie, with her being pregnant. It's a different situation than it was for the rest of us."

"I dunno. From what you said about his reaction when Sofie was mentioned," Jude pointed out acutely, "it sounds like he couldn't have watered it down."

"Mmn. You're probably right. I do feel sorry for her."

This was an out-and-out lie. Sally envied Katie more than she had ever envied anyone in her life. Not only the pregnancy, but Michael's reaction to it. Who could have known that Michael would take to impending fatherhood so well? He was already reading baby books and working out how to convert the box room into a little nursery. If it had always been that easy . . . if the announcement that you were pregnant was enough to convert Michael into a devoted long-term boyfriend . . . would Sally, she wondered, have thrown away her pill packet and waited for her first missed period?

No, she thought. Impossible. Horribly practical thoughts flashed through her head: she would have had to pop one pill out a day and flush it down the toilet. Michael would have noticed if the packet was missing from its customary place on the shelf above the sink. Did pills even flush down the toilet? Maybe she would have had to carry one through to the swing bin in the kitchen every morning and bury it at the bottom of the rubbish.

It wouldn't have worked then, anyway. Sally had been Katie's age when she went out with Michael, and there was no way that she had been ready then to take on the responsibility of a child. Though it had broken her heart when Michael left her, it was him she wanted, not his baby, and the idea of getting pregnant to keep him would never have entered her head. Or, to be more accurate, it was Michael as her wonderful, incredible-in-bed, confident lover she wanted then, when she was young and wild, not Michael as domesticated parent and husband. Now it was different. Sally had settled down. She had a flat of her own and no one to share it with. The idea of moving across the street into Michael's, painting the box room in bright primary colors, made the pieces of her still-broken heart melt into her rib cage with a hot guilty pleasure. No, she corrected herself. She wouldn't move into Michael's. Sally had property too: they could sell both their places and afford something bigger, with a proper bedroom for the baby . . .

"So when does Sofie arrive?" Jude was saying.

Sally was glad she wasn't there in person with Jude, who would have immediately spotted that she was drifting away into daydreams. She pulled herself back with an effort. It was hard; these thoughts were constantly swirling round her mind nowadays. She even dreamed them sometimes. "Next week," she said.

"Bloody hell. I can't wait to meet her," Jude said with relish.

"Me neither," Sally responded. It was true. She had always had a burning curiosity to see the mythical Sofie for herself. But she couldn't help envying Jude a little, however, for being less directly involved, and thus able to enjoy the drama of it so much more.

"So how did Katie look? I mean, what did everyone say at the time?" Jude probed.

"She looked poleaxed," Sally said, cheering up slightly at the recollection. Just before Stephanie had mentioned Sofie's name, Katie had given Sally a very smug, possessive smile, and Sally had taken great, if wicked pleasure, in seeing Katie so stunned. "Michael finally said, 'Oh, Katie, haven't I told you about Sofie? She's an ex of mine from years and years ago. It'll be great to see her.' And then Stephanie changed the subject, very tactfully, but that made it worse, of course, because Katie could see what a big deal it was because Stephanie was treading on eggshells . . . Shit." Her attention had been drawn to her computer screen, which was flashing with an urgent incoming work message. "Got to go. See you tonight? You at home?"

"Yup. Want to have dinner? I've got a big frozen pizza."

"No pepperoni?"

"Sal, you *know* I never get pepperoni because you won't eat it, do me a favor . . ."

"OK, see you later. Got to go."

Sally hung up. Jude clicked her headset to OFF and noticed someone approaching her desk. She looked up the length of smart gray suit, maroon shirt, dull burgundy silk tie—he must have had a meeting with clients today—to Paul's shining fair head. She knew exactly why he was here. It was an open-plan office, and Jude only had to mention Sally's name on the phone to have Paul wander over. Like the CIA listening stations that were tuned to pick up linked words like "president," "capitalist imperialist," and "blow him to pieces" in phone calls all over the world, Paul's antennae were tuned to any variation of "Sally." He had it bad—so bad he wasn't capable of making the slightest effort to conceal it.

"So how's your friend Sally doing?" were the first words out of his mouth. He fiddled with his tie and did his best to sound casual, but it was as unconvincing as a soap actress auditioning to play Desdemona.

Jude stared at him thoughtfully. This was the third time that Paul had tried to talk to her about Sally. He had obtained Sally's number from her the Monday morning after the party and, Jude knew from Sally, rung her several times, only to get either the answering machine or a polite brush-off from Sally herself. So he had turned his attention to Jude instead, hoping to pick up any useful Sally wooing tips from her. And Jude had basically ignored him, because Paul was no longer of any use as a stalking horse. Even if Michael did become so insanely jealous that he realized Sally was the woman of his life, what good would it do, with Katie pregnant? What kind of a happy ending would that be?

If Paul had been quickly discouraged, Jude wouldn't even have considered a Plan B. But now she thought: Well, what harm would it do? Michael's going to be a father. He and Katie'll probably get married once the baby comes. Sally can't spend the rest of her life waiting for him anymore. She needs someone else—someone as persistent as Paul, who doesn't give up easily . . .

In a flick of Jude's pen, she rewrote Paul's role as Transitional Boyfriend. She would just have to make sure she didn't give Paul carte blanche to pursue Sally to the point of insanity. She needed to spur him on, to give him a sense of mission, but she didn't want him seeing himself as James Bond, License To Stalk.

"She's OK," Jude said, "but she's a bit distracted at the moment . . ."

"Oh dear." Paul perched on her desk, looking concerned, having picked up the uncertainty in her tone. "Is she all right?"

"*Well,*" Jude began, about to launch into a bowdlerized version of recent events, tailored to make Paul feel that Sally needed rescuing. He was just the kind of man who would love the opportunity to saddle up his white charger for a damsel in distress. Briefly, she felt guilty at the way she was using Paul. It wasn't kind. She was throwing him into a snake pit. But then, faint heart never won fair lady, did it? And besides, it was Sally whom Jude cared about. It might be cruel of her to manipulate Paul in this way, but she couldn't look after everyone. Paul would just have to take his chances.

Chapter
Nine

*K*atie had put her foot down for the first time with Michael. He had wanted to go without her, and she had absolutely refused to let him. She had made a huge effort with her clothes and hair, even putting on some lipstick. She was still nauseous, but the actual vomiting was gradually becoming less frequent, thanks in part to the flat Diet Coke, which seemed to be helping. So she had put on a few of the pounds she had lost, and looked much healthier. Her skin was a little less sallow, too, she thought. The red lipstick didn't look too grotesque.

She fidgeted from foot to foot, looking at the clock every few minutes, even though she knew it wouldn't help. They had been here for over an hour. Two trains had arrived already and they had watched all the passengers get off, Katie with her heart beating madly, as if she were waiting to meet her nemesis. Well, perhaps she was. Michael too was unusually excited; he couldn't stand still. Fidgeting like Katie wasn't enough for him; he was pacing up and down the long waiting area, hands shoved in his pockets.

She looked at him striding back and forth and, to reassure herself, called up all the lovely things he had said and done recently. Stroking her belly, telling her he couldn't wait for it to grow, laughing at her when she worried about getting too fat and unattractive for him; he had pushed her back on the bed and gone down on her till she came and came, and then kissed her, with the taste of her still on his mouth, telling her that he would always love the way she smelled and tasted and felt, she would always be his Katie, who was having his baby. Reading extracts from the baby books out to her with great seriousness, almost like a schoolboy with a new craze. It wasn't even the baby stuff that reassured her the most: it was all the things that had made her love him from the beginning, the way he had been, immediately, so physically affectionate, hugging and cuddling her all the time, with none of the embarrassment about being seen embracing in public she usually expected from men. Being unable to stay away from her, right from the start, ringing her all the time, wanting her with him, giving her a key to his flat almost as soon as they got back to London. How easy it was to be with him. She had never had such instant relaxation with a man before, as if she had known him all her life, just not met him till that moment. And he was great with her friends, too. She had told Michael jokingly that he would be able to get on with a dead dog if she introduced them. Michael said he drew the line at maggots.

Katie checked the clock for the hundredth time. Five past four. Then she looked over at the display board. Yup, another half-hour had passed; the next train had just arrived. She felt suddenly sick to her stomach with anticipation. What if . . . *What if, what if, what if?* she repeated crossly. What good did wondering do? She would just have to wait and deal with whatever the situation turned out to be.

"Katie! Next train in! Maybe it'll be this one!" Michael called.

"It's about bloody time," Katie muttered. "I know it was supposed to be the three o'clock."

"What?"

"Nothing." She forced herself to blow him a kiss.

The first passengers were beginning to trickle through the barriers of passport control. As before, Katie scanned them anxiously, imagining the worst. God, some of these women were impossibly glamorous. She rejected all the ones with smart jackets and silk scarves tied around their necks, or the streaky blond clotheshorses in tight trousers and spiky heels. But even with those eliminated, there were plenty of petite, striking brunettes. In miniskirts, trendy jeans, bright suede jackets, and cute little pull-on woolly hats, they came out one by one, carrying woven shoulderbags, pulling dinky patterned suitcases, pretty, smiling, and confident, each of them Katie's worst nightmare.

As soon as Katie realized she was pregnant, she had begun to notice all the other women who were too, all the bulging tummies and swollen breasts and mothers with squirming infants in strollers. Suddenly they were everywhere, a pregnant army multiplying by the day, till it felt like she couldn't leave the house without three enormously swollen women waiting on the front steps to greet her merrily. Now, watching the prospects from Paris stream out onto the station forecourt, all she could see were endless ranks of possible brunettes. Her gaze immediately discarded anyone who didn't fit the profile. And yet she completely failed to pick out the right one. Just as she was staring with a mixture of envy and hostility at a particularly pretty girl with her dark hair in bunches and a big portfolio slung under her arm, Michael shot forward to embrace another girl whom Katie hadn't even noticed. They hugged for what seemed like hours. As they finally pulled back, the girl's face came into view. Katie was transfixed with shock.

"Katie! This is Sofie! My two favorite girls!" Michael cried happily, slinging Sofie's big, shabby canvas duffle over his shoulder. It had dwarfed Sofie, but on Michael it looked like a handbag. He pulled Sofie over toward Katie.

"Sof, this is Katie! God, it's so great to see you again!"

He enfolded Sofie in another enormous hug.

"Hello, Katie," Sofie said when Michael finally released her. "It is very nice to meet you."

She leaned in and planted two little kisses on Katie's cheeks. Katie mumbled something back. She hoped it sounded friendly; she had no idea what she was saying. The sight of Sofie had left her speechless.

Chapter
Ten

"*Y*ou look great," Scott said. "Hey, I brought you these."

Shyly he handed her a bouquet of flowers. From the garage down the road, Jude was willing to bet; she recognized the paper in which they were wrapped, a gaudy, generic red and white print. Still, where else was he going to get flowers from around here? The Caledonian Road wasn't exactly full of glossy floral boutiques where they custom-designed bouquets for you. Scott was lucky he hadn't been mugged on the five-minute walk from the petrol station to Jude's flat. Carrying something as soppy as a bunch of flowers in this area marked you out as an easy target.

"They're really pretty," she said. "God, I know I've got a vase somewhere . . ."

She went into the kitchen to search through the cabinets. If she had been Sally, she would have three or four to hand; Sally was the House Beautiful member of the partnership. Jude was almost about to stick them, in desperation, into an empty wine bottle when an association of ideas reminded her that her mum had left an old glass carafe under the sink, which Jude had never got round to throwing away. Triumphantly she brought it out, rinsed it with detergent—it was both dusty and slimy—and popped the flowers in it. They didn't look as good as they had in the bouquet. Jude wasn't much at flower-arranging. Not enough posh genes, probably. If she'd been christened Camilla, she would have known how to arrange flowers at birth.

She carried the flowers back into the sitting room and put them on the coffee table.

"Thanks," she said, kissing Scott. His arms tightened around her and she tangled her hands into his hair, soft and newly washed for her benefit. To her surprise she realized that Scott was kissing her deeper and deeper, his tongue slipping past her lips, his groin pressing hard into hers. One of his hands slid up to the back of her head, holding her mouth against his, while the other was moving down to her buttocks, squeezing them, keeping her, there too, exactly how he wanted her. Jude responded with great enthusiasm. Scott was usually a touch repressed about this kind of thing; passionate though he was in bed, their kisses on greeting and leaving each other were often quick flicks on the lips rather than this kind of deep, thorough embrace, surely much more appropriate for a couple who hadn't been going out that long and still couldn't spend a night together without having sex. She used her considerable strength to grind herself back into him, feeling her insides beginning to loosen, her underwear dampening. Scott tasted deliciously of mouthwash; he must have gargled, or had a mint, just before arriving here.

"Fancy a quickie before we go out?" he whispered against her mouth. "Right here?"

You mean "on the sofa," Jude thought sardonically. You'd

break your back if you tried to fuck me right here. Still, she appreciated the thought.

He bent his head to kiss her neck exactly where she was most sensitive, which drew a gasp of pleasure.

"Ah—oh, Scott—"

He was now licking and blowing on the place which, he had recently discovered, sent Jude into ecstasies.

"Come on," he muttered into her neck.

"What's got into you?" Jude gasped. It hadn't been what she had meant to say, which was something along the lines of "Oh God, that's so *good!*" The exclamation just popped out from nowhere.

Scott paused for a moment. "I missed you," he mumbled, sounding embarrassed. "We haven't seen each other for a bit— I've been working—and—well, I missed you."

He kissed her mouth again, hard, and Jude felt herself flushing with pleasure. Not just physical reaction, either. This was the first time Scott had ever admitted missing her. It felt like payback for all the times she had moped by the phone, waiting for it to ring and knowing that it wouldn't, because she was waiting, whereas if she were off on a date with somebody else it would be ringing frantically enough to vibrate its little buzzer off.

After their fight at the party, she and Scott had made up quickly enough. Jude had been embarrassed and apologetic, but Scott had barely considered that she had done anything she needed to say sorry for: people got a bit silly and argumentative sometimes when they drank, was his attitude, and if it was only a one-off, there was no need even to mention it. He had been deeply cool, in fact. And now he was actually saying that he'd missed her. Trumpet fanfares rang in her head. She knew not to make a big deal about it, though.

"I missed you too," she said into his mouth. She pulled off his leather jacket and dropped it on the floor behind him, where it fell with a heavy thud, jingling with the keys in his pockets.

"Yeah?" Scott said enthusiastically, taking this for a green light on the quickie front. He started unbuttoning her shirt.

"Shit, no, I don't know—what's the time?" Jude mumbled, trying to turn Scott's wrist around so she could see his watch.

"Time to be doing it on the carpet," Scott said, sliding the watch-wearing hand under her shirt, which performed the double function of not letting her see the display and also distracting her thoroughly. He squeezed her breast gently but firmly till she moaned.

"No, we're supposed to be there at eight—"

"It's just a drink, we can be a bit late—"

"No, it's dinner—"

"It's *what?*" Scott's hand froze on her breast.

"It's dinner—Katie's cooking—"

"Ah, fuck!" The hand slipped down and out of her shirt. Scott's face was a picture of disappointment. "I thought it was just you and me this evening—I mean, I thought we were just dropping in there for a quick one—"

"Like what you're doing right now?" Jude teased. "Dropping in for a quick one—"

"Well, if we don't have time—"

He looked so crestfallen that Jude melted. Besides, he was being nice, though he didn't want to be; nobly renouncing sex on the carpet because it might make them late for dinner with her friends, whom, as she knew perfectly well, he could happily have lived without seeing for the rest of his life. It was the combination of Scott's niceness and her now raging libido that made her pick up his hand, slide it back on top of her breast—lifting her bra away from her skin so he could make full contact—and say: "Better make it quick, OK? None of your half-hours on the job—"

"I promise . . ." Scott sighed, his hands shooting round her back to undo her bra. "I promise, five minutes at the most, in and out, no messing about—"

"I'll hold you to that—" Jude was unzipping his trousers.

"Aah . . ." Scott moaned, the unmistakable sound of a man whose penis is being gripped for the first time that session by the hands of his lover. "Aah, Jude, you can hold me any way you want . . ."

"You two are so late," Sally said, mock-disapprovingly, holding the door open for them. It was impossible not to know what they had just been doing; Jude was glowing with post-coital languor, her hair tangled and her mascara smudged under her eyes, while even Scott's usual calm, controlled expression had softened into something more relaxed, maybe even a little smug. And their clothes looked as if they had been thrown onto them from a considerable distance away.

"Scott was just telling me how he thinks I ought to wear skirts more," Jude said, keeping as poker-faced as she could.

"I do actually think they'd suit you," Scott said defensively. "You have nice legs."

Jude and Sally's eyes met, brimming with amusement, an expression in which many things were combined. Mirth at the blindness of men, for a start: Jude's legs famously went straight down from her thighs to her feet like tree trunks. They weren't large, her legs; they simply didn't go in and out the way most people's did. Thus they looked fine in trousers, and weren't too noticeable when she was completely naked, or in a swimsuit. But a skirt, no matter where the hem fell, indicated the problem inexorably, making her legs look like twin stumps. That Scott hadn't spotted Jude's lack of ankles yet indicated a typical kind of male shortsightedness, but also a niceness about him, for which Sally and Jude's look also conveyed appreciation. He wasn't one of those awful men who pointed out all your weak spots to make himself feel better.

And finally, of course, the two of them were amused by the knowledge of how Scott's comment had originally been made; skirts were much better for quickies. Even if you were wearing tights. Sally and Jude knew each other so well by now their connection felt almost psychic sometimes.

"We brought some wine," Jude offered, holding out a bottle.

"Mmn, lovely," Sally said sarcastically, examining the label. "Isn't this the one someone brought you for that party you had last year? And we never drank it because he said he got it from the petrol station?"

Jude devoutly hoped that Scott didn't realize she knew where his flowers had come from. "Is dinner ready?" she said quickly, to change the subject. "We're starving."

"I bet you are. Hi, Scott," Sally added, remembering that she hadn't greeted him properly. Sally's good middle-class manners always amused Jude considerably. "No, we're just getting drunk—that is, me and Mikey are. Katie's in the kitchen panicking because all the guests are late."

"God, I'm sorry," Scott said contritely, taking off his jacket and hanging it on a peg by the door. "It was my fault. Jude said we were running late."

The sight of him removing a piece of clothing sent a thrill of remembered sexual excitement through Jude, like a silent string being plucked. She hoped dinner wouldn't run too late. She was looking forward to sex with Scott all over again as a nightcap.

"No problem," Sally said, leading them through to the sitting room, where Michael's rickety old dining table had been set up in the center. Katie's decorating magic had been at work again; the room was soft with candles, and a glass bowl in the center of the white-covered table gleamed with shiny stones and floating white flowers.

Jude looked around eagerly for Sofie, but she was nowhere to be seen. Only Michael, rising from his favorite big squishy armchair to kiss her. He hugged Jude with as much enthusiasm as if he hadn't seen her for years, and nodded at Scott over her shoulder. "Hi," he said.

"All right," Scott responded. After that they both took a drink and pretended that the other one didn't exist.

"Sofie's gone AWOL," Sally announced. "She left Stephanie's over an hour ago and she's not answering her phone. We think she went in the wrong direction from King's Cross."

"It's really easy from King's Cross, though," Katie called from the kitchen, "the bus stop is just where you come out of the tube . . ."

Michael waved all this away. Clearly they had been in the middle of this discussion before Jude and Scott arrived. He was, Jude noticed, disproportionately anxious. After all, Sofie was in her late thirties, spoke English, and must be able to take care of herself.

"Perhaps we should just start eating," Jude suggested, disingenuously, as she had the post-coital munchies and her stomach was rumbling thunderously. "I'm sure she'd hate to think of us all sitting round waiting while the food gets cold."

"Oh, *could* we?" Katie popped out of the kitchen, wrapped in Michael's barbecuing apron, which went round her one-and-a-half times, making her look like a child dressing up in her parents' clothes. "I'm so worried the lasagne will be burned if I keep it in the oven any longer—"

Just then the doorbell rang, luckily for Katie, as Michael had been about to object fiercely to this procedure. He rushed to answer the door and Katie hung back, her gaze nipping from Jude's face to Sally's, desperately curious to know whether their first reaction to Sofie would tally with her own.

It was like the moment in a Hollywood blockbuster when the star, after twenty minutes of carefully calculated build-up, is finally discovered, dressed as a cowboy or a diner waitress or a convict; after the frisson of seeing that famous face smeared in mud, or under a uniform cap, but still breathtakingly lit by star quality, the audience relaxes into their padded seats, reaching for their soft drinks, secure in the knowledge that now the Star has arrived on screen the story will kick into full throttle. Katie, in the kitchen doorway, had a view of the entire scene. Deep down, she was furious with herself for feeling like an extra. Here she was, living at Michael's, pregnant with his baby, dinner cooked by her in the oven: how much more in possession could she be? She had even managed not to snap at Sally for answering the door to Jude and Scott, or at Michael for letting her (Sally had said that she recognized Jude's ring, which, considering that they were in Michael's flat, had nearly caused the top of Katie's head to explode).

And yet Sofie's entrance immediately reduced Katie to a bit part in what was now her own home.

Jude and Sally were gawping at Sofie, who was kissing Michael neatly on either cheek, fending him off with one small hand when he went for his patented big hug. She pulled back and took off her leather jacket, which, besides being too big for her, looked as old and battered as if it had spent the past twenty years being thrown loose into the cargo hold of one airplane after another. Michael rushed to take it from her.

She looked around the room, but not with curiosity—rather as if she were placing all the bodies within it, like the furniture, so she could see where to walk without tripping over someone.

"This is Sofie, everyone," Michael announced proudly, coming to stand behind her, his hands on her shoulders. This made Sofie look even tinier than she was. And skinnier. French-women might be legendarily slim, but Sofie was almost gaunt. Her cheeks were sunken hollows, her bones looked brittle as a chicken's, and under her eyes were big dark bruised circles, signifying bad circulation, or possibly malnutrition.

"Hi, Sofie, I'm Sally," Sally said, stepping forward, and unsure whether to shake Sofie's hand or kiss those fragile cheeks. Sofie offered no help; she just stood and gazed at Sally as if she were an exhibit in a museum. Finally Sally planted a couple of quick near air-kisses on Sofie and stepped back.

Jude didn't think she was capable of doing the double-cheek Continental kiss, especially if Sofie wasn't even helping. Jude was a working-class girl from North London, for God's sake. And she knew Scott would rather die.

"I'm Jude, and this is Scott," she said with a smile. She had been tempted to say "my boyfriend," but restrained herself womanfully. She didn't want to push things, after all. "Nice to meet you. We've heard so much about you."

"*Ah oui?*" Sofie said. But she didn't seem that interested in finding out exactly what.

"Sofie, a drink!" Michael said bluffly, pouring her a red wine. "And dinner's ready! Shall we all sit down?"

"Did you get lost coming from the station?" Sally asked, pulling up her chair. "We thought that was what might have happened."

Thank God for Sally, Jude thought. Without her to make some conversation they would have been lost.

"No, *pas du tout*," Sofie informed her. "It is that I have not been to this quarter before, and I am interested. I walk round and see the people and the buildings."

"God, you must be the only person to find King's Cross interesting!" Jude said. "Everyone who lives here just keeps their head down and gets out as fast as possible."

"*Au contraire*. As I say, I am interested," Sofie said, sipping her wine. "I am interested in every place, no importance how sordid. I like to look, always. It is for my art."

That, naturally, threw a wrench into the conversation. Not

only had Sofie called their area of residence sordid—which was very different from someone who lived here, like Jude, saying it was a hellhole—but, being English, they were all made deeply uncomfortable with people mentioning their art casually over the dinner table. A pause ensued, filled by Katie coming through from the kitchen with an enormous serving dish of lasagne.

"God, Katie, how much did you make?" Michael exclaimed. "Even I couldn't eat half of that!"

"I think I got into a muddle with the quantities," Katie said, visibly frazzled. "I doubled some by mistake, so then I had to double it all." She looked at Sally. "It's the recipe from Michael's mum's—Stephanie's"—she added quickly, defiantly, to show Sally that she, too, called Michael's mother by her first name—"cleaning lady. The one Michael likes for Sunday lunch. I thought it would be the perfect thing to make."

"Lovely," Sally said politely, catching Jude's eye and wondering if they were both thinking the same thing. When they first met Katie, she had been a lively, fun girl-about-town, bubbly and bright, just as a twenty-four-year-old should be. Now she seemed hell-bent on transforming herself into a parody of a fifties housewife, cooking her man's favorite recipes while his bun rose in her oven. Katie was trying much too hard.

Katie heaved the enormous aluminium dish onto the table. Sally recognized the container as the roasting dish Michael had bought, years ago, when he had planned to cook Christmas dinner and then forgotten to buy a turkey. To her knowledge, this was the first time it had ever been used.

"It looks very nice," Scott observed.

"It's a bit burned on top, I think," Katie said, casting a vindictive look in Sofie's direction. "It was in the oven for ages longer than it should have been."

It was a wasted gambit. Sofie clearly had no sense of any personal responsibility toward the slightly scorched lasagne. She just sat there, calmly, next to Michael, sipping at her wine, her thoughts seeming many miles removed from anything as mundane as food.

Jude was baffled by her appearance. She had always assumed that Frenchwomen were chic. Or that, if not chic, they were elegantly wasted, like Jeanne Moreau or Anouk Aimée, with a strong sense of personal style. *This,* she thought, was the matrix? *This* was what had prevented Michael from getting seriously involved with another woman ever since? Sofie's dark hair was lank, straggly, and pushed back casually behind her ears. She wore no makeup but some mascara and a dark red lipstick that made her skin look even sallower and her under-eye circles darker than they were. And her clothes! She was wearing a long-sleeved dark green T-shirt under a sort of pinafore dress made of black crêpe which hung painfully off her sharp collarbones. Over the flat front of the dress hung a string of green beads which looked as if she had bought them for 20p—or the equivalent in Euros—at a jumble sale. Jude would never previously have believed that the French had jumble sales; she would have assumed they were above that kind of shabbiness. Well, with Sofie before her, she would have believed that they had car boot sales as well. That was how awful Sofie looked. If this was an example of what the young, avant-garde French artist about town was wearing, Jude was more than ever glad to have been born on this side of the Channel.

"So tell us about your art, Sofie," Sally finally managed. She cast a resentful glance at Jude and Scott, who were bearing none of the burden of this conversation whatsoever. Sally hated awkward silences; her parents had trained her to talk fluently to adults from an early age and held her responsible whenever a pause ensued. Sally would have disemboweled herself with a butter knife rather than sit through a long, uncomfortable silence. At least that would give everyone else something to talk about.

It was a clumsy question, she knew. Any self-respecting English artist would have curled up in embarrassment rather than respond to it. But it turned out to be the only subject in which Sofie was remotely interested.

"I make drawings of myself," she said, with more enthusiasm than she had previously shown. "Mostly naked. In different positions and in front of different landscapes. It is a constant attempt to explore the meaning of my . . ."—she reached for a word—*"femininité,* and to make a comment on the mystery of the woman's body."

Katie, cutting into the lasagne, paused momentarily to favor Sofie with a glance that labeled her so clearly a pretentious wanker that Jude, intercepting it, nearly burst out laughing.

"Is that why you walk around different, um, areas?" Sally persisted bravely, struggling hard with the impulse to brain Jude, who was snuffling next to her, with the closest wine bottle. "To put them in your drawings?"

"No, *pas du tout,*" Sofie answered, staring at Sally as if she were a moron. "I like to experience different places to have them enter my subconscious. I keep myself constantly open to new . . ."—she searched for the word—"sensations. But I must remain always passive. That is the . . . *qualité éssentiel*—"

"Essential quality," Michael supplied helpfully.

"Oui, the essential quality of the artist. The passivity."

Since nobody had anything remotely socially acceptable to say to this, it was fortunate that a distraction was provided by the first serving of lasagne, sliding off Katie's serving spatula and onto the plate with a series of squashy, liquid slurps that could have served as the soundtrack for a hard-hitting documentary about Irritable Bowel Syndrome. Katie stared at the plateful in horror. The lasagne was leaking as if it had been punctured. A watery pale red juice was already filling up the bottom of the plate.

"I thought I'd *over*cooked it!" she wailed. "It was in the oven for so long!"

It did seem particularly unfair that the lasagne should have been burned on top and runny underneath. Jude, whose cooking skills were confined to boiling pasta and shoving frozen pizzas into the oven, took this fiasco as a clear lesson never to go trying recipes that were clearly out of her league.

"I think it might have been doubling the recipe," Michael said unhelpfully. "Maybe you did get some of the quantities wrong."

Katie was on the verge of tears. Her face, already flushed from standing over the oven, now had a hectic spot of red on each cheek, and her breath was coming fast. This was not one of those evenings when you can laugh gaily at a culinary disaster and reach for the takeaway pizza menu; there was more loss of face involved in this for Katie than the entire island of Hong Kong trying simultaneously to honor their ancestors.

Sally, as always, came to the rescue. "I'm sure it'll taste lovely!" she said, bravely commandeering the first piece. "It's just a bit—juicier than normal, that's all. Come on, Katie, I can't start before everyone else is served, and I'm starving."

Katie's spatula-holding hand, which had been shaking ominously, paused, steadied itself, and then dipped into the enormous tray of lasagne once more. Her resentment of Sally was growing exponentially, however. How dare Sally be the one to rescue her? Every muscle in her body was trembling: she wanted nothing more than to flick a giant serving of over-juicy lasagne into Sally's pink-embroidered lap.

"Remember to give Mikey loads," Sally added, giving him a spiky smile. Katie wasn't the only person at the table nourishing increasingly deep feelings of resentment. "It's his favorite dish.'

Chapter
Eleven

"*O*h my God, what a *disaster*—"

"I *know*. I could barely get that down, it was like eating pasta soup—"

"Lucky there was loads of ice cream—is anyone still hungry, by the way?"

Jude was, actually, but not quite enough to look like a pig in front of Scott by scarfing down biscuits. Besides, she was still hoping for more sex imminently, and knew from misguided past experiences that trying to make passionate love with a full stomach could lead to all sorts of personal humiliations.

"I'm OK," Scott said.

Jude knew he wasn't, really. He would much rather have gone straight back to Jude's than drop into Sally's for a post-mortem on the evening. If he and Jude had been more estab-lished as a couple, it would have been easy enough for him to say he was going to watch the football, say, or the news at Jude's, while she and Sally enthusiastically rehashed the dinner party in all its gory details. But if Jude suggested that now, she would seem to be taking him for granted. It couldn't be done. Scott would just have to sweat it out. The thought of skipping the gossip with Sally never crossed her mind.

"How *did* she get the lasagne like that?" Jude marveled.

"Probably too many tinned tomatoes," Scott said. "That's the most common problem with lasagne. People panic because they think there isn't enough sauce, so they chuck in another tin at the last moment. Never works."

"I didn't know you could cook!" Jude marveled.

Scott looked embarrassed. "I've been so busy these last few months . . ." he mumbled. "I haven't cooked you dinner yet, have I?"

"No," Jude said firmly, feeling cheated.

"We all finished our lasagne!" Sally announced triumphantly. "We are so good! I can't believe we all finished our lasagne!"

Sally, Jude realized, was drunker than she had previously thought. Well, Sally had heroically borne the weight of the dinner party on her slender shoulders; if she needed to self-medicate with alcohol to help her in her efforts, Jude wasn't going to throw the first stone.

"Michael had seconds," Scott observed.

"Mikey always has seconds," Sally confirmed. "Except with women, of course. Mikey doesn't like seconds of his girlfriends. He wants new"—she hunted for a word—"new dishes all the time."

"Did you notice that Sofie didn't even *touch* her lasagne?" Jude said.

"So *rude,*" Sally said. "I couldn't *believe* it."

"No, zank you, I do not eat murch in ze evening, I weel just blow ze smoke of my Gauloises in everyone's face eef that is fine weez you," Jude mimicked.

It would have been bad enough if Sofie had declined to eat before the serving of lasagne had been put in front of her; but the look she had given the plateful, the way she had pushed it, delicately but firmly, to one side and requested an ashtray, would, in Jude's opinion, have been grounds for Katie upending the entire runny tray of half-cooked pasta over Sofie's lank hair. It had needed a wash, anyway.

"And what about her *clothes?*" Jude continued.

"I *know,*" Sally agreed, leaning forward with the deeply serious expression her pretty face always assumed when fashion was the subject under discussion. "She looked like a refugee from a war zone. That *pinafore.*"

"Those *beads!*"

"I know!"

"And her hair was all greasy . . ."

"Do you think," Sally asked, her voice growing even more serious, her lean forward more pronounced, "do you think she was gorgeous once? When Mikey first knew her?"

Jude pondered this. It didn't take long. "No," she said definitively. "If she had a bit more weight on her it would help . . . but no, I don't think so."

Jude watched the wobbling glass in Sally's hand with considerable nervousness. At least it was only half-full. That was the plus side. The minus was that the other half of it was in Sally.

"Becaushe"—Sally was slurring now—"becaushe I jusht don't see what Mikey ever shaw in her. Do you? Do you, Jude? She's sho—I thought she was going to be incredibly gorgeous,

didn't you? Incredibly shophisticated . . . lots of black eyeliner . . ."

Sally's head was as unsteady on her neck as one of those
wobbly dogs you still saw hanging from truckers' rear-view mirrors, and her eyes were glazed with red wine varnish, but she
was still one of the prettiest girls Jude had ever seen. Jude knew
exactly what Sally meant. She, too, had expected something
devastatingly glamorous from the mythical Sofie. Something
that would explain everything about Michael's failure to con-
nect for any length of time with all the women who had been
and gone through his love life. Out of all the ones Jude had
met, Sally was unquestionably the prettiest, the best put
together; and though that was a shallow way to choose a girlfriend, Sally had everything else, too: the great sense of humor,
the friendliness, the intelligence. Little Katie couldn't hold a
candle to her yet in any of those departments; she was too
young still, too unformed. And any prettiness Katie had was
due to her youth; her features were nothing to write home
about.

"And that artist crap!" Sally finally, to Jude's relief, noticed
the glass in her hand and put it down on the coffee table. Then
she picked it up again and took another long swig. "Paintings of
hershelf naked, how shelf-obshessed is that!"

"Sofie does have something going on," Scott observed
almost apologetically. "Since you girls were wondering."

"You're *joking.*"

As women always are, Jude was deeply thrown by her
boyfriend finding a female sexy who was the complete opposite
to her, physically, mentally—Jesus, in every way possible. If

Scott, who was going out with a five-foot-nine bobbed blonde who could barely have got Sofie's tiny little T-shirt over her head, let alone her torso, fancied Sofie, what did that say about his taste in women? And Scott and Jude's relationship?

"You think *Shofie's shexshy?*" Sally exclaimed, though the way in which she stumbled over the last two words diluted her amazement to some degree.

"Not personally," Scott said, quite as calmly as if Jude hadn't gone all tense and Sally weren't staring at him as if he had confessed to a weakness for threesomes with a rent boy and a donkey. "I can see the attraction, though. That mad-chick thing. And the way she seems perpetually off on her own cloud. As if it'd be a real challenge to get her attention."

"And men *like* that?" Jude said incredulously.

But just then she remembered a girl she'd been at school with, who had been a boy magnet for reasons none of the other girls had ever been able to see. She slouched; she had a long horse face; she threw herself on the closest sofa at parties and sulked, barely even making eye contact with anyone; and yet the boys had queued up in front of that sofa for a chance to chat her up. Maybe Sofie was one of those. The girls you couldn't spot, the stealth missiles of dating, the ones whose competition you didn't worry about until it was too late, because they slipped right under your radar. You were busy looking out for the gorgeous blondes, and the sulky cow went and nabbed the guy you wanted while your back was turned for a moment.

"It's the mad-chick thing," Scott elaborated. "Someone who could freak out at any time. There's an element of risk. It's like the bad-boy thing for women."

"Sho we're too shane. Me and Jude. Ish that what you're say-ing?" Sally said combatively. "We should be more fucked-up?"

Sally, Jude thought, could not be more fucked-up than she was at that moment, at least in a physical sense.

"I mean," Sally was continuing, "you have a lovely girl-friend—lovely—Jude'sh my besht mate, aren't you, Jude, I love you—she's sho lovely," she said, turning to face Scott with such abruptness that she nearly fell off the sofa, "lovely, *lovely* Jude, and he jusht wants shome fucked-up chick—it makesh me sho *angry*—"

"Come on, you," Jude said firmly, rising to her feet. "Time for bed."

She pulled Sally to her feet. Sally swayed back and forth like a sapling in a typhoon.

"Need a hand?" Scott asked.

"No, it's fine. Tell you what, why don't you take my keys—they're in my jacket—and let yourself into mine? I'll be over in a second."

It took a little longer than that to take Sally's shoes off, settle her under her duvet, and place a large glass of water and two aspirin on the bedside table, within easy reach but not so close to the edge that Sally might knock them off in, say, a drunken stagger to the toilet. Sally was extremely docile, and curled up dutifully in bed, requiring only to clasp Jude's hand tight for a few minutes and tell her again what a lovely girl she was and how lucky she, Sally, was to know and love such a lovely girl.

Jude examined herself in the living-room mirror before returning to her own flat. Straight dirty-blond hair, clear gray eyes, widish cheekbones, and a no-nonsense chin. She looked unquestionably sane. Even her clothes—her blue fitted shirt and black stretch trousers—were sane. Well, of course they were. Sensibly chosen. That was what all the fashion magazines recommended if you had a pear-shaped figure. She sighed. Maybe it was her own light drunkenness that had made her feel suddenly insecure. Scott wouldn't have talked like that if what he secretly wanted was some mad arty chick liable to cut all his precious sweaters to pieces on a whim. He seemed perfectly content with her. He'd brought her flowers, hadn't he? And yet Jude felt the desire ebbing away from her like a tide that would take a long while to come back in. It wasn't fair of her to punish Scott for being honest, for answering a question that had stumped her and Sally. And yet she just didn't feel like sex anymore. She was tired and wanted to go to sleep.

It was the curse of Sofie. Sally would have a stinking hangover tomorrow, and Jude wasn't getting laid again tonight. She shuddered to think what was going on across the street with Michael and Katie. Sofie had left early, and though one might have thought that the atmosphere would lighten up once she had gone, that had been far from the case. Michael had been too busy fussing round Sofie, making sure she knew how to get back to Stephanie's, to realize that Katie was steaming with anger and neglect, clearly dying to point out to him how badly he had behaved toward her that evening.

Jude pulled back the curtains and looked over the street at Michael's front window. The lights were still on downstairs. Jude saw Michael's large silhouette moving around in the living room, slotting the leaves of the dining table under one another so he could slide it back against the wall. He paused when this was done and walked to the window, leaning his forehead on his hands against the glass. The light was behind him and Jude could not read his expression, but his posture signified helplessness. Katie was doubtless banging dishes around in the kitchen while shouting at him. A cozy domestic tableau. Jude found it hard to drag her gaze from Michael's figure, his slumped shoulders and sunken head. She caught herself hoping for Katie to storm through from the kitchen, throwing the lasagne dish at him.

Jude ticked herself off. She really was treating this like a soap opera. And yet she was involved in it too, she was one of the actors, even if in a minor role; the confidante to the heroine, like a Restoration comedy. Sally was the heroine, Katie the ingénue, Sofie the woman of mystery. And Michael was the hub around which they all turned.

Chapter
Twelve

Katie had an hour and a half to kill after work before she met Tash and a couple of other friends for dinner. She did what she had always done before in those circumstances: she went shopping on Oxford Street. Only this time, it was with an entirely different focus. No trendy high-street boutiques or discount shops where you could pick up great T-shirts for a fiver. She caught the bus to Marble Arch and went to Mothercare.

Katie wasn't showing yet, and every time she entered a maternity shop she felt like a fraud. It was full, always, of women pushing strollers or walking slowly, their bellies slung low and full, one hand to the small of their back.

Katie wished that she had shoved a pillow down the front of her trousers before entering Mothercare. She wanted to button-hole the women with the most obvious bumps and tell them that she was pregnant too. "It's just early, and apparently I won't show for ages . . . but I'm due in December, a Christmas baby . . . I'm just not showing yet. Isn't it great?" And of course, that would only make them think she was a lunatic; the women with strollers would immediately pull them closer, protectively, in case she tried to steal their baby.

She couldn't wait for her stomach to start swelling, for her breasts to get bigger. Well, "bigger," who was she trying to fool? She caught sight of herself in a mirror: yup, still flat-chested as a boy. They hadn't suddenly popped out during the afternoon. This was the way she'd been in school, every morning jumping out of bed and checking herself in the mirror, hoping that today would bring better news.

Rows and rows of tiny little shoes and socks. Why was it always the tiny shoes that made your heart turn over with tenderness? She fingered a miniature little pair of bovver boots, black plastic with Velcro buckles around ankles that looked scarcely larger than her thumb. Longingly she slid a finger inside one, imagining little baby feet filling them up.

Her phone beeped. It was a text message from Tash: *where r u?*
Mothercare, Katie texted back.
Ooh, baby clothes!!!!!! b there 5 mins.

That was good, Katie thought. With Tash here, she could talk in a carrying voice about being pregnant. Then she caught herself and had to laugh. How sad was that?

All the books—and the doctor—had said not to tell people till you had passed the first trimester, till the risk of a miscarriage had abated substantially. But Katie didn't care about that anymore. She was absolutely sure that this baby would be fine. Look at the way she'd been vomiting. That was supposed to be a good sign, a healthy baby rejecting anything it didn't completely feel sure about. Thank God it seemed to have subsided, though. She put her hand on her big shoulderbag automatically, checking for the bottle of flat Diet Coke she now carried everywhere with her.

Coming in front door, where r u? Tash texted.

Look up. Katie leaned over the mezzanine balcony, waving at her. Tash whooped, waved back, and jumped on the escalator. She was always like that. Even if she had seen you yesterday she acted as if you'd been separated for years. She hurtled off the escalator and hugged Katie.

"Hey! Hey, baby!" Tash patted Katie's tummy. "God, you haven't got anything like a bump yet."

"It's early," Katie said, aware of a couple of women turning to look at them, feeling a pleasant rush of satisfaction. "Your tits come up first, apparently."

"You wish," Tash said. "God, that'll be funny. Katie with tits."

"I know. I bet I spend the whole time just staring down at them."

"So what do we need to get?" Tash said bouncily. "You should make a list of what you need. We could throw you a baby shower. I mean, you'll need a lot of stuff."

"I know. Me and Michael are going down to see Mum and Dad next month, and they're going to sort us out some things. They have a secondhand shop in the village for prams and stuff."

"Your mum will've organized everything," Tash prophesied. "You know what she's like. God." She stopped dead by a display of embroidered socks. "What did she *say?* How did she take it? You never told me!"

"Oh, she's really happy," Katie said, fingering some socks covered in strawberries, which looked barely large enough to fit over her big toe. "She had me when she was pretty young, as well. And, you know, Michael has a good job, his own place, all that stuff parents like. They're not so happy about him being freelance, but that got sort of canceled out by him doing computer programming—that sounds so respectable and secure. I didn't tell them it was game design, of course."

"She doesn't mind him being older?"

"God, no. Dad's ten years older than she is. They're dying to meet him."

"I bet."

Tash caught sight of Katie and herself in a mirror, and swung Katie round too. "Look! Isn't it weird that you couldn't tell which one of us is pregnant? I still can't get over you not looking any different!"

Katie rolled her eyes. Tash was well-meaning, a great friend, but she could be really immature sometimes. "Tash, it's not like you get a big red 'P' sewn on your T-shirt as soon as the sperm meets the egg, you know." She smoothed one hand over her stomach.

They looked, she suddenly thought, like schoolgirls. Tash, big and bubbly, with her plaits and trendy gathered top and bright blue eyeshadow, Katie so small and boyish-looking in her T-shirt and camouflage trousers.

"Wait till my tummy's hanging out and I'm living in horrible trousers with elasticized waists," she said grimly. "You'll know then who's pregnant."

"Ich," Tash said in disgust. "Elasticized waists!"

Katie smiled maliciously. "Come on," she said, grabbing Tash's hand. "Let's go and look at maternity clothes. That'll really freak you out."

Chapter
Thirteen

Paul had left four messages on Sally's answering machine. Well, to be precise, he had left three hang-ups and then, finally, a message.

"Sally? This is Paul. Jude's colleague. Um, we met at Portobello Market, and then the party . . . I know you said you'd be very busy these next few weeks, but I was wondering if you'd have the chance at all to find an evening free. Maybe I could take you to dinner. Anyway, give me a ring sometime. I left my number before but it's 7836 8204. Um, look forward to hearing from you."

She was distinctly annoyed. A juicily promising, flashing red number four had turned out, yet again, to be just Paul, again and again and again . . . And it was so obvious that he had kept hanging up, hoping to get hold of her and not the machine.

She sighed and deleted his message. And the hang-ups. She liked him—he seemed very nice and friendly, and very good-looking—she just didn't have time for this right now. The question of when she had ever found time to answer one of the many men who had rung her up over the years did not occur to her.

She hung up her coat and crossed the room to the window. Her curtains were still open, and before closing them she looked down to Michael's flat to see if his lights were on. They were. Normally she would immediately have reached for the phone, to see what he was up to. But now, for all she knew, Mikey might be out; it might be Katie in there instead. Sally almost shivered as she drew the curtains and turned away from the window. The idea of Katie being in residence in Michael's flat was more than she could bear.

Jude wasn't back from work yet. Sally could always tell, passing Jude's door, at least when night had fallen. Jude's front door hadn't been hung very well; there was always a telltale line of light underneath it and one small perfect shaft in the top center, through the peephole, indicating that Jude was home. She reached for the phone to leave a message on Jude's machine, asking her to come round. Sally hoped Jude wasn't seeing Scott tonight. She really needed her company.

There wasn't a dialing tone on the line. But before she could turn the phone off and on again, she heard a cautious "Sal? Sal, is that you?"

"Mikey?"

"Hey! That was odd!"

"What happened? I didn't even hear it ring!"

"Me neither. I just dialed your number and there you were."

"I was just about to ring you," Sally lied.

"We're psychic," Michael said comfortably. "What're you doing?"

"Just got home."

"Yeah, I know, I saw your light come on. Katie's out to dinner with some of her friends, and I'm bored. It's odd being here alone. I've sort of got used to having someone else here."

"Mikey, you *always* hate being in the flat alone," Sally said firmly. "That's why you're round with us all the time."

This was true enough, but she had an extra reason for affirming it so strongly: she didn't want to make Michael think it was Katie's absence, in particular, that was affecting him.

"Well, can I come over?" Michael was unstoppable when he wanted something. "I could pop round to the Chinese and get a takeaway. It's probably my turn to bring dinner."

Probably my turn, Sally thought ironically. Michael had to have at least ten meals with her and Jude before he remembered to bring anything in the way of provisions himself. But she was too happy with the prospect of his company to tease him.

"Lemon chicken for me," she said. "And some mangetout."

"Oh, I'll get loads of stuff, we can pick," Michael said comfortably.

Shit. This meant that her fridge would be stuffed with leftovers for days, and of course she would eat her way through them. Greasy delicious noodles and rice, fatty sweet-and-sour pork, deep-fried chicken wings. When Michael went to the local Chinese he seemed compelled to buy one of practically everything on the menu, to the extent that even he couldn't manage to finish the lot.

By the time Michael arrived, loaded down with plastic bags like a mule, there was lounge music playing on the stereo, the paper was open to the TV listings, and Sally was curled up on the sofa in her nice comfy pajamas, sipping a beer.

"It's open," she called.

"I wish you wouldn't do that," Michael complained, locking the door behind him.

This dialogue was so familiar that Sally didn't even bother to answer. Jude, too, was always telling her off for opening the door when Jude buzzed without even bothering to look through the council-provided peephole; she would just swing it open, dripping wet from the bath, to pad back and get in the tub again so that Jude could sit on the loo and chat to her. Sally would point out that no one else ever rang her doorbell; Jude would insist that you *never knew,* grinding her teeth in frustration, and nothing ever changed.

Sally indicated instead the plates, cutlery, chopsticks, and bottles of soy and chilli sauce arranged on the coffee table.

"Feed me, feed me," she chanted. "I'm starving. Oh, and there's beer in the fridge."

"I brought some, too," Michael said virtuously.

"Great. Did you remember my lemon chicken?"

"I got *everything.*"

Sally surveyed the bulging bags.

"God, you did as well. Excellent."

There was a specific pleasure in pigging out with a man. If you did it with another woman, both of you were required to moan gloomily about how fat you were getting, how your stomach was swelling by the minute, how repulsed you were by yourself. With a man, especially one a lot bigger than you were, you could, for one mad evening, free from any normal rules about carbohydrates and saturated fats, lay into as much fried rice as your burgeoning Buddha belly could take. Sally and Michael worked their way through quantities of dumplings, deep-fried beef sticks, chow mein, and many, many other bulging containers offered them by the Jade Garden, and subsided, half an hour later, near-comatose.

"Another beer?" Michael suggested.

"I couldn't. Really." Sally lay back in an old pose of hers, propped up by pillows in the corner of the sofa, hands to her stomach. It didn't occur to her, mercifully for the happiness of her mood, that someone glancing at her might have assumed from this that she was pregnant. She reached languidly for the remote control and flicked through that evening's paltry TV offerings.

"Game show?" she called. "In-depth documentary on the state of the NHS? Investigative program on . . . um . . . second-hand car salesmen? Crappy film on Channel Five?"

"You know our tastes, Watson. Apply them," Michael said from the fridge, which he was busy stacking with foil cartons of leftovers. "Shall I put the rice in the oven?"

"Mikey, you *know* I don't like you doing that, why do you always ask—?"

"Because it gets crunchy in the fridge overnight—"

"I know that's why, but why do you always *ask* when you know I think it's unsanitary—"

"Because I hope against hope that one magic evening you'll have changed your mind and see the light—"

"Well, I haven't. Put it in the sodding fridge."

"I expect it's good we have *one* thing we don't agree about," he said contemplatively. "Otherwise we'd just be too smug. Squash up."

He settled onto the other end of the sofa, wedging the corner pillows more firmly behind his back and stretching his long legs onto the coffee table. Reaching for Sally's, he picked them up and slung her calves across his lap.

"There, nice and cozy. Where are we up to?"

"The family on the left is going for a sports car, but if they lose, everything they've won so far goes to the family on the right. Including the once-in-a-lifetime holiday on the *QE2*."

Michael sighed, a deep, satisfied sigh that seemed to have been drawn right up from the soles of his feet.

"Bliss," he said happily.

An hour later, Jude knocked on the door, and to a shouted "Come in," opened it. She popped her head in. Two abstracted "Hey, Jude's" greeted her. It was such an old joke that Jude didn't even notice it by now, and no more did they.

Sally and Michael were on the sofa, backs to each arm, legs stretched out in front, a blanket over them, and a big tray on top of it.

"Picking up the pack . . . and laying down three queens," Sally said, flicking through the discard pile to extract the third queen she needed for the set.

"Damn. I thought you only had one."

"More fool you."

She snapped them down with great satisfaction.

"Oh, and last card," she announced.

"Bollocks." Michael rifled with frustration through his huge hand of cards. "I am in so much trouble."

"Jude, there's some leftover Chinese in the fridge if you want it," Sally said, remembering Jude's presence with an effort.

"No, I ate. Thanks."

"Want a beer?" Michael said.

Jude did. But Sally and Michael were so cozily tucked up, so engrossed in their card game, that it felt as if they had a force field around them, pushing her back and out of the flat. It was like walking in on a pair of lovers deep in intimate conversation: no matter how much they encourage you to stay, you know that all they want is to snap back together again, eye to eye, mouth to mouth.

"No, I'm a bit tired," she said, not completely lying. "I'm going to get an early night."

"There's nothing on the box," Michael said. "We gave it up as a lost cause—hah! A run!"

He put it down triumphantly.

"I picked up a video from the rental place," Jude said. "That new thriller with Brad Pitt."

She knew Sally had wanted to watch it. But Sally, still absorbed by the game, said only: "Ooh, cool, I'll keep it on for tomorrow when you've finished with it, and take it back, OK? Mikey, you can't put that there . . ."

"Right. I'll drop it in tomorrow morning. Night," Jude said, closing the door behind her to a couple of casual "Night's" as Sally argued with Michael about discard protocol.

She let herself into her own flat and flicked the TV on straight away to make it seem more inhabited, more welcoming. She couldn't hold any resentment against Sally and Michael; she knew they would have been perfectly happy if she'd taken a beer and some Chinese food and lain on the rug reading a book while they finished their game. It wasn't their fault that their intimacy, on full beam, was so strong that it tended to blind them to anyone else's existence. Jude, like Sally and Michael, was an only child. She assumed this was one reason why the three of them had been so drawn to one another. So she had had no experience of sibling rivalry till now. This was exactly what she was feeling. It wasn't jealousy in any sexual sense. It was the third child in a family envying the almost wordless closeness of the other two, wanting to join in their game and being fobbed off with promises.

The feeling went so deep and was so shameful she barely admitted it to herself. She processed it, in fact, by projecting it onto Katie, imagining how Katie would have felt to walk in on Sally and Michael in that state of intimacy. Michael took his friendship with Sally so much for granted that even Katie would have got only that vague, happy-to-see-you-but-not-really-available-right-now "Hello." For Katie, Jude reflected, it would be worse, almost, than catching Sally and Michael in bed. The sight of them so engrossed in each other to the exclusion of all else . . . there was a domesticity in that, a settled contentment, that would be almost as threatening to Katie as the sight of Sally and Michael making the beast with two backs. Sex, after all, didn't endure; not the passion in sex. But the kind of intimacy Sally and Michael shared would last forever.

Chapter
Fourteen

*S*ally came out of Boots with a calorie-counted sandwich wrap and a can of diet fizzy drink and turned right, heading toward Regent's Park. She loved Boots. It was so reassuring that, after a few nights spent finishing off all that Chinese food Michael had so selfishly left in her fridge, she could do penance at the altar of its Shapers section, where even the water, bizarrely enough, was labeled LOW IN CALORIES. With the hand that wasn't carrying the plastic bag, she squeezed low down on one hip, feeling for a love-handle. She was definitely a bit squishier. Oh well, her trouser waistband should be loosened up again by a few days of abstinence from anything too sinful. She reflected briefly on her vocabulary. Every woman was a Catholic when it came to dieting.

It was a beautiful spring day, the kind that England does so well: clear blue skies, a balmy breeze, and a gorgeous expanse of greenery up ahead, branches fluttering delicate new leaves in a tremulous excitement at the prospect of the new season. Everyone on the street actually looked happy; people strode along with an appropriate spring in their step, smiles on their faces. The rarity of days this perfect in London meant that when they came, the whole city delighted in them as one. Sally reached the top of Baker Street and waited for a moment at the traffic lights, turning her face up to the sun in complete happiness. She was debating where to eat her sandwich. She wasn't that hungry yet; maybe she would stroll through the park for half an hour before finding a nice tree to sit under, or a bench, if there was one she could have to herself. It was always better to walk first and eat afterward. That way she felt pleasantly virtuous when she did finally yield to the temptations of her sandwich. Her offices were so close to the park that, whenever the weather permitted, this was her lunchtime routine. It was a way of getting exercise without having to join a gym.

She would walk round the pond, she decided, up to the Rose Garden, loop back, and then find a nice spot to eat her wrap, with the pond glittering on one side and the majestic white Nash terraces on the other, gleaming faintly pinkish in the sun. Later in the year, in June and the early part of July, she always had her lunch in the Rose Garden; it was so beautiful, that long formal walk blooming with full-blossomed, rich-scented roses. But April was for looking at the crocuses, which were planted in banks along the lake, white, purple and yellow, the first touch of color in the park this year.

She took the long route around the lake, crossing back at the bandstand to make sure she got in at least a thirty-minute walk. The sun bounced off the water and glistened off each blade of green grass—dazzling, but not hot enough to make her temples contract. It was hypnotic. She swung her plastic bag and walked along briskly, enjoying herself so much that she took an extra detour when the lake was past, looping up to the left so that she could walk down the whole length of the Rose Garden avenue. The fountain was playing at the base of it, bright water dancing in the sunlight, splashing off the gray stone. It was so pretty that for a moment she wondered whether to sit down on one of the benches that lined the avenue and eat her sandwich there; she had already worked up an appetite. No, she told herself firmly, she was going to get the whole walk in first: rules were rules, and her trouser waist was tight . . .

And then, right down at the end of the avenue, next to the fountain, she saw Mikey, sitting on a bench. She would have recognized him anywhere: the large shaved head, his big frame, and that comfortable sprawling way he had of arranging himself on a seat. Mikey was more secure in his own body than any man she had ever known, despite its manifest flaws. It was one of the factors that made him so attractive: women picked up on it immediately and felt at ease with their own bodies around him, as if it permeated them through osmosis. If you could make a woman feel instantly good about her own body, you had practically won her over already.

For an instant she speeded up her steps; there was nothing she would like more than to enjoy this gorgeous day with Mikey, sitting on a bench in the sun. Then she saw there was a cardigan over the seat next to him, clearly a woman's, and she stopped dead in her tracks. Katie was with him.

Sally had several options at that point. Turn on her heels; keep going, and exchange a few friendly words with Mikey and Katie; or cut right through the paths winding around the rose beds and take a more circuitous route back to the lake. What she did, however, was to slip onto a bench just where she was standing, far enough up the avenue so that neither Mikey nor Katie would notice her, but close enough so that she could observe them. She was suddenly consumed with a desire to see how they behaved in private, when they thought they were completely anonymous. And before Katie returned from wherever she had gone, Sally could pretend that Mikey was waiting for her, that it was her cardigan lying on the bench, that she was the one who would stroll back to him and curl up against his big body and reach her head up for a kiss . . . Memories of their time as lovers flooded in on her so fast that she was swamped by them. She remembered exactly what it felt like to have his mouth on hers, his arms around her, the warmth of his body heating her skin, and she actually heard a tiny moan escape from her lips. Her body was infused with pain and she felt suddenly as exposed as if she were naked. She wrapped her arms around herself and tried not to cry.

Mikey was leaning forward as if he had spotted Katie. Sally's head turned, too, but all she could see was a heavyset girl in jeans and a T-shirt coming quickly back up the avenue, her hands cupped in front of her as if she was holding something. From the playground hidden behind the rose garden, the shrill happy screams of children rose and sank, wild as seagulls, a constant background noise. The girl had a heavy dark mane of hair, long tight black curls like bunches of grapes falling over her shoulders. Thick white skin, somewhat pitted, Sally observed, as if she had had bad acne when younger. Though it couldn't have been that long ago; she was definitely a girl, still in her teens. She was laughing, and as she reached Mikey she held her hands out to him, and he bent over them, seeming to drink.

Sally realized the girl must have gone to the water fountain, and sure enough, after Mikey had lapped at her cupped hands for a few seconds she drew one over the back of his neck and scalp, letting drops of water dampen his skin. He was laughing too, and now he pulled her toward him and buried his head in her stomach, kissing her, or maybe making those kind of bubbly noises that people do on babies' tummies to send them into giggles. It wouldn't have occurred to anyone but Sally that this was what he was doing, but she recognized it, because that was something he had loved to do with her . . . The girl was laughing and pushing at Mikey, and finally she knocked him away and jumped onto the bench, and he put both his hands into her heavy hair, pushing it back from her face so he could kiss her.

Sally actually thought that her heart would stop. She had no conscious awareness of the next few minutes. For all she knew she could have fainted on the spot. When she became aware again of herself, she was holding her can of soft drink. She had no memory of having opened it, and yet it was so light it must be empty. Her mouth was sticky and sweet with the chemicals.

She only had to turn her head slightly to see Mikey and the girl. She knew they wouldn't notice her. Mikey was a little shortsighted and would never recognize her at this distance. Besides, he was clearly much too busy staring into the eyes of Miss Teenage Acne Queen 2003 to notice anything short of Sally emptying a bucket of water over them. As one did to break up dogs. Carefully, as if afraid of crushing it, Sally put the empty can back in the thin plastic bag. Her movements were slow, her limbs feeling as heavy and unmanageable as if she were very old. As her arm brushed against the wooden slats of the bench, their warmth shocked her. She felt clammy and cold, and despite the drink, her mouth was dry.

Her emotions were so strong and so confused that it took her a long time to distinguish them. And the one that came last, the one that truly shocked her, was completely unexpected. It was an awful, burning joy. As if this fulfilled something for which she had been waiting a long, long time. It was something she had not felt since the happiness of being with Mikey. Her heart, again, was full.

Chapter
Fifteen

"*S*o what are you going to say to him?" Jude asked finally.

She poured them some more wine. Pizza Express Chianti, thin as vinegar, but with a twelve percent alcohol content, which was really all that mattered right then. They were so keyed up they could have drunk antifreeze without noticing, as long as it softened the edges.

"*Say* to him?" Sally echoed, picking up her glass.

"Well, yeah!" Jude stared at her. "You're going to tell him you saw him canoodling with a fifteen-year-old, right?"

"She wasn't *fifteen*," Sally demurred. "More like nineteen. I mean, she was clearly legal."

"Great," Jude said, reaching for a breadstick. "One less thing to worry about. Michael may be shagging around on his pregnant girlfriend, but at least he won't be done for statutory rape. Whoopee!"

Once she had opened the packet, though, she just broke the grissini slowly into little pieces, leaving a pile of crumbs on the tabletop. Her appetite had evaporated. Sally had insisted they sit down and order before she told Jude the momentous news she had promised on the phone. It had been the sensible thing to do; Jude was very grateful she had some wine immediately available on hearing Sally's revelation. But now she didn't know if she could manage to eat anything, let alone an American Hot. She felt terrible. What surprised her was that Sally's reaction did not seem to parallel her own. Sally's eyes were sparkling, and she was attacking a breadstick with gusto, her small white teeth sinking into it as if it were a juicy bone and she a dog that hadn't eaten in days.

"I don't know why . . ." Sally said finally. "I didn't think—I mean, why do you think I should talk to Mikey?"

"To tell him to stop!" Jude said so loudly that the people at the next table turned their heads. "He can't do this to Katie!"

"He *is*," Sally pointed out, and Jude could not help noticing that Sally pronounced these two words with a degree of satisfaction.

"Well, he can't do it anymore!" Jude's voice was lowered now but her tone was just as emphatic. "There's a baby on the way! He's only been going out with Katie for a few months!"

She knew the two objections were scarcely of equal value, but she was so upset that the words just seemed to fall out of her mouth. Behind her she heard the scrape of a chair as the people at the next table tried to edge closer to overhear. She turned her head and gave them such a stare of menace that they whipped their gazes away and pretended to be deeply enthralled by the menu.

"He *will* do it," Sally corrected. "That's what he does. He can't stay with someone for long, you know that, Jude."

"So what do you mean—he's going to leave Katie for this girl you saw?"

"I don't think so," Sally said thoughtfully. "She wasn't at all his type. No, I think he's just having a fling."

"Do you think he'll stay with Katie?" Jude was open-mouthed.

"I don't know." Sally shrugged. "He's very happy about the baby . . ."

"So what you're saying," Jude said incredulously, "is that Michael's just going to keep on shagging around, same old same old, while poor Katie's sitting there at home with the baby?"

Sally leaned a little toward Jude, planting both her elbows on the table and propping her face in her hands.

"But, Jude, what did you think would happen? Did you think Mikey would suddenly reform his wicked ways just because Katie's pregnant? I mean, people don't change overnight like that."

Jude felt incredibly naive. Not only that: she was shocked to realize how much she was out of the loop, had, on this showing, always been out of the loop. She had been doddering along in some pathetic, cloudy fancy of Michael basically being a good person who had lost his way, who would eventually come to his senses and settle down with Sally one day. And all the time Sally had been watching the same events and interpreting them very differently—and probably correctly. Michael, on Sally's showing, was irreformable. Jude had been living in a fantasy world, where things happened like they did in bad American films or the sitcom to which Sally had always compared their situation, the comically errant ex-boyfriend finally seeing the error of his ways and laying his heart at Sally's feet. She had thought she knew Michael and Sally. Now she realized that, in many ways, she didn't. It made her feel suddenly very lonely. She took a long drink of her wine.

Thank God she had never told Sally she thought that she and Michael would end up together. Her efforts to start that ball rolling by using Paul to make Michael jealous seemed pathetically childish in retrospect.

"Do you really think—" she started, and heard how weak her voice sounded, how she was almost pleading with Sally to give her a softened version of the truth. She didn't want to think of Michael like this.

"Mikey's always left one girl for another," Sally said simply. "There's always someone new on the horizon, even if it doesn't work out. Remember before Katie he was having that fling with that Brazilian girl?"

"Always?" Jude tried to remember.

"The only time there wasn't someone was with me," Sally said, an edge of pride creeping into her expression. "You know, I told you, we had a big fight because I started talking about moving in together, getting a place of our own, and he said he wasn't ready, and I said it didn't look to me like he'd ever be ready, he just kept on stringing me along . . . I was right, then," she added. "But he was too, he just wasn't ready."

"But from the sound of it, he'll never be ready," Jude pointed out. "I mean, he's got Katie installed with a baby on the way and he's *still* not ready—"

"Oh, Katie isn't right for him," Sally said dismissively.

The pizzas arrived, hot and steaming. Jude remembered the Pizza Express pizzas from her youth as being larger than the ones they served now: these seemed as compact as saucers. She could never decide whether they really had shrunk or whether her youthful memory just painted them as enormous, as it does with everything adult-size. Still, right then it was irrelevant. She had no appetite at all. The thought of spicy pepperoni made her stomach turn. She picked at the crust while Sally sliced into her Quattro Stagioni, thin ribbons of cheese separating reluctantly under the knife.

"I still think you have to talk to him," Jude insisted reluctantly. The wine was going to her head. She knew she should eat something, that she was in mild shock, but it was impossible.

"It won't make any difference," Sally said through a mouthful of cheese and mushrooms. She wiped her lips. "He'll just roll his eyes and say, 'Sal, you know what I'm like, it doesn't mean anything.'"

"Well, then, you should talk to Katie."

"To *Katie?*" Sally set down her slice of pizza. "Are you mad?"

"At least warn her about what she's getting into . . ."

"We talked about this before! You know, about how you can't warn people, they have to go through the experience themselves. If some ex of Mikey's had warned me about him it wouldn't have changed anything. I'd still have gone out with him. You don't just fall out of love with people because someone else tells you they have problems."

All this was true: but Jude noticed that Sally sounded distinctly defensive.

"She's *pregnant,*" Jude pointed out, zooming in on the flaw in Sally's argument. "There's going to be a *baby.*"

"I know what being pregnant means," Sally snapped. She

seemed completely unaware of the ears behind Jude, straining to catch every nuance of their conversation.

Annoyed as Jude was, she could scarcely blame them; this was juicier than an entire field of Florida oranges. "Well, that changes things! Don't you think?"

"She'd just think it was sour grapes," Sally said, demolishing the rest of her pizza slice with gusto.

This was so true that Jude was momentarily stumped. More, she thought it was truer than Sally even realized. Jude hadn't just been slow to appreciate the real depth of Michael's problems with commitment; she was being slow now, slow to pick up on the fact that Sally was, in a deep hidden part of her, relishing Katie's defeat. Katie hadn't been able to keep Michael faithful for even a few months, and the glow on Sally's face, the sparkle in her big dark eyes, reflected that directly. Jude might have been nourishing many illusions about Sally and Michael, but so, on this evidence, was Sally. This was such a horrible conclusion that Jude felt completely helpless, and unable to extend any help to Sally, too, who sorely needed it.

"Did Paul ever ring you?" she said eventually, trying in this feeble way to signal that she thought Sally's romantic focus should be, with this new revelation, miles away from Michael.

"Paul?" Sally looked for a moment as if she couldn't even remember who this was. "Oh yeah." She cut more pizza. "He leaves messages every now and then."

"So you haven't rung him back?"

Sally shook her head. She still had some lipstick on, even after half a pizza. Her mouth wasn't greasy and her nail polish was immaculate. Jude had often said about Sally that she could

travel on the tube all day, wearing white gloves, and keep them
as clean and unstained as they had been when she'd put them
on that morning. She had always envied Sally's pretty perfec-
tion—still did, if she were honest. But now she saw it also as a
symbol of Sally's distance from reality, from the messy compli-
cations that any human relationship inevitably entailed.

"Why not?" Jude said daringly.

"Why not?" Sally was surprised. "Well, why should I?"

"Because he's nice, he's really keen on you, you might have
fun . . ."

Sally took another bite. "I—" She seemed to have difficulty
coming up with a reason. "I didn't feel like it."

"But you want to meet someone, right? I mean, you don't
want to spend your life alone."

"I just didn't want to go out with Paul."

"How do you know? You didn't even give him a chance!
Why didn't you at least go out to see a film with him?"

"I didn't feel like it, OK?" Sally said sulkily. "Why are you
going on about him all of a sudden?"

"Because you never go out with anyone! Men ask you out all
the time and you never say yes!"

"They do not ask me out all the time. That's ridiculous."

"They would if you gave them half a chance."

Sally shrugged.

The wine had gone thoroughly to Jude's head by now. She
hadn't eaten since an early lunch and now she was almost dizzy
with alcohol and daring. It gave her the courage to push forward. In no other circumstances would she have been able to
say to Sally: "You don't want to go out with Paul or anyone

because you're still waiting for Michael! It's almost like you're *married* to him, and you don't mind him cheating because you know it's you he loves . . . but, Sal, look at what he's doing to Katie, he'd do that to you too if you ever got back with him, you can't trust him, you have to move on and go out with someone else—"

"He would *not!*" Sally interrupted furiously before she realized what she was saying. Then she looked horrified. She shoved her plate away from her. "I didn't mean—I'm not *waiting* for Mikey . . . Fuck, how can you say something like that? You're my friend, you're supposed to be supportive . . ."

As if there were some sort of friends' contract you signed when a certain degree of intimacy had been reached, Jude thought with a small detached portion of her brain.

"I just—" Sally was almost panting, torn between an effort to get the words out and a strong resistance to admitting that there was any truth in what Jude had just said. "I just—"

Suddenly she stood up and grabbed clumsily for her bag. "I can't—I can't talk to you right now, this is complete crap." She gulped. "I'm so *angry*—"

She turned on her heel and stormed out, knocking into several occupied chairs as she went and not apologizing to a single person. It was completely unlike Sally; but then everything that evening had been unlike Sally. Jude relieved her bruised feelings by turning round and snapping at the people behind her "What are *you* looking at?" so vindictively that they buried their heads in their pizzas and started mumbling disjointed phrases of conversation to each other in a pathetic effort to pretend they hadn't heard a word of the fight at the next table. Jude wanted desperately to run out after Sally, but what would she say? The only thing that would calm Sally down would be a complete retraction of her last words, and Jude couldn't do that—she was, despite her misery at having upset Sally, secretly proud of herself for finally speaking a truth she had wanted to say for years. When the waiter passed their table next, Jude asked for the bill.

"Do you want me to box that up for you?" he said, looking down at Jude's untouched pizza.

The dramatically appropriate gesture, of course, would have been to say "No," leave the American Hot sitting on its plate, and charge out empty-handed, her head swimming with cheap wine. But Jude was not dramatic by nature. And good common sense told her that, for all her lack of appetite now, she would be even hungrier in a few hours, once the adrenaline of the confrontation had worn off.

"Yeah, thanks," she said.

She looked at Sally's Quattro Stagioni, which was only half-eaten. Sally hadn't even touched the part with ham on it, which was Jude's favorite. She always had ham rights when Sally ordered the Quattro Stagioni. Maybe Sally had a point about that friends' contract after all. Jude was going to have to pay for that as well as her own, and she might as well reap the benefits. She pointed to Sally's plate.

"And could I get a box for that one too?"

Scott, as usual, was working late in the office of Stock Shots. Jude found him at a computer, busy tinkering with digital images. Views of London were arranged in rows on the screen, mostly high shining glass and steel towers: Docklands, the City, the glass gleaming against gray skies scudding with clouds. There were some photographs, too, of the London Eye, its carriages hanging from the wheel like great oval fruit. They were beautifully done, each image clear and sharp and precise. Jude complimented him and he shrugged.

"Catalogue stuff. There's no art to it."

"They're really good, though."

But Scott obviously didn't want praise for something he considered so run-of-the-mill. Jude looked round the small office, at some of the photographs blown up for the catalogues, hung on the walls. Glossy and glamorous, yes—they weren't art, Scott was right. But they were still technically brilliant, each layer of landscape with just the right amount of focus, the image Scott had intended to highlight given perfect definition, light shimmering around them in an almost three-dimensional effect. She wished he would let her compliment him. It was hard going out with someone who wasn't content with what he was doing professionally. Any time she tried to tell him how talented she thought he was, he brushed her off. And he really was good. She had been trying for months to find a way through this wall Scott put up around himself, to make him realize that, even though he might not yet have achieved what he wanted to, she was proud to be with someone who was so gifted. But he always made her feel as if she were artificially trying to boost his ego; the compliments bounced off his defenses and fell flat at her feet like damp squibs, and she felt stupid for having attempted them.

"So you brought me pizza?" he said, changing the subject, as he always did when his work was under discussion.

"It's more leftovers, really."

Scott opened the top box. "This one isn't even touched," he said. "God, it's small! Did you get the dieting size?"

Jude felt a momentary flush of pleasure. "You *see,* I knew I was right," she said, staring into the big flat cardboard boxes, in which she had heard the pizzas sliding around on her bus ride from Baker Street like imperfectly packed Frisbees. "They *are* getting smaller."

"Makes it easier to put them in the microwave," Scott said, seeing the bright side. "Shall I heat 'em up?"

"Yeah, OK."

He looked at her narrowly. "What's wrong? You sounded funny on the phone."

Jude sighed. She had wanted to confide in Scott, had been incredibly happy to hear his voice actually answering his mobile, rather than the answer service picking up; but now she felt stupid, interrupting him at work like this.

"It's Sally," she said finally. "We had a big fight."

"Really?" Scott, halving the pizzas to make them fit in the microwave, raised his eyebrows. "I always thought you two were joined at the hip."

"That's why it's so shitty that we fought." Jude sighed again. She wished she'd thought to pick up a bottle of wine on her way. "Sally spotted Michael in Regent's Park this lunchtime, snogging some teenager."

"Michael whose girlfriend's got a baby coming?"

Jude noticed that Scott sounded more ironic than surprised.

"Yeah."

"So what did Sally do?"

"Nothing."

"Hmmn." Scott shut the microwave door and pinged the buttons. "And what's she going to do?"

"Nothing."

"Hmmn."

"Don't keep saying that! Don't you think she should do something?"

"Like what?"

"Talk to Michael! Tell him he can't behave like this!"

"But, Jude, he *is* behaving like this. She's not going to change him."

"But we can't just stand back and let him screw up his and Katie's and the baby's lives like this!"

Scott looked serious. "I don't see what anyone can do," he said gently.

"Warn Katie!" Jude said immediately.

"How do you think she'd react to that?"

Jude pulled a face. Her tipsiness in the restaurant had abated considerably; it had only been a couple of glasses of wine, after all, and the news about Michael had abetted her light-headedness. Now that the alcohol was ebbing from her system, the energy it had lent her was fading too. She felt suddenly very tired.

"Of course she won't *like* it," she admitted. "But I think she needs to know. I mean—" She hesitated. It seemed like such a terrible thing to say. And yet Katie's decision to keep the baby had surely been based on how happy she was with Michael . . . "It's not too late for her to get an abortion, if she wanted. I mean, this puts things in a different perspective."

Scott was as uncomfortable with this as Jude had known he

would be. He wriggled and shrugged and said "Umph" a couple of times, and, when the microwave rang, looked immensely relieved to have something to do, rushing over to it and pressing a large quantity of what had to be unnecessary buttons. What comfort men found in any kind of technology.

"Did you talk about that with Sally?" he said finally.

"No, she was too weird. She was almost . . ." Jude could barely get the word out, it felt so disloyal. *"Gloating."*

"Jude," Scott said, pulling the pizzas out of the microwave and setting them back in the boxes, "I really think you should back off from all of this a bit."

"What?"

"Well, it's not directly to do with you, and it sounds like such a big mess—"

"Not directly to do with me!" Jude was incredibly indignant. "I mean, no, it's not me snogging Michael in the park, but—these are my *friends!* What do you expect me to do?"

"I just think the more you get tangled up in it, the worse it'll get—I mean, the more upset you'll get—"

"I can't help that! I care about them!"

Scott sliced into some pizza. Deliberately avoiding Jude's eye, he addressed his slice instead as he said, "Do you realize how much time you spend talking about them?"

"What do you mean?"

"Well, it's always Sally and Michael this, Sally and Michael that—sometimes it's hard to get a word in edgewise—"

Jude felt an explosion of anger in her head, like a white flash. "So you're saying I'm boring? Is that it? I just witter on about my mates the whole time?"

"No!" Scott looked cross, his brow furrowing in frustration. "You're deliberately misunderstanding me! I'm just saying that you act like they're the center of your life, that's all."

"Well," Jude said vindictively, "at least they always have time for me. No wonder I hang around with them so much—they make me feel like they actually *want* to see me."

"That is *really* unfair!" Scott said between clenched teeth. "You *know* how hard I'm working! I do my level best to make all the time for you I can. And when I do see you, we have to spend hours discussing what Sally and Michael have been up to, how their lunch went with Katie and Michael's mum, what annoying thing that Sofie idiot said yesterday evening, what Katie's been doing to the baby's room—and whenever I do get a night off I usually get dragged round to hang out with them too, as if I didn't feel I was hanging out with them every night of the week as it was—"

Jude wanted to throw the pizza box at his head. The only thing that discouraged her was its flimsiness. A meat axe would have been a lot more satisfying.

"That's my *life!*" she yelled. "They're like my *family!*"

"No they're not, Jude, they're your *friends.*"

"They're *like* my family!"

"Well, you still can't do anything for them! You can't sort out this mess they've got themselves into! You have to step back a bit and let them get on with it, instead of throwing yourself into the middle of it all the time!"

"I'm not doing that, I'm trying to *help!*" She took a deep breath, so enraged it felt as if she were inhaling 151-proof alcohol so she could blow it out, set it on fire, and torch his face.

"And what would happen if I did step back? Would you have any more time for me? I bet you bloody wouldn't! But it would be easier for you, because I wouldn't be out all the time, I'd be sitting at home waiting for whenever you could be bothered to ring me! You just want to see me when it's convenient for you, you're married to your work, anyway"—damn, she wished she hadn't used the m-word, it made men so paranoid, but it was too late now, all she could do was ride over it and keep going— "and you won't even let me be supportive of it, or tell you how good I think it is! You push me away whenever I try! I want to be needed by *someone!*"

This felt so true and so sad that it stopped her in her tracks. It was like all those torch songs where the singer lamented that she had so much love to give and nobody to give it to. In horror, Jude looked at Scott and saw the embarrassed, uncomfortable expression on his face. She wanted to curl up and die. The anger vanished in a second, and she knew that her face now mirrored his own. She couldn't bear it. Standing up, pushing her chair back so roughly the casters squeaked on the floor, she grabbed her bag and ran for the door.

Behind her she could hear Scott calling, "Jude, come back— Jude—"

Blinded by rising tears, she fumbled at the security lock on the door and by a miracle got it open. She was hoping, of course, that he would come after her, but her stubbornness made her run as fast as she could, clattering down the lino-covered stairs, slamming the main door behind her, out into the streets of Soho and ducking round the corner to evade pursuit. She had heard him calling after her as she ran down the stairs, which meant he had followed her out onto the landing, but once she was in the street she knew she was alone. Why would he bother to chase an emotional lunatic down three flights of stairs? This way, she thought bitterly and unfairly, he got all the pizza for himself.

She walked over to Tottenham Court Road and waited for the bus. Every few minutes she checked her phone, making sure it was on, in case either Sally or Scott was trying to ring her. It was, and they didn't. The bus arrived almost immediately. Ironic: when she was in a hurry she had to wait for ages, and when, as now, she was dreading going home, it mocked her by being punctual for once. If Sally was home, she would hear Jude coming in. They always heard the lift and recognized the sound of each other's front doors opening and closing. And Sally wouldn't come over to Jude's, not after that scene. What if Jude tried to knock on Sally's door—she couldn't use the keys, not when they'd fought—and Sally told her to go away? Jude couldn't bear the idea. The bus swayed and creaked through the dark night streets and Jude fantasized about staying on it till the end of the line. She had managed to get the best seat of all, the one on the top floor, back left, the only one on any bus that was built into the wall so it felt like a sofa, nice and squashy, tenderized by all the bottoms that had sat on it over the years. She curled up on it, as best as a tall and not unsubstantial girl can do, and closed her eyes. She had a Travelcard; maybe the bus conductor would just let her ride the Number 10 back and forth, from Archway to Hammersmith, till twelve-thirty, or whenever the last bus went. Hiding out from everyone. Or rather, everyone's absence.

*   *   *

She felt like a criminal as she stepped out of the lift. Like a burglar. As if Sally would burst out of her own flat at any second, screaming at her, and Jude would have to run away before she called the police. It was ridiculous how guilty she was feeling for having told Sally the truth. There was no light on under Sally's door, for which Jude was hugely grateful. She sneaked into her own flat and as the door closed behind her she felt more lonely than she had ever been. Could she really have alienated Sally and Scott forever? Best friend and boyfriend gone in one night? What kind of monumental, crashing idiocy was that?

Then she noticed the light flashing on her answering machine. No matter how scared she was that it was Sally ringing to tell her never to knock on her door again, she practically ran over to the machine, hoping against hope.

"Hey, Jude, it's me. Scott. Um, I'm sorry I got you so upset. I didn't mean to. Um, and I know I haven't had much time since we got together. Sorry. It's work, you know that, there's nothing I can do about it, but I don't want it to make you feel . . . um, well . . . anyway, I was going to tell you, but there's this job that might be on the cards, I might have to go to Florida in a couple of weeks, and I was wondering . . . the job's only for a couple of days but I was thinking we might make a week of it, you could come out with me and we could have a bit of a holiday together, would you like that? I don't know if you could get time off work, but it would be nice . . . um, I'll know in a couple of days, so I'll give you a call . . . anyway, hope you're OK, and call me soon, OK? Um, yeah. Well. Anyway. Bye then."

Happiness flooded through Jude like a warm wave of hot chocolate with whipped cream on top. Scott still wanted to see her. Not just see her, go to Florida with her! She could have hugged herself.

And yet, no message from Sally. One out of two. Despite her joy, she couldn't help wondering how she would have felt if the message had been from Sally instead, wanting to make up. Would she have been just as happy? And she realized that she would.

Chapter
Sixteen

"*G*od, that was the worst yet—"

"Oh, come on, it wasn't as bad as the Liquid Lasagne night—"

"I'm sorry, I have to disagree, being forced to look at all those awful drawings and find something nice to say about *every single one* was my personal lowest point with Sofie so far—"

"What about the ones with the *cucumber?*"

"I know, I thought I was going to crack up—"

"I was trying so hard not to look at you, I knew that would send me over the edge—"

"Oh *God—*" Sally was laughing so hard she had to stop by the side of the street, bent over with the giggles.

"Zis is my investigation into my relationship wiz my sexualitee, in wheech I am using ze phalleec symbol to explore my penis envee . . ."

"Please, no more—"

"Unfortunatelee zee vibrator shop was closed, so I was forced to use zis cucumber instead. Eet was a leetle cold from the fridge, but because I am French and veree strange I found zat strangely enjoyable . . ."

"Ow! Jude, please, it hurts . . ."

Jude did an imitation of Sofie in the drawing in question, holding the cucumber against her lower stomach with a soulful expression on her face, which sent Sally into fresh spasms of laughter.

"Oh God, they might hear me—" she said through her hiccups.

"Nah, don't worry, Sofie's still droning on about her penis envy, they won't hear anything over that."

"Aah. Ugh. Oh."

Sally slowly straightened up and wiped the tears of laughter from her eyes. "That really hurt," she said reproachfully. "I couldn't breathe at one stage."

"Don't shoot the messenger. Oh look, we can cross."

"The thing is," Sally said as they dodged traffic across the road, "that some of those drawings were actually good. Well, not *good* exactly, she's so self-indulgent, but—"

"She's a good drawer. Draw-er," Jude said. Discussing art or literature with Sally always made her self-consciously aware of how little cultural background or vocabulary she had compared with Sally or Michael. "I mean—"

"Draftsmanship," Sally said. "She has really nice lines, some of it was really pretty. I just wish she wouldn't keep drawing *herself*. I don't think she's got any real distance or perspective on herself."

"Well, obviously," Jude said, taking this at its most literal meaning. "But, you know, I sort of admire her for not making herself look all gorgeous. If I was drawing myself I'd definitely tart up all my weak points."

"Whereas she didn't even try to make her tits look bigger or her tummy look smaller," Sally said rather vindictively. "Do you have your keys—oh, good."

Jude was unlocking the main door.

"But I know what you mean," Sally continued. "And it's unfair of me, because we always complain about women in magazines being airbrushed and liposuctioned, and then when some French arty-farty does drawings of her potbelly and her tiny tits, we tick her off for not being a supermodel."

"Though I do think she could do something about her pubes," Jude said, pressing the button for the lift.

"I *know!* I mean, I think it's really sexist to expect women to shave down there, or wax, or whatever, but if I had hair going down to my *knees*—"

"There were only a few curls at mid-thigh, let's be fair," Jude said in fake consideration for Sofie, which just made them giggle harder.

"How did Mikey put up with that?" Sally said wonderingly. "He's always going on about women's body hair. Once I hadn't depilated for a week, and I was wearing sheer tights, and he said seeing all my hairs pressed up against them was like some sort of biology exhibit under glass."

"Ick. I don't know why you don't just shave every morning in the shower. It gets to be such a routine you don't even think about it."

"I don't have enough hairs, it's not worth it. You know how I am."

Sally stuck out one perfectly smooth arm for Jude's examination.

"It's nice now, but I know it means I'll be a bald old lady," she sighed. "Oh well, I can have a nice set of wigs."

They stepped into the lift and silence fell; they had temporarily exhausted the topic of conversation. This wouldn't have been anything to worry about normally. Jude and Sally were used to their companionable silences. But, with the state of tension that currently existed between them, it was an instant pall of awkwardness. They averted their eyes from each other and stared ahead at where the display for the floors they were passing should have been; Jude could not remember it ever having worked. You quickly learned to recognize your floor when the lift door opened by the particular pattern of graffiti on the opposite wall.

As the doors creaked open, Sally muttered, "Well, night, then," and turned toward her own flat.

"Yeah, good night," Jude returned, not to be outdone.

Her heart sank. She had been hoping that the camaraderie of this evening would have softened Sally toward her; there was nothing like uniting against a common enemy to make people forget their differences. Jude had been almost certain that Sally would ask her in this evening. Of course, she could always have asked Sally over to hers, but she felt that it was Sally who had to make the first move, because it was Sally who had been injured by Jude. It wasn't that Jude thought she needed to be ritually forgiven. But she was scared of suggesting that they make up, only to be rebuffed by Sally asking her incredulously how she, Sally, could ever truly be friends again with someone who had been so rude and thoughtless.

The morning after their fight, Jude had found a white envelope lying on her doormat, pushed underneath the door by

Sally on her way to work. Eagerly she had ripped it open, and only when she had extracted the piece of paper inside, wrapped around a twenty-pound note, did she realize that Sally writing to her, rather than dropping round, was not the sign of reconciliation for which she had been hoping. Sally's note was short: she apologized for storming out and sticking Jude for her half of the bill, and enclosed some money to make up for it. Despite her disappointment, Jude couldn't help smiling. It was so Sally. Those inbred good manners of hers.

She hadn't yet told Sally about Florida. Not just Florida, the Keys! Key West, Key Largo . . . They were flying into Miami, renting a car and then driving down the Keys, stopping where they felt like it. Half the anticipated pleasure was lost, though, without being able to gloat over it with Sally, get advice on the best fake tan, be reassured that her bikini didn't make her look like a white whale in drag . . . Their relations were so tenuous, being confined to the times Michael came round, or invited them over—as tonight—that opportunities for confidences were rare. It was ridiculous: when Michael was around, the girls put on a front that nothing was wrong. If he dropped in, Sally would tell him to knock on Jude's door and see if she was in. If he invited them over, Sally would communicate this to Jude, usually by texting her mobile so they didn't have to speak. They were like a married couple on the verge of divorce, putting on a good show for the neighbors. And Jude couldn't find a way out of it; every time it happened, the more difficult it seemed for them to recover the old easy friendship. She had hoped so much for that to happen tonight. Seeing Sally over those drawings of Sofie, obviously as close to cracking up with laughter as Jude was, she had thought that this would break down the barrier between them. But she had clearly been wrong.

And Jude was reluctant to tell Sally about the holiday with Scott—Only ten days now! She couldn't wait!—for another reason too. After all she had said to Sally on the subject of her feelings for Michael, telling her now that she and Scott were getting closer would be like rubbing salt in the wound. I, Jude, have the right to criticize your patheticness from the lofty heights of my own Successful Relationship. Yah-boo-sucks. But she would have to tell Sally that she was going away. She couldn't just disappear for a week.

Suddenly Jude wondered whether, after all, she could. If she just vanished for a week, wouldn't that make Sally realize what she was missing, and prompt her toward a reconciliation? She knew that this idea was almost like trying, say, to spur an ex-boyfriend into a fit of jealousy that would prompt him to come back to her. And she couldn't work out whether that meant that Scott was right, that her relationship with Sally and Michael was unhealthily close. But people had to get close to each other, didn't they? What was the point of life otherwise? An only child, with no family experience to guide her, Jude felt as if she were stumbling in the dark. She hadn't had siblings to fight and make up with, she had never learned that sort of profound, inbuilt trust that came with knowing you were tied so deeply together that you could never break those bonds, but had to renegotiate them instead, time after time. She longed for that.

And constantly she wondered, as if she were a rejected lover, whether Sally was feeling the same sense of loss at their absence from one another's lives.

Chapter
Seventeen

Sally still couldn't tell, from looking at her, that Katie was pregnant. It made it easier for Sally to pretend that Katie wasn't, that this nightmare wasn't really happening. The morning sickness had settled down; Katie wasn't running to the toilet every five minutes, and though she was sitting in a corner of the pub where people around her were being careful not to smoke, and only drinking Diet Coke, which she stirred with a straw to get the bubbles out, these were signs that weren't immediately noticeable. With a force of will Sally could still imagine that Katie was just another one of Michael's disposable, identikit girlfriends. And that was exactly what she was trying to do.

She knew she was being an ostrich, with not just her head, but as much of her body under the sand as she could manage. Most of her time was spent desperately attempting not to think about it. It was incredibly difficult, especially since she no longer had Jude around for distraction; Jude had changed from being her bulwark to a major part of what Sally was trying not to think about. If she let herself realize what was going on, she was well aware that soon the weight and mass of all the things she was trying to suppress would bounce back with increased force and whack her over the head. With a sort of resigned hopelessness, though, she had effectively decided that this would happen when it chose to; right until it did she would go on valiantly pretending that everything was just the same as before. It was a pathetic kind of comfort, but it was all she had.

She looked as good as ever, except when she was alone. Sally had always had a considerable amount of self-control, not to mention pride, and when she was out with friends she was always bright and funny and pretty and well-groomed and all those qualities for which she was known. It was just in private that she looked at herself in the mirror and saw the sad expression in her eyes and the drawn skin over her cheeks. But that was easy to fix. A delicate film of pale yellow eyeshadow to counteract the red tone of her eyelids, black eyeliner to make her eyes stand out, and a touch more blusher than she normally wore, to hide how pale she was. No one seemed to have seen any difference. It was one of her few consolations.

"Wow! I can't believe how many people came!"

Siobhan plopped herself down on the seat next to Sally.

"They're all glad to see you go," Sally said, clinking her glass with Siobhan's. "Congratulations!"

"Oh, we'll be back before you know it. I wish we could have afforded to go for a year. Everyone says six months isn't really enough."

Siobhan and her husband Bill had packed in their jobs, rented out their flat, bought two round-the-world tickets, and were off to Australia in five days.

"You never know," Sally said consolingly. "You might find

some amazing business opportunity in Thailand and never come back."

"Yeah. Or suddenly find God and become missionaries and get kidnapped by terrorists in the Philippines."

"Well, if you make it out alive you can always write a best-seller about it."

"And then they might make a film about us," Siobhan said excitedly. She fingered her long red hair. "I want to be played by Nicole Kidman."

"What about Bill?"

Siobhan laughed and looked over at her husband, who was at the bar, chatting to Michael and a couple of other guys. "Maybe Joe Pesci? He's no heartthrob, is he?" she said fondly. Bill was short and balding. "My little potbellied pig. We're hoping he'll lose the tummy with all the traveling."

"Go to India," Sally suggested. "Don't wash the fruit and eat stuff from the street stalls. It's the miracle diet. You can lose a stone in a week. Of course, it comes out from both ends like a fountain and your bottom gets really, really sore, but you do get to see your hip bones jutting out like steel girders."

She was speaking as lightly as she could, and Siobhan laughed again, but it was unexpectedly hard for Sally. Seeing the love Siobhan had for Bill, a wonderful guy but scarcely the most prepossessing specimen of masculinity, made Sally all the more acutely aware of her own loneliness. And it echoed the feelings she had for Michael, who, though more physically imposing than Bill, and possessed of the kind of charm that made any woman instantly aware of him, wasn't exactly handsome either. Sally, who had always gone for conventionally good-looking men before Michael, had been amazed to discover that she didn't at all mind him having a belly, actually found it hugely endearing. It felt as if he had permanently changed her DNA in some way. It wasn't that she now eyed up tall, bald, slightly portly men. It was worse. She couldn't look at anyone but Michael.

"Bill has this dream of getting a job as a roustabout on an Australian bush station," Siobhan was saying. "I don't know if he even knows what a roustabout does, he just thinks the word sounds cool . . ."

Sally let Siobhan rattle on about their plans, taking in just enough so that she would know what to answer when Siobhan finally wound to a halt. She was thinking that Siobhan, besides her curly red hair and white Irish skin, bore absolutely no resemblance to Nicole Kidman; Siobhan, of course, had meant it as a joke, a gentle self-tease about her own lack of beauty. But, dumpy and pudge-faced as Siobhan was, she had found someone who made her happy, someone enough in tune with her for them to be able to decide to put their careers on hold and throw caution to the winds for the sake of a big adventure together. She and Bill had been happily married for five years now, while Sally hadn't even been able to persuade Michael to move in with her. And Sally was ten times prettier than Siobhan. All those fashion magazines that were Holy Writ to her, all the precision-tuned clothes shopping and personal reinterpretations of the latest trends, what good had they done? Sally, without false modesty, knew how much other women envied her looks and her style; they told her so, ooh-ing and aah-ing over her latest outfits and haircuts. And yet it was tubby little Siobhan, in her unflattering baggy jeans and over-tight T-shirts with silly slogans, who'd found the love of her life, while Sally sat on the sidelines, watching hers get another woman pregnant. Was it easier if you knew you weren't that physically attractive? Did you just happily settle for what you could get and thank your lucky stars for it, instead of feeling that you deserved exactly what you wanted, because you had followed all the rules society dictated you should and were, by its beauty standards, a raving success?

God, if Siobhan could read one fraction of Sally's thoughts she would throw the beer she shouldn't be drinking (because it didn't help with her tubbiness problem) over Sally's lovely new sweater and never speak to her again. And Sally wouldn't blame her. She was all too aware that Katie's pregnancy was making her a monster of selfishness and evil wishes. Only the other day she had caught herself hoping that Katie might miscarry—it wasn't quite the end of the third month, so she wasn't out of the woods, and first pregnancies did often miscarry, didn't they?—and then been shocked at her own capacity for hate. While, of course, a nasty secret little part of her brain still continued to wait every day for a sobbing phone call from Mikey, recounting how Katie was sitting on the toilet, crying her eyes out, as their baby slid out from her and swirled away down the drain, together with their relationship . . .

"Yeah, New Zealand's supposed to be fantastically gorgeous," she said to Siobhan, who had paused, "and think of all that lovely wine!"

It was more than enough. Siobhan launched off again and Sally was alone with her endlessly churning thoughts. It was like one of those tortures in the Greek myths: she felt as if she'd been sentenced to a snake in her brain, perpetually gnawing away at its own tail, but never consuming it. She knew she needed to snap out of this and find another perspective. How she wished she could talk to Jude. But Jude would tell her she ought to ring Paul, and Sally had a resistance the size and shape of the Great Wall of China to going out with another man. Somehow that would symbolize her being finished with Mikey. And she couldn't do that. She still believed that if she hung on long enough it would work out. What did it have to take, she wondered, before she would give up that hope? The birth of Katie's baby? (She insisted on thinking of it as "Katie's baby," despite Michael's obvious participation in its creation.) Michael and Katie's marriage? The announcement of Katie's second pregnancy?

"Are you OK?" Siobhan said, staring at her. "You look a bit funny."

"Just a bit light-headed, I think," Sally managed to say. "I didn't have much at lunch and the vodka's going to my head a bit."

"Have some crisps." Siobhan pushed one of the packets over to her. "We got loads. I've been hogging them. Ooh, and talking about traveling, have you heard Jude's news? It's so exciting! Key West sounds so romantic . . ."

Sally had no idea what Siobhan was talking about. Still, there was no way she was going to admit to the existence of a rift between herself and Jude. "Yeah, it's great," she said, smiling brightly.

Her heart was beating fast. She hated Siobhan having Jude's

news before she did. She was Jude's best friend, after all. Or was she still? Had Jude dropped her? She had always assumed that she and Jude would make up when they were ready—but what if Jude didn't want to? Had she decided to cut Sally out of her life?

She looked over at Jude, who was standing at the bar. By chance Jude had happened to be glancing her way, and their eyes met. Jude ducked her head awkwardly, then turned away, continuing her conversation with a couple of Siobhan's work colleagues, swiveling a little so that Sally could now only see one shoulder and part of her profile.

She's fed up with me, Sally thought. She's completely sick of me and my stupid problems, she's going away with Scott—she assumed Scott was involved in the trip, because of Siobhan's use of the word "romantic"—and then she'll move in with him and never want to see me again. The hurt she felt at Jude not having confided this wonderful news, that she and Scott were going on holiday together, was almost as bad as the hurt she felt every time she looked over at Katie. She knew how much this would mean to Jude. Sally tried very hard to be happy for her, and failed.

"Cheese and onion?" Siobhan said. "Or barbecue flavor?"

Sally could have slapped her.

"I have tried to use other people in my work," Sofie was saying. "I have experimented for many times to include other physical forms. But somehow there is never the correct symmetry. I try, I try and finally I make myself admit that the symmetry, it is not there, because I am fundamentally not interested in the figure of the other. My own body, that is what interests me. I must concentrate on that."

She made an elegant little throwaway gesture.

"So you basically do drawings of yourself?" asked Gary, a work colleague of Bill's.

"Yes, that is correct. Because I am the subject in which I am interested. Only myself."

"Riiight," Bill said, clearly trying not to sound too amused by this and failing dismally.

"It is a fascinating discovery for me," Sofie said, becoming almost animated. "At first I think, all human life is of interest. So I experiment with many, many subjects. All of course with myself in the drawing too, you understand. But then I realize, no, one must be honest with oneself, I am the only subject that I succeed in realizing with real . . ."

She looked at Michael. *"Clarité?"*

"Clarity," he said.

"Clarity. And affection. The affection, I have it really only for my own body. So then I decide to draw only myself, naked of course, and it is a revelation. Suddenly my art becomes exalted."

Jude, eavesdropping behind the group, heard one of those Sofie-silences fall and couldn't help grinning to herself. She had been thinking: I must remember all this for Sally, she'll love it, and then realized that she and Sally were no longer really on those terms. Still, maybe if they traveled back together tonight—no, they'd probably share a cab with Michael and Katie—well, waiting for the lift, she could relate this latest example of Sofie's magnificent solipsism to Sally and maybe it would take too long, if she spun it out, so when they reached their floor she would still be in the middle of the story, and Sally would ask her in so she could finish it . . .

Jude knew, even before she looked, that Bill and Gary would be staring at Sofie with their jaws dropped nearly to the floor, while Michael would be beaming happily at her.

"Didn't you say you had a show lined up, Sofie?" Michael said, prompting her to recount her achievements just as a spouse coaxes their other half to tell their latest success, proudly showing them off in public. What made him think Sofie needed any prompting was completely beyond Jude.

"Yes, I am talking to many galleries," Sofie answered. "They are all very attracted by my work."

Bill mumbled something to Gary that Jude didn't hear. But she didn't imagine it was that flattering to Sofie.

"But some of them do not have room for me. So then I must decide between some others. I think though it will be in the summer. I am very excited."

Sofie announced her excitement as composedly as if she had been telling them about making a cup of tea. She was wearing another one of her super-drab outfits that evening, a droopy old tweed dress over heavy woollen tights and clog-like shoes. A chunky amber necklace hung half-in, half-out of the neckline of the dress, and her hair, as always, looked as if she had given it a good rinse in olive oil before coming out. The circles under her eyes were twin bruises. And yet Gary was now starting to ask Sofie questions in that tentative, polite voice people use when they are romantically interested in the person they're talking to. Lots of head-ducks and foot-shuffling. Bill, rolling his eyes at

Jude, peeled away from the group, and she followed him a little further down the bar.

"That woman is unbelievable," Bill said when they had put enough distance between them and the others. The bar was noisy; they were having to raise their voices, so just by leaning in and talking close to her Bill was able to be completely discreet. *"Unbelievable."*

"You have to see it as entertainment," Jude advised. "If you take her seriously you go mad."

"I can't believe Michael doesn't see through all that pretentious bullshit!" Bill said, irritated. "He's usually the first one to take the piss out of people."

"Sofie's got a spell on him," Jude said.

Bill shrugged. "Maybe you're right. Bloody hell, though. I mean, I'd heard him mention her before in hushed tones and from the way he talked about her I thought she'd be this cross between Juliette Binoche and Emmanuelle Béart. I was looking forward to some top-class French totty. And look what the cat dragged in!"

"Gary doesn't seem to mind," Jude said, indicating him. He was inexorably moving in on Sofie, having managed, with careful choreography, to lean one elbow on the bar and get her to turn to face him, thus isolating her from the rest of the roomful of people. Sofie seemed quite happy to be talking to an audience of one. From the time Jude had spent observing her, she had noticed that Sofie was contented as long as she had any kind of audience. It was when people tried to talk about anything other than her that she looked bored, with a weary, existentialist ennui that only the French can pull off effectively.

Bill pulled a face. "One born every minute, eh?"

"My—Scott says that some men like mad women," Jude said. "I mean, not just women who don't care about them, but really loopy ones."

She relished the guilty pleasure she took in saying "Scott says." She had caught herself before saying "My boyfriend," feeling that this might be tempting fate; but she was aware that nowadays she did overuse the first phrase. She couldn't help it. It was awful; she knew she ought to be an independent woman responsible for her own opinions without needing to bolster them with reference to a man; but sometimes it was just so lovely to be able to say "Scott says," in a casual way, pretending it didn't make any difference to her one way or the other that she was quoting her boyfriend . . .

"Well, she certainly is that," Bill said dismissively. "So far up her own arse she's talking out of her stomach."

As if in a reflex to remind himself of his own marital happiness, he turned to smile fondly at Siobhan, who was still in lively conversation with Sally. Jude would have envied this before. Now she almost basked in it, as if the current success of her relationship with Scott was slowly but surely giving her a passport to the world of contented couples.

Jude's eyes lingered on Sally for a moment. They had made eye contact before, but Jude had been too embarrassed to do anything normal like smile or raise her eyebrows; instead she had just turned away to hide the flush of anger that had risen in her, the anger that everything had changed, and she and Sally were much further away from each other now than the mere distance across a wine bar.

*   *   *

It was a midweek night at the bar, prime relax-and-unwind time for all the workers with offices nearby, and the place, groaning under the extra strain of the twenty or so people gathered to give Bill and Siobhan a good send-off, was packed. Sally didn't know how long the girl had been there; when she caught sight of her she was standing in a corner, staring at Michael, looking very out-of-place in this crowd of well-groomed twenty- and thirtysomethings in their smart work clothes. She was wearing a big baggy sweater that looked as if her grandmother had knitted it from the wool of her own goats, and her thick dark hair was held off her face by a tie-dyed scarf, the kind that tourists buy for five pounds on Carnaby Street. The exposed ears were heavily pierced, rings and studs running up both lobes and around the rim of the ear in a style that hadn't been fashionable for years. No makeup: her only other accessory was a heavy scowl. Maybe that was because she knew she didn't fit in here, Sally thought. She looked like a throwback to the seventies, her heavy breasts swinging under the jumper as if she had just been organizing a bra-burning in the street outside. And yet she was very young; you could see that in everything about her, from her hesitant, yet somehow aggressive posture, to the fact that she hadn't yet learned how to hide her feelings in public, like a child who wriggles and kicks the furniture when she talks to you, communicating physically her discomfort at having a conversation with a grown-up.

Her skin's terrible, Sally observed. I wonder if a facial peel would help? And then, with horror, she made the connection—bad skin, all that dark hair, the heavy body—and identified this girl as the one she had seen in the park with Mikey just a couple of weeks ago.

Sally froze to the spot. What should she do?

It was odd that that had been her first response; after all, this was so clearly none of her business. But what was the girl doing here? Mikey couldn't possibly have been so crass as to invite her, could he?

She looked over at Michael. He hadn't seen the girl; he was leaning over Katie, saying something that made her laugh. Katie had that little friend with her, Tash or Trish; she had probably asked her along because she too was nervous about making conversation with adults all evening and wanted some backup. Sally caught herself being a bitch again, and grimaced. Still, her bitchiness was scarcely the main problem right now. She waved at Michael, attracting his attention, and, dropping a kiss on Katie's head, he made his way through the crowd to where Sally was standing.

"What is it, Sal?" he said comfortably. "You looked all urgent. Something important?"

"No—it's just—"

Sally couldn't get the words out. She realized that to warn Mikey of the girl's presence would be to admit that she knew all about his affair, or fling, or flirtation, or whatever it was, and suddenly she didn't want to admit to that, to having kept his secret. That seemed to cast her in the role of a mother, say, or an older sister, staying quiet or warning him as necessary. And besides, she didn't want to say it. It was as if it would change everything between her and Mikey, for reasons on which she had no grasp. Despite the way she had been gloating about the girl's existence, now, confronted with what she had been hoping for, she wanted it all to go away, for them to continue in the old Michael/Sally/Katie triangle, painful as that had been for her. The introduction of a fourth element made the whole pattern instantly unstable. It had never happened before. Now anything was possible.

"What?" Michael said, seeing her distress. "Ah, sweetheart, what is it?" He stroked her cheek. "Look at this worried little face! Come on, tell me, it can't be that bad. Is it about your fight with Jude?"

"How did you know about that?" Sally said, completely taken aback.

"You must think I'm an idiot! You two are always thick as thieves, and now every time I see you, you're barely talking to each other. I knew something was up ages ago. Come on, spit it out. I bet it's nothing. I'll talk to Jude for you if you like. She'll be as keen to make up as you are."

It hadn't been much of a reprieve; since of course the fight had been about Mikey and the girl, Sally had swung full circle back into exactly what she had been trying to avoid. Her face must have shown such distress that Michael, making calming noises, pulled her into his arms for a hug, patting her shoulder reassuringly and whispering in her ear that it wasn't that bad. In the strong warm circle of his arms, his body pressing against her with such instant familiarity, Sally was almost convinced for a few seconds that everything would turn out all right after all. She breathed in Mikey's smell, felt the fibers of his T-shirt against her face, his belly comfortingly firm and round against her, and pretended that everything else was just a bad dream.

"This is her, isn't it! This is Katie!"

The voice hardly registered with Sally; she didn't recognize it, and was anyway so distracted and lulled by Mikey's warmth that any outside sound seemed momentarily miles away. But it acted on Mikey like a bucketful of cold water. He jumped, and pushed Sally away simultaneously in a reflex that nearly sent her off-balance. She took a step back to stop herself from falling. The girl was very close, aggressively imposing herself between Sally and Michael, and despite the hostility emanating from her as clearly as if her hair were bristling up like a cat's, she still looked awkward and uncomfortable.

"Viliama, what are you *doing* here?" Michael said, more shocked than scared at this stage. "I thought you had evening class all this week."

"So I didn't go," Viliama said furiously. "I know you go out with your *girlfriend*"—she spat this word out as if it were burning her mouth—"and I follow you from your work."

She turned to Sally.

"He loves me!" she said. "Me! He tells me so! He loves *me!*"

The tone wasn't confident or elated. It was as angry as if she were shouting a slogan at a protest march: "Sally Sally Sally, OUT OUT OUT!" through a handheld megaphone.

Sally started: "But we're not—I'm not—"

She found it hard to get the words out, to admit to this awful Viliama creature that she, Sally, wasn't really Mikey's girlfriend. Despite all the potential for nastiness in this situation, she still couldn't help feeling a warm glow of pride at Viliama's mistake. And then, stumbling over the words, she caught Mikey's eye. He was shaking his head, looking panic-stricken. What was he trying to tell her? What didn't he want her to say?

And then she realized. He wanted her to lie to Viliama, to say she was his girlfriend, so that this scene could just be played out between the three of them without involving Katie. The bar was so noisy and crowded that maybe Mikey was actually hoping he could move Viliama away, have a screaming match with her and Sally and then pack her off before Katie even got wind of what was happening.

Sally stared at him in disbelief. She was determined not to say another word. Let Mikey dig himself out of this hole; she wasn't going to lift a finger to help him.

The silence seemed to last for minutes, the three of them standing in close proximity, isolated from the rest of the loud laughing population of the wine bar. Then Viliama said angrily to Mikey: "So tell her! Tell her that you love me! You say you want to tell her, so here we are!"

"Viliama," Michael managed desperately, "this is really not a good time . . . it's not a good idea . . . look, why don't we go outside and talk—"

"No!"

Sally had to admire Viliama's persistence. This was someone who didn't need any self-assertiveness classes. She could have given lessons.

"I want to talk to her!" Viliama continued, advancing her head toward Sally in the manner of a snake, extending her neck and shoulders so that her head jutted aggressively forward. "I want her to know about us!"

Michael shot an anguished glance at Sally. "Well, she does now. I mean, you've said what you wanted to say. Why don't we—"

"I want to stay here! I want to meet your friends! I don't let you send me away!"

Sally sensed that Viliama had been planning this scene for a long time, had rehearsed over and over again what she was going to say and do. She seemed as certain of her course as if she had plotted it on a map. What she had conceived of as her final destination, however, was more than Sally could imagine.

"Well," Michael said, hedging, "it's just a bit difficult right now. You know I told you this is someone's leaving party, it's not really the best time for you to meet people, why don't you and I go and have a drink somewhere else and we can talk about things and I can—"

"No! I go nowhere! I stay here with you and your friends and you tell everyone that you love me!"

Despite the horror of this situation, Sally couldn't help, in an awful, twisted way, respect Viliama's persistence. Perhaps it was her youth that gave her such bloody-minded confidence. Sally knew better than anyone what a comprehensive net of enchantment Michael could throw over a woman, convincing her that she was his one and only focus. Viliama had clearly been completely swept away by him and taken that as assurance that his feelings matched her own.

"Mikey!"

Bill, who by now was a few sheets to the wind, had come up behind Michael and was hugging him affectionately. "We're going to miss you guys . . ." he said in maudlin tones. "We're going to miss you guys so much . . . why don't you all come with us, why don't you pack in your jobs and come with us, we could all go round the world together, it would be such a laugh . . ."

Bill's short podgy arms hardly met around Michael's torso, yet Bill was clutching onto him as if he wouldn't stand upright without the support of Michael's large body. Any other time it would have been hilarious. Given the explosive nature of the situation, however, Sally was too petrified to be amused.

"You are a friend of Michael's?" Viliama said loudly. "Good. Hello, I am Viliama."

She stuck out her hand. Bill, his head propped awkwardly against Michael's shoulder, regarded her owlishly and flickered his fingers at her without letting go of Michael.

"Hello, I'm Bill, nice-to-meet-you," he said. "This is my party! Mine and Siobhan's! We're going away! We're going all the way round the world!"

Rather than being fazed by this, Viliama ignored it. Perhaps she hadn't understood all of it; her English was clearly basic, and Bill was slurring heavily.

"I love Michael!" she announced. "I love Michael and he loves me!"

"I love Mikey too!" Bill said happily. "We all love Mikey!" He stared at her. "*What* did you say your name was?"

"Viliama," she said, for the first time a little taken aback.

"Viliama, Viliama—is that like *William?*" Bill said. "Is that like being called *William-a?* William-a!" he chanted. "Or like . . . what is it . . . *Wilhelmina?*"

He started giggling uncontrollably.

"It is a very . . ." Viliama began, looking angrily at Michael for support. "I do not know the word! It is a name used in my country many times!"

"Common?" Michael suggested desperately.

"Yes, it is very common in my country," she said, scowling at Bill. "But that is not important, what I want to say is that—"

"And where's that?" Bill was still giggling. "Where's your country? Me and Siobhan are going to lots of countries—"

"Serbia!" announced Viliama, still angry.

"Ooooh, scary," Bill said. "Scary scary scary. No, we don't want to go to Serbia, that's much too scary. And no sun. We want the sun," he said confidingly, looking at Sally. "But Siobhan says we'll have to wear lots of sunblock. On my head. I have to wear sunblock. Have to be careful not to burn."

He loosened one hand from Michael's waist and patted his balding scalp. This movement unbalanced him and made him stagger slightly. Michael caught hold of him to steady him, saying to Viliama, "Look, Bill's a bit pissed, I'm just going to find somewhere for him to sit down . . . take him back to his wife . . . Hold on a bit, can you?"

He asked this much as a fox cornered by hounds might ask them if they'd be OK hanging on for a few minutes while he just popped over to the next burrow for a last cup of tea before being torn to pieces. If he had managed to sound authoritative, Viliama might have yielded, but the cravenness of his approach indicated his weakness all too clearly.

"No!" she said. "You stay here and tell *her*"—she shot out a jabbing finger at Sally, who flinched—"that you love me!"

Michael's large brown eyes implored Sally, with every fiber of his being, not to give the game away. He mouthed "Please" at her desperately. Meanwhile Bill was slipping down under Michael's steadying arm. He toppled toward Viliama, who caught his shoulders, more in a reflex, it seemed, than any generous impulse to prevent him hitting the floor.

"So!" a voice behind her shouted. "So this is him!"

It burst into a tirade of unintelligible angry words. Viliama blanched. A furious-looking young man shouldered past Sally to face Viliama, still shouting at her. He couldn't have been more than twenty, stocky and muscular and good-looking in a rather brutal, manly way. His short forehead was mostly obscured by tight springy dark curls of hair, which grew practically down to his thick single bristly eyebrow. This in turn was lowered by a deep scowl, half-obscuring his eyes. His jaw was thrust forward aggressively and his fists were clenched.

Viliama started shouting back at him in the same language—Serbian, Sally assumed. The young man aimed a fist at Bill. Viliama, shouting even louder, shook her head violently and pointed with one hand at Michael. The young man swiveled to face Michael. Meanwhile Viliama's gesture had fatally loosened her grip on Bill, who hiccupped, flailed around, and sat down heavily on the floor between them.

"You! I tell you now!" the young man yelled at Michael. "Viliama is mine!" He whacked his chest with one clenched hand. "She is mine!"

"That's OK," Michael said, holding up his hands and backing away. "She's yours, that's fine, no problem, mate—"

"No!" Viliama screeched. "No! I am not yours! I love Michael and he loves me!"

Sally shot a panicked glance around. There was no chance

that this scene would not attract the attention of practically everyone, no matter how noisy the wine bar had been. Already the other conversations were hushing themselves to listen to this slice of high drama.

"You try to take her from me!" the young man yelled.

"No," Michael said, "no, really, we're just friends—"

"Liar!" Viliama screamed. She launched into a torrent of Serbian, now directed at Michael, and finished by slapping him across the face. It was a good solid smack, and Michael's head jerked back with the impact. "Liar! You love me, you say so! You tell him, you tell all people!"

The young man made a sound like "Aaaah!," stepped forward over the slumped Bill, and punched Michael in the face. He reeled back. Viliama tried to grab the young man, shoving her face up against his and yelling at him in Serbian. He shoved her aside. She caught her foot on Bill and went flying, rescued from a nasty fall by a man at the next table who had jumped up just in time. Everyone was now backing away from Michael and the young man, apart from Bill, who was still on the floor, rubbing his leg and looking dazed.

"What the fuck's *happening?*" Jude said, catching Sally's arm and pulling her back out of harm's way.

"Chickens coming home to roost." Sally was light-headed.

"*What?*"

"That's Mikey's fling and what looks like her boyfriend—"

"Oh my *God!*"

They both looked around the room for Katie and saw her on her feet, coming toward Michael, confused and scared. Gary, who had come over from the bar, tried to grab the young man's arm and was thrown off violently. The young man squared up to Michael again, fists raised. Michael was backing away as fast as he could. The young man reached out and grabbed at Michael's shirt, catching him by the collar, and with his free hand punched him in the stomach. Michael doubled over. Katie screamed and would have run toward him if Tash hadn't got in her way.

"No, Katie, the baby! The baby! Get back!" she cried.

"Mikey, Mikey!" Katie shouted, tears running down her face. "Get off him, you bastard!"

Viliama might have been one-track-minded, but she wasn't a fool. She cast a furious glance at Sally and stormed over to Katie.

"So *you* are Katie!" she yelled. "So now I tell you that Michael loves *me,* not you! I am Viliama and he loves *me!*"

"For fuck's sake, she's pregnant, get away from her, you mad cow!" Tash shouted back, imposing her body protectively between Katie and Viliama.

Viliama's jaw dropped. She stared at Tash and Katie, completely taken aback by this revelation. Gary courageously made another attempt to grab the young man, who threw a wild punch that caught him on the shoulder. Gary cannoned into the people standing behind him and in the confusion the young man snatched a beer bottle off a nearby table. He stood there for a moment, brandishing the bottle over his head. The people nearest the door ran for it, stampeding over each other.

"Dragan! No!" Viliama yelled.

Michael was still bent over, clutching his stomach. The young man took one step forward and smashed the bottle over

Michael's head. Blood ran from his scalp. Katie wailed hysterically.

"Jesus fucking *Christ!*" Jude said.

The young man, now holding the broken bottle in his hand, paused momentarily, as if debating whether to hit Michael again. Everyone was paralyzed, apart from Viliama. She darted forward, picked up a small stool and whacked the young man smack in the face with it. He tottered, the bottle falling from his hand with a clash of breaking glass, and was promptly restrained by Gary and a couple of other men, who grappled him to the ground and sat on him.

Sirens could be heard outside. The bar staff must have rung the police. The bar was suddenly very quiet. The only sounds were Katie's sobbing, the panting breaths coming from the pile of men under which Dragan had almost entirely disappeared, and the sirens, getting louder and louder. Sally looked toward the door and saw that all the people who had evacuated the wine bar had their faces squashed up against the glass outside, staring in at the free show.

"Mikey! Are you OK? Mikey!"

Katie broke free of Tash and ran toward Michael, kneeling down beside him and embracing as much of him as she could. Viliama, still holding the stool, stared from Michael to the young man, her expression agonized.

"Oh my God, what's she going to *do?*" Sally said frantically, as Viliama took an uncertain step toward Michael and Katie, wielding the stool. "Katie—the *baby*—"

"Put down the stool," the biggest bartender, emerging from behind the bar, said to Viliama. "Come on, love, put down the stool, it's all over. You did a great job. The police are here now."

And then the bar was suddenly lit up by flashing red and blue lights from the police cars parked outside, and police officers were flooding in, filling up the room. The bartender, taking advantage of the distraction, wrestled the stool away from Viliama, who was too dazed to resist. Paramedics were bending over Mikey. Sally's head was spinning. It was only after a couple of minutes that she realized she was clinging onto Jude, sobbing into her shoulder, as Jude, crying too with relief, hugged her back as tightly as Sally was clutching at her.

Chapter
Eighteen

"*M*ichael Glinn?" said an exhausted-looking nurse in a grubby tunic and trousers, reading off a clipboard on the desk.

"It's *Gwynne*," Jude said, jumping to her feet. "*Gwynne*. Here he is. God, two hours' wait and they can't even get his name right!" she muttered to Sally.

"Can you come over here, please?" the nurse said, clearly reluctant to walk one step further than he had to.

Cursing under her breath, Jude helped Michael to his feet. Katie, who had been dozing on Tash's shoulder, woke up at the sound of Michael's name and jumped up too, still half-asleep and a little unsteady on her feet.

"What time is it?" she said, looking at her watch. "God, it's nearly one o'clock! How long have we been waiting?"

"I can't believe you saw the guy who hit him at once, and we had to wait nearly *two hours* till you could bother to look at the *victim*," Jude said angrily to the nurse and the woman behind the reception desk.

"I told you before," the receptionist said in a hostile tone, "we take people in order of the seriousness of their injuries."

"He got hit with a bottle!" Jude said. "He has blood all over his head!"

It was all wasted rhetoric: she and the receptionist had had exactly the same exchange several times during the long wait to get Michael seen by someone in Casualty. Still, it comforted her somehow. The shock of the bar fight had affected everyone differently. Once they'd got Michael to Casualty, Katie and Sally had collapsed, thoroughly worn out by emotional strain. But Jude had got angry. She still felt as if she had bucketfuls of adrenaline pumping through her veins.

"He's been punched in the face and had a bottle broken over his head," she said to the nurse combatively.

"What kind of bottle?" the nurse asked, tilting down Michael's head to take a look at the now-crusted wound on his scalp.

"Beer."

"Good." He touched around the wound gently with his fingers. Shouldn't he be wearing plastic gloves? Jude wondered.

"Good?" Katie said, coming over to stand next to Michael, though careful not to make any physical contact with him.

"Doesn't do as much damage as a wine bottle," the nurse explained laconically. "Did he lose consciousness at all?"

"I don't know," Katie said. "He looked really stunned."

"Michael?" the nurse said. "Does this hurt?"

He touched Michael's nose. Michael shook his head slowly. "Not much."

"You'll have a black eye, but your nose isn't broken. The head wound's superficial. What we need to worry about is concussion. Did you lose consciousness at all?"

"I don't know," Michael said. "I don't remember much. My head went very swimmy."

He raised one hand to touch his head in reflex, and winced as his fingers grazed the gash in his scalp.

"Hold still," the nurse said, pulling up one of his eyelids. "Hmmn."

"What?" Katie said anxiously.

"We're going to put some stitches in this cut, and then we're going to do some tests to see if he's concussed."

"What does that mean? What if he is?" Katie blurted out.

Michael managed a twisted smile. "Don't worry, Kates," he said. "It's not brain damage or anything."

"Pity," Jude muttered to herself.

"If he's concussed we'll need to keep him in overnight," the nurse said. "Just in case. No need to panic. It's just a routine precaution. He'll be fine."

He yawned unreassuringly.

"Come on then, let's start sewing you up," he said. "And try to find a doctor who's a bit more awake than I am."

"Will it take some time?" Jude said.

"I could lie to you," the nurse said, "but I won't. We're pretty busy right now. It might take quite a while."

"Katie, I think you should come back with me now and spend the night at mine," Tash said firmly. She too looked very tired: interviews with police, the journey to Casualty, and then a long time spent under fluorescent lights, on chipped orange plastic chairs that had been factory-molded to the contours of no bottom that could ever have existed in nature, was not a late-night entertainment calculated to put a spring in anyone's step.

But her small round jaw was set hard, and every time she looked at Michael—which she avoided as much as possible—enough fire shot from her eyes to have scorched someone less emotionally Teflon-plated than him.

"Oh Tash, are you sure?" Katie said in a small sleepy voice. "You don't have a spare bed."

"We can share. Or I can sleep on the floor. It's fine. But you're coming back with me."

"You don't want to come back to ours?" Katie said feebly. "We've got a spare bed."

"No," Tash said between clenched teeth. "No way are you going back there tonight. Come on."

She looked like a plump avenging angel in a tight Hello Kitty T-shirt, baggy jeans, and pigtails. The force of her will, set against Michael's enfeebled state, was quite enough to overpower Katie.

"Well, OK. I *am* really tired," Katie yielded. "Mikey . . ."

She looked up at him, for the first time seeming to take in the enormity of the situation, the fact that this wasn't just the consequence of a nasty bar fight. It was as if, up to now, her concern for Michael and the emotional exhaustion of all the high drama they had gone through had temporarily obscured the real issue at stake: his infidelity. Now that the matter-of-fact pronouncement of the nurse had reassured her about Michael's injuries, that left her with nothing but the realization that her boyfriend had been cheating on her with a teenage Serbian. Her face crumpled like a used tissue, her soft, youthfully rounded cheeks suddenly seeming lined and worn under the harsh lights. Her mouth drooped and her red-rimmed eyes filled with tears.

She made a gesture to reach over to kiss Michael goodbye, and then checked herself, suspended clumsily between two postures, too tired and worn out to make a decision about what she wanted to do: kiss him or pull away from him.

Tash made the decision for her. She put one chunky arm around Katie's fragile shoulders and practically dragged her away without a word of goodbye to anyone. As she guided Katie toward the door she bent her head to hers and whispered what sounded like words of encouragement.

It was a poignant sight. They could have been a pair of teenagers, overcome by circumstances of adult weight and depth. Jude watched them go and realized guiltily that her thoughts were divided between pity for Katie and overpowering relief that she herself wasn't caught in such an awful situation. It was one of your worst nightmares: a baby on the way, and an unfaithful boyfriend. There is always a part of us that takes comfort in the misfortunes of others, and Jude found herself leaning heavily on that consolation. She had Sally to look after, of course. But she was relieved, too, that she wasn't in Tash's position. At least she didn't have to see Sally through what Katie was suffering.

The nurse was leading Michael away. Michael hadn't tried to say goodbye to Katie; he looked utterly knocked out by what had happened. He didn't even turn to wave at Jude and Sally.

"We should wait and see what they say about him," Sally said. "Will you tell us about the concussion?" she called to the nurse.

"Yup," he said. "It'll be a while, though. We need to get him sewn up first."

They disappeared down the dirty corridor. God, Jude thought, watching them go, the state of the NHS was depressing. The floors were filthy, the staff running on four hours' sleep a night, and worst of all, from her point of view, the hot drinks machine in the foyer couldn't have worked for decades, judging by its condition. It was hanging at an angle, where some frustrated customer, denied their ersatz cappuccino, had doubtless tried to rip it off the wall. The area around the refund button was heavily dented. Someone had probably punched it, broken their fingers and then had to wait for three hours to get them set.

"You were lucky we didn't have any stabbings tonight," said the receptionist as Sally and Jude sat down again. "That's always the longest wait."

"Great," Jude said. "Look on the bright side."

She shot a glance around the other occupants of the waiting room, but they were too demoralized, or in too much pain, to see any humor in this exchange.

"How're you doing?" she said to Sally.

"I don't know, really. It's all so weird. I feel so dazed I don't know which end is up."

"I know," Jude said.

It was the first time they had been alone together, having a proper conversation, since their fight at Pizza Express, and Jude was determined to bury any hatchet that might still be sticking up out of the ground. She had decided to talk to Sally as if that argument had never happened, and so far it seemed to be working.

"I don't know what I think about anything anymore," Sally said, brushing the hair out of her face and trying to sit up straighter on the nasty plastic chair. She wiggled, trying to tilt it back, before she remembered that the chairs were all soldered together on a single long metal strip. "God, I'd kill for a cup of coffee."

"Yeah. They ought to get Nescafé or someone to sponsor coffee machines. And Coke or Pepsi or someone for soft drinks. I don't care if it'd be selling out the NHS, anything's better than having to wait hours without even a bit of caffeine."

"Not Nescafé." Sally's liberal middle-class conscience reared its head. "Remember about them selling baby milk in the Third World?"

"All right," Jude said impatiently, "Maxwell House or someone. Anyway."

Sally sighed. "I'm so confused . . ." she said. "I got really messed up seeing Mikey with that Viliama girl, close up, actually talking to each other—well, her shouting at him. They were such an unlikely couple. I mean, even for a one-night stand, let alone having an affair or anything. She was really—this sounds awful, but she was really ugly, and podgy, and badly dressed— shit, I sound like such a superficial bitch. I know I'm a bitch, you don't need to say anything. But I just kept thinking underneath it all how desperate Mikey must have been to cheat on Katie if he had to settle for someone like Viliama. He must have grabbed hold of the first thing he saw. Mikey's usually so fastidious, he likes them pretty and slim and all that—I'm not saying he should or shouldn't, it's just a fact. And she's—well, I bet her underarms look like she's got bits of shag carpet glued under there. She doesn't look like she's ever heard of a razor, does she?"

"You think he was desperate to cheat on Katie?" Jude said, picking the salient point out of this incoherent tirade.

"Yeah! He must have been! And in such a hurry that he couldn't even bother with quality control! He just grabbed at the first escape route he could find."

"Mmmn," Jude said. She was terrified that Sally was going to use this deduction as simply more evidence that Katie wasn't right for Michael, without blaming the real culprit for anything but temporary bad taste in women.

"It's pathetic," Sally added. "He's pathetic."

"Well, yeah," Jude agreed, greatly relieved.

"He was just using everyone. That poor Viliama cow was obviously convinced he was in love with her. He must have *told* her he was in love with her, which is obviously a complete lie. And Katie—he was very happy about the baby, and now look at him. And you know what? He picked someone to cheat on Katie with who was a complete nutcase. A psycho teenager with a jealous boyfriend."

"You think it was a death wish?" Jude joked.

"No," Sally corrected herself. "Well, not quite. I think it was him wanting subconsciously to make sure that the affair would come out sooner rather than later. He must have seen how possessive Viliama was, he must have known she'd throw a big scene. I bet she did plenty of those in private. He deliberately picked someone who was going to blow up in his face."

"As it were," Jude said, wiggling her eyebrows suggestively.

Sally giggled, the first in a very long time. Jude was hugely proud of having made her laugh.

"But you see what I mean?" Sally said, when the giggles subsided.

"You've been doing a lot of thinking about this."

"I had a lot of stuff to sort out. Oh my God, I haven't told you the worst bit."

Sally leaned toward Jude and lowered her voice slightly; there wasn't any need for it, since no one in the waiting room knew them. It was simply a reflexive instinct when confiding a particularly juicy piece of gossip.

"When Viliama first came up to us, Mikey was hugging me, and she thought I was Katie. She kept saying, 'He loves me, not you.' And Mikey wanted me to go along with it. Pretend I was Katie."

"*Fuck,*" Jude said, so loudly that even the receptionist, who must have been used to the worst extremes of human behavior by now, shot her a reproving look.

"Yeah. He kept shooting me these imploring glances. I think he was trying to get her out of there before Katie could see."

"But you said he was subconsciously trying to get her to make a scene and have it all blow up in his face."

"*Subconsciously,*" Sally corrected. "*Consciously* he'd have been desperate not to have Katie know about Viliama."

Just then Viliama herself stomped round the corner of the corridor and into view. Sally and Jude jumped and looked at each other nervously. Had she overheard them? Were there any loose chairs she could hit them with?

Immediately behind her came Dragan. At least, they assumed it was Dragan, as his face was so heavily bandaged that they could hardly see his features. He said something to Viliama, who immediately snapped back a retort at him before he had finished talking. She was looking round the waiting room, clearly in search of Michael. Catching sight of Sally, she shot her a nasty glare, her eyes sweeping over Jude, who felt, once Viliama's gaze had moved on, rather as if she had had a close brush with a flamethrower.

Her survey of the waiting room completed, a disappointed Viliama muttered something to herself and stalked toward the exit. Dragan followed after her, his voice rising angrily. She ignored him till they were outside. Through the floor-to-ceiling glass window, Sally and Jude saw her swivel abruptly, point one finger at him and launch into a stream of what they could only assume by her manner was highly charged invective. Dragan made some attempts at protest, but she beat him down, stabbing her finger into his chest repeatedly to emphasize her points. Finally she stomped off, Dragan hurrying in her wake.

"She seems to be taking the moral high ground," Sally said.

"Well, he'd be in the nick if it weren't for Michael saying he didn't want him done for assault," Jude said.

"I was pissed off at the time, but I've got to admit now I see why he did that," Sally reflected. "Can you imagine a court case coming up?"

"I wonder how much damage she did him with that stool," Jude said.

"His nose was definitely broken."

"Maybe they did an operation to separate his eyebrows while they were at it," Jude suggested, and they both broke into laughter.

"So glad I'm not the only bitch here," Sally said, smiling at Jude.

"I don't want us to fight anymore," Jude blurted out, surprising herself with the naivete of this comment.

"Me neither," Sally said immediately. "Especially not over Mikey. He's not worth it."

Wow, Jude thought. That's a big change.

"I can't worry about him anymore, or keep his secrets," Sally said resolutely. "I've decided he's messing up too much. He's got to sort himself out. Nobody can do it for him."

"What do you think will happen with him and Katie?" Jude asked. She meant this as a trick question, and waited with bated breath to hear Sally's response.

"Fuck knows," Sally said, to Jude's great relief. "Fuck knows if she'll take him back after this. But the baby—ah, I can't even think about this right now. It's too awful. I don't want to think about it anymore. Or at least for a very long time."

They looked at each other in silence.

"Are you thinking what I'm thinking?" Jude said.

"Why are we even *waiting* for him?" Sally said. "He might be hours yet!"

"Shall we just go home?"

They stood up and made for the door.

"What about your boyfriend?" the receptionist called.

"He's not my boyfriend," Sally said firmly. "And he can make his own way home."

She turned to Jude.

"And now you've got to tell me all about your holiday," she said a little shyly. "Siobhan said you were off with Scott in a couple of days, it sounds really lovely . . . did you get a new swimsuit?"

Chapter
Nineteen

"*I* can't believe you came to Florida to take photos of *dinosaurs,*" Jude said.

"Are you joking? This is brilliant! I'm going to do a whole series!"

Scott, kneeling, fiddled with his camera and shot another couple of photographs of the large fiberglass Tyrannosaurus Rex, which was incongruously planted in front of the tiki barbecue hut. The sun beat down on Jude's head, and she retreated a few paces to a bench in the shade. Scott seemed oblivious to the heat; he was entirely focused on the looming monster in front of him.

"*I* can't believe they didn't even mention these in the guidebook," he said.

"They don't have much space for entries."

"*Still*—how could they possibly leave them out?"

Jude and Scott had found this motel by chance, as they had all their other accommodation. It wasn't busy season in the Florida Keys, and they had spent a leisurely few days driving from one end of the Keys to the other, stopping wherever took their fancy. They had started out at the bottom, in Key West, where Scott had been taking photographs of a luxury yacht that was moored there, and now they were on their last two days, which they had decided to spend hanging out in Key Largo, a much smaller, sleepier town than the bustling Key West, to chill out and work on their tans. Key West was lots of fun, but its beaches were tiny and crowded, and they had wanted a certain amount of peace after getting drunk every night and partying it up. The Sunset Cove had sounded small and sweet and had its own beach, with kayaks and pedalos and a little pier, and they had been given a bungalow with a beach view—well, if they squinted out of the window with their heads tilted to the right to avoid the view of their rental car. But its main claim to fame, which Scott rightly pointed out should have been included in any self-respecting guidebook, was the fact that its small grounds, with roughly pebbled paths meandering between the shacklike bungalows, were strewn with enormous painted fiberglass sculptures of animals. So far they had come across one Tyrannosaurus Rex, two raptors, one deer, one elephant, and a couple of what Scott thought were meerkats. He was completely enchanted by them.

"Dinosaurs and palm trees," he said happily. "Have you ever seen anything so tacky?"

"You know what's missing?" Jude said. "Flamingos. There ought to be flamingos. We're in Florida, after all."

"Mmn, you're right. Still, that would be more obvious. They've definitely gone for the left-field approach."

Scott stood up, brushing some dirt from his knees.

"I'm going to shoot the meerkats now," he announced.

"Well, fascinating as it is watching the artist at work, I think I might change and jump in the sea," Jude said.

"Very good idea. I'll join you in a bit. Hey, where are you going?"

Jude, already heading off toward their bungalow—Bayview, as it was slightly optimistically called—stopped in her tracks. "I told you, I'm going to jump in the sea—"

"Oi, kiss first," Scott said, coming over and dropping a kiss on her lips. They were both hot and sweaty after the drive, and he tasted of salt and suntan lotion. "Sorry not to come with you, I can't not take a few shots of these things right away—"

"No problem," Jude said, stroking the back of his neck. "You take your time. I'll be on a lounger by the sea when you need the key."

He kissed her again and she strolled down to Bayview, trying hard not to let a gigantic smirk come to her face, and failing completely. She couldn't remember ever having been this happy. In the mirror of the tiny cramped bathroom she surveyed herself.

Without vanity, she knew she had never looked so good. Her eyes were shining, her whole face seemed to be lit up with happiness, and her skin was glowing pale gold with the sun, a few small freckles dotting her nose. Her blond hair was thick with pale streaks—helped along by a special spray that Sally had found for her—and she felt slim and gorgeous, contented for once with every square inch of her body. Her suntanned legs actually looked relatively decent and she didn't even care that she could squidge her stomach with both her hands. It was brown. What did she care how big it was?

She unpacked quickly, strewing most of her things over the floor. Scott, for all his tidiness at home, had turned out to have a very relaxed attitude when he was on holiday. She had been worried he would think she was a slob, but when you were on the move every two days you couldn't unpack everything and put it away neatly in drawers, could you? She didn't know if it was because they were on holiday, or the uninhibiting effects of the constant sun, but Scott seemed much more relaxed here, much more easygoing and open to public displays of affection. It was exactly what she had hoped for.

They had even been through one of the best couple-bonding tests on holiday. Scott had eaten some bad fish at a restaurant two nights before, had his bottom glued to the toilet for several hours, and finally emerged weak as a kitten and in need of looking after. Luckily there was a microwave in their motel room and Jude found some boil-in-a-bag white rice at the local pharmacy—why did they call them "pharmacies" when they were so much more like supermarkets?—so she was able to feed him that till his stomach settled down. The initial self-consciousness about the roiling state of his bowels had quickly settled down: in fact, he had been shouting jokes about it through the bathroom door after the first hour or so. Jude had thoughtfully shoved a magazine under the door for him to read and turned up the volume on the TV so they wouldn't be embarrassed by the noises he was making.

Pulling on her bikini now, she couldn't help smiling at the memory. It was ridiculous the things that could make you nostalgic.

It was just lucky she hadn't eaten the fish too. Both of them desperately competing for the same toilet bowl wouldn't have been endearing at all . . .

They were almost halfway through the bottle of suntan lotion. Arranging herself contentedly on a lounger, she smeared herself with it from head to toe. So far she hadn't burned, and the danger period was probably over, but it was boiling hot here and she dreaded going bright red and peeling, identifying herself as obviously as a British holidaymaker as if she had been wearing a pair of Union Jack boxers on her head and complaining because the local restaurants didn't serve fish and chips.

Scott wasn't doing quite as well on the tanning front, but then he was a man and cursed with the macho attitude that didn't let him keep reapplying suntan lotion. Real men only put it on once, no matter how long they were in the sun or how many times they went into the sea and washed it off. His back had been lobsterlike the first couple of days, but the red tinge was gradually ebbing now. Jude lay back, closed her eyes and listened to the soft lapping of the sea just a few feet beneath her. She must have fallen into a doze, because she heard Scott's voice through a thick hazy fog of happy semi-consciousness.

"Hey," she said, stirring. "Done all your photos?"

"For now. I want to do more, though. At night. Sort of do them by day, when they look really tacky and funny, and then at night I can shoot them so they loom up at you and look scary instead. It'll be a great contrast."

She opened her eyes. He was kneeling next to her and his face was lit up with excitement. "You need to put some more suntan stuff on your forehead," she said sleepily. "And your nose."

"Yes, ma'am."

"God, you look really happy about those dinosaurs!"

"I found some antelopes too," he beamed.

"Excellent."

"Wait till you see these photos, Jude. I want to see if I can get them into a show."

"Oh, Scott, that's great . . ." She heaved herself into a sitting position and leaned over the lounger to hug his shoulders awkwardly. He embraced her with fervor.

"I'm so glad we came," he said.

"Because you found some big fiberglass animals?" she said, fishing for compliments.

"Yeah, that's the only reason."

He squished her tightly.

"No, it's just being such a great holiday. I wasn't sure how it would go—you know—" He cleared his throat awkwardly. "Well, you never know how you're going to get on, do you? But we're having such a good time . . ."

"Yeah," she said, trying not to sound too excited by this. The result was that her "Yeah" came out almost dismissive. She corrected it immediately, putting more enthusiasm into her second one. "Yeah, we really are."

"You're crap at paying compliments," Jude said a little drunkenly.

"Bollocks!" Scott slid an arm round her.

"Yes you are," she said, smiling contentedly. "Remember when I pretended to jump into the convertible, and you said I looked like Daisy from *The Dukes of Hazzard?*"

"Well, you did."

"And I said she was much prettier than me, and you said no

she wasn't, and I said, come on, Scott, she was *much* prettier than me, and you said, well, now she's old, because that TV show was on decades ago, so you're definitely much prettier than she is now, because she's ancient by this time? That was the worst compliment I've ever heard in my life!"

"It was your fault," Scott said firmly. He didn't back down, or let himself be bullied, even teasingly, and she liked him for it. "You should just have said 'Thank you,' and let it go at that."

"Hmph." Jude patted her rounded, very un–Daisy Duke tummy contentedly. "That was a *lovely* dinner. They should put those lobsters on the tourist posters."

"They were *enormous.*"

"And all that crab and cheese."

"I'm really going to miss that crab and cheese in London," Scott said wistfully. "I've got used to it by now."

"Oh, don't talk about rainy old London," Jude said, hugging his arm. "Only one more full day here, I can't bear it—"

"Shhh."

Scott bent down and kissed her.

"My fault for talking about London," he said. "Sorry."

They turned into the entrance to the Sunset Cove. The fiberglass deer, lit up by the colored fairy lights strung through the palm trees, were mind-bogglingly surreal.

"I don't feel like going to bed yet," Jude said. "Why don't we go and sit in that hammock for a bit?"

This was another world-class feature of the Sunset Cove: the three gigantic hammocks, or swings, or whatever they called these things in Florida, set right on the beach. Under thatched roofs hung huge wicker contraptions, like enormous baskets with sides that sloped up very gently, padded with thick green mattresses. They were big enough for Scott, who was nearly six foot, to recline in them with only his shins coming off the end. You couldn't be on a romantic holiday without having sex in one of those.

Jude was hoping to coax Scott into this: she had already learned that he was a touch shy about sex in unusual locations. On a near-deserted beach in Marathon, one of their earlier stops, she had proposed a shag in the sea, and had been surprised when he had refused, despite the fact that there was no one else around but a couple far down the shore who looked as if they were doing exactly that. She was crossing her fingers that if she could get Scott into the hammock and start messing around, he would, especially with a few rum runners inside him, be so carried away he wouldn't care too much that they were in the open air. After all, the wicker walls of the hut were very wide, and the thatched roof low enough that it offered a lot of concealment. If they were discreet, no one should be able to realize what they were doing.

"Feeling romantic?" he said, squeezing her affectionately.

Yeah, right, she thought, but didn't say aloud. Right then she was thinking with a much lower portion of her anatomy than her heart.

"Mmmn, this is lovely," Scott said, climbing into the wicker swing. "Fresh sea air, the best hammock in the world, and thou."

Jude, stretching out beside him, reached up to kiss him, strategically letting one hand rest, as if casually, on his stomach. Her calculation was that if she could get his penis out of his trousers, and into a state of excitement, then he would probably not insist on putting it back again long enough for them to return to Bayview and finish what they had started. But she took it slow. They rolled toward each other, sinking luxuriously into the center of the hammock, and kissed, gently at first, then deeper, mapping each other's lips with their tongues, the light sea breeze stroking over their exposed skin. Scott wrapped Jude's hair around his hands, caressing her scalp in the way he had already discovered got her wriggling with excitement. It was dark out here on the sea front and she could scarcely see his face, which added somehow to the thrill, as if they were anonymous lovers who just happened to know what turned the other one on.

She had left her hand on his stomach, and now she pushed up his T-shirt, stroking his skin in slow small circles at first, then more insistently, playing her fingers underneath his belt as he offered no resistance, feeling the soft line of hair that led down to his groin. He groaned and untwined one hand from her hair, moving it down and closing it around hers.

"Jude—no—" he said, but she sensed it was only a token resistance.

"No, let me go on—" she whispered into his mouth, and slipped her hand down further, playing with the waistband of his boxers. He groaned again, still trying to stop her, and then her hand molded around his penis, half-erect under the soft cotton, and he sighed and his hand fell away from hers, coming up to find one of her breasts. She gasped, pushing herself into his palm, and closed her hand tighter around him, feeling him hardening under her fingers. She had him now. He wouldn't make her stop.

"Oh *God,*" Scott moaned as his penis came out into the night air.

With one hand closed on him firmly she began to stroke. He fidgeted beneath her, pulling up her skirt, reaching up between her thighs, and then his fingers slid into her. It was so good it spurred her on. She bent down, careful not to dislodge his fingers, and took him in her mouth.

Scott gasped, and his hand went slack for a second, but then took up the rhythm she needed, and she bore down on him, controlling him with one hand, the other pressed awkwardly against the mattress for balance. The wicker was creaking heavily, and she was worried her knees were going into spasm, not to mention her mouth, but then Scott's stroking fingers hit their mark and she came so hard she forgot about any muscle cramps and sank her mouth even deeper onto him, and suddenly his other hand, which was buried in her hair, clamped on her scalp, and he made a feeble effort to push her away, but she held on for dear life as his penis jerked and his hands went limp and she felt him flooding into her mouth. They had been having so much sex over the past few days that there wasn't that much. She held on and swallowed and then, when she was sure he had done, she relaxed and let him slip out of her mouth.

She took a long breath and then slowly slid up to lie beside him, their heads again touching.

"That was wonderful," he whispered.

"Good," she said, her face suffused with smugness.

"I wasn't sure—I didn't even know if I'd get an erection, outside like this—but God, that was wonderful."

"Good," Jude said again, grinning with self-satisfaction like a mad fool. There was something so powerful and sexy about doing that to a man, especially one you cared about as much as she did for Scott; she wondered if this was what men felt like after they fucked a woman, this triumphant feeling of having reduced your mate to a quivering, happy, boneless wreck.

"Was it good for you?" he asked.

"*Oh* yeah."

"Because I was thinking . . . since we're here now, and your skirt's up round your waist, and my hand happens to be feeling its way into your knickers—"

He suited the action to the word.

"I was just wondering if you wanted to come again . . ."

Jude was beyond coyness or even any playful banter. She pushed her hips against his fingers, dragged his head toward her, shoved her tongue in his mouth and abandoned herself completely to what he was doing.

"I take it that's a yes," Scott mumbled, as best he could with her tongue down his throat, and got on with the task in hand.

Chapter
Twenty

"Sal! Hey! I'm back!"

Jude knocked a rat-a-tat-tat on Sally's door. She was about to fish in her bag for the key when Sally opened it—looking, to Jude's surprise, more than a little embarrassed.

"Hey!" she said, kissing Jude. "I forgot you were due back today! How was it?"

"Great! I sent you a postcard, but you probably haven't got it yet."

"Ooh, look how tanned you are—"

"I brought us some rum," Jude said, brandishing the bottle. "I thought we could make rum runners."

"Oh, great . . ."

Sally, who had been partially blocking the door, took the bottle and said a distracted "Thank you." Jude barreled inside, too keen to relate all the exciting moments of her holiday to pick up on the fact that Sally's welcome hadn't been delivered with the full-blown enthusiasm she had been expecting. As soon as she was inside, however, she realized that something was up. There were two wine glasses on the coffee table; the living room was lit mostly by candles, creating a romantic atmosphere, which Sally wouldn't have bothered with if she were on her own; and just then there came the unmistakable sound of a wine cork popping in the kitchen.

"Is there someone here?" Jude said stupidly. She stared at Sally, realization sinking in. "Is it *Michael?*"

"No, no," Sally said, blushing. "I haven't seen him since that night at Casualty."

"Then—"

"Hi, Jude," said Paul, emerging from the kitchen. He too looked as if he were blushing, though it was hard to tell across the room by candlelight.

"*Paul!*" Jude took the whole situation in at one glance. "Um, hi! How are you doing?"

"Oh, good, thanks. Sally and I just went to see a film."

"Oh, what was that?" Jude was very grateful for this conversational bone.

"The new Spielberg. We didn't think much of it, did we, Sally?"

"No, not really. A bit heavy-handed."

That was not a phrase Sally had ever used in Jude's hearing. She must be quoting Paul. Curiouser and curiouser.

"Would you like a glass of wine?" Paul offered.

Jude knew she ought to go. But she was bursting with news, and she wanted to wind down after the long flight.

"Maybe just half a glass," she said, compromising between her own needs and Sally's obvious self-consciousness. "Then I should go and get as much sleep as I can."

"Do you want a sleeping pill?" Sally said with telling eagerness. "I could fish one out for you if you want."

Right, Jude thought. Get a sleeping pill down me now with some red wine and you'll be hoping I'll pass out in twenty minutes.

She wasn't taking this personally. Sally hadn't been seeing Paul when Jude left, just over a week ago; this could only at best be a second date. It was the first time Sally had ever, for the whole time Jude had known her, entertained a man at hers with wine and candles. No wonder Sally was feeling deeply awkward about the situation.

"We picked up some melatonin in Florida," Jude said, accepting a glass of wine from Paul. He had taken her at her word, and only half-filled it; clearly he didn't want to encourage her to stay long, either. "It's supposed to help you sleep. I'm going to take two and pass out."

"Should you take them now?" Sally suggested helpfully.

"No thanks," Jude said, grinning. She couldn't help enjoying teasing Sally a bit. "I've still got to unpack. Don't worry, I won't stay long."

Sally launched into a confused series of protestations that Jude was welcome to stay as long as she wanted, accompanied by Paul mumbling much the same thing. It was like a badly written aria for soprano and tenor. If Jude had been feeling more energetic, she would have joined in. She imagined this with much amusement as Sally and Paul gradually ran down to a halt.

Soprano: "You must stay! Stay! Do not go away!"

Contralto: "No no no, I will go! No no no, now I go!"

Tenor (pianissimo): "Obviously it's not my flat or anything, but do at least stay and finish your wine, it's quite a nice South African Cabernet Shiraz . . ."

Jude sank onto the armchair, leaving the sofa tactfully for the burgeoning lovers, so they wouldn't be stranded on different pieces of soft furniture when she did take her leave.

"So how was Florida?" Sally said brightly.

"*Brilliant,*" Jude said with a contented sigh. She launched into a description of the Keys, and had just got as far as the Seven Mile Bridge, in which Paul, as an architect, was taking a polite interest, when there came a fuzzy beep which was their ancient intercom system announcing that someone was ringing the bell downstairs.

Sally looked at Jude in absolute panic. Jude, taking in the situation immediately, said quickly: "Bloody kids. Are they still ringing your bell at all hours?"

"Bit late for kids, isn't it?" Paul said.

"You'd be surprised round here," Jude said dourly. Another difference between rich architects who lived in posh areas of Notting Hill and people like herself who had grown up on insalubrious council estates.

The bell rang again. Despite Jude having provided her with a perfect excuse, Sally looked as hunted as if it were the Grim Reaper downstairs doing practice swings with his scythe while he waited to be buzzed in.

"Ignore hi—*them,*" Jude corrected herself swiftly. "They'll get bored and go away."

The bell stopped ringing. Sally relaxed slightly.

"So what's in rum runners?" she said in what Jude recognized as her making-social-conversation-while-her-mind-was-elsewhere tone. "They sound great!"

"You serve them in these enormous glasses," Jude began.

"You can put all kinds of stuff in them, there's this 151-proof rum they float on the top sometimes and set fire to—God, I had one of those the first night and I nearly passed out in my starter, it was so strong—they call them appetizers in America, starters, but they're *enormous,* you should see the portions they give you over there—"

The phone rang. Jude knew exactly who it was, and so, by her manner, did Sally, who was doing a great impression of a heroine in a thriller being stalked by a serial killer.

"I'll just leave that," she said nervously. "We're having such a nice chat, why spoil it—"

Jude realized with horror that Sally had forgotten that the machine would pick up. Sure enough, after five rings the phone stopped; Sally looked unspeakably relieved; and then Michael's voice filled the silence, tinny through the speakers, but unmistakable: "Sal? It's me, Mikey. I just rang your bell, your lights were on, I thought you might be in the bath or something and not hear the bell—pick up if you're there—Sal? Sal, I really need to see you. Katie's walked out on me and she won't answer my calls, she's staying with Tash and she won't let Katie see me—I don't know what to do—Sal, I really need to talk to you . . ." He sighed long and gustily. "Look, ring me, OK?"

He tailed off on a dying fall, and silence seemed to surge in and fill the room, replacing the sound of his voice.

Sally was staring at Jude in mute appeal. Jude gathered up all the confidence that a blissfully happy week with Scott had given her and rose to the challenge.

"Poor Mikey," she said, infusing her voice with just the right blend of pity and detachment. "I feel so sorry for him. He's made such a mess of things with Katie. But he's got to find her and try to sort things out. There's no point just leaning on his friends like this. I'm sure he's leaving exactly the same message on my machine right now."

"Has he had a fight with his girlfriend?" Paul said.

"Yeah, a bad one," Jude answered, seeing that Sally was still incapable of speech. "He's been an idiot, basically. But, you know, there's nothing we can do about it."

She waved her hand in dismissal of Michael and gave Paul a big smile to signal the relative unimportance of Michael's problems.

"So where was I? Oh yeah, rum runners," she said.

Twenty minutes later the atmosphere had calmed down enough for Jude to judge that it was time to leave the new lovebirds to bill and coo together. She rose, citing jet lag, and Sally saw her to the door.

"See you tomorrow night?" she said. "I want to hear all the juicy details you couldn't say in front of Paul."

"Lots of those," Jude said, with a naughty smile.

"Thank you SO MUCH," Sally mouthed, kissing her goodnight. They hugged tightly.

"Night, Jude," Paul called from the sofa.

"Have fun!" Jude mouthed back to Sally. She stared for a moment at the door as it closed behind her, hoping that Sally and Paul would at least snog tonight, that the evening hadn't been ruined romantically by Michael's intrusion.

Unpacking, she gave her Florida souvenirs pride of place. Two shot glasses from Key West, the sheet of room rates from the Sunset Cove (two of the rooms had actually been converted

Airstream trailers, and Scott had been very disappointed to find out they were taken. Maybe next time, he had said casually, glancing sideways at Jude to see how she took this) and three large postcards from the motel, showing the dock in better days, when it had been freshly painted and you could actually read the name of the motel along the pier. The three thatched hammock huts were dotted along the dock. Jude put a finger on theirs, and beamed smugly. She even found herself reading through the sheet of room rates (Bayview: 1 Queen Bed with Small Kitchen; Seaside: An Airstream Trailer with 1 Queen Bed and a Fold Down Futon) with a nostalgic tug at her heart. Like Scott's food-poisoning trauma, it was absurd how the smallest things could make you go all gooey when you were in love.

Chapter

Twenty-one

"God, I still stink of chlorine. I'm going to have to have another shower," Sally said, sniffing her arm.

"Oh, I quite like it," Jude said. "Reminds me I've just managed to do something healthy for a change."

Sally snorted. "Healthy! All you wanted to do was show off your tan! You were the only person in the whole pool in a bikini!"

"I have a brown tummy," Jude said happily. "I was the only person in the pool with a brown tummy. After nearly two weeks. That tan-maximizing cream really works."

"You should be ashamed of yourself, flaunting your holiday in front of those poor deprived people. I hope your hair goes green from the chlorine," Sally said malevolently.

Jude's hair was still lightly damp at the roots: the council-provided hairdryers at the pool were so weak she'd have done better to use the hand dryer. She didn't mind. It reminded her of Florida, coming out of the sea to let her hair dry gradually in the sun. There was a light breeze wafting down the Caledonian Road, considerably more polluted than the one off the Keys, but it lifted her hair gently, and she tilted her head and let all those petrol fumes run through it.

"Nah, I won't go green," she said. "Some jealous cow gave me this crappy lightening spray before I left in an attempt to sabotage my lovely holiday, but if her evil plan had worked I'd have known by now."

Sally ignored this last comment. "Swimming was nice. We should do it more often."

"I know. I've lived here all my life with a pool only five minutes' walk away and I've hardly ever been there. Seems a waste."

"It's not too bad, for a council pool. I just worry about all the kids weeing in it."

"That's why there's so much chlorine," Jude said. "They're trying to burn up all that wee."

"Or at least stop you tasting it."

"Mmn, maybe we should change this conversation right now before we start making excuses never to get in the pool again—Sal, look!"

"What?"

Jude was pointing across the street, to Michael's house.

"I don't want to see him," Sally said quickly. "I'll just nip into the newsagent's till he's gone. If I see him he'll get hold of me again, you know I can't resist Michael, he'll just pour on the charm and I'll end up feeling sorry for him; and I made a resolution that I wasn't going to see him for at least a month, to give Paul a chance—"

"Yeah, yeah, I know—" Jude cut through Sally's torrent of words. "It's not Michael. It's Katie."

"*Katie?*"

Katie had just come out of Michael's front door. She moved slowly down the path to the front gate, hampered by the fact that she was carrying two big cheap bags printed with a garish checked pattern, the plastic kind sold in 99p stores, ostensibly for taking dirty clothes to the launderette. In practice they were more often used by very poor people who couldn't afford even cheap suitcases. You saw them at Victoria coach station, bound up with string and brown tape, carried by skinny, desperate men wearing mismatched clothes from Oxfam smelling of other people's sweat. Those checked bags were one of the most instant indicators of poverty Jude knew, and they made Katie look destitute.

"She's moving her stuff out," Sally said, as Katie hefted the bags through the gate.

"Should we go and talk to her?" Jude really wanted to: more, if she were strictly honest with herself, out of nosiness than any real concern for Katie. Her curiosity was rampant.

They exchanged glances. Jude saw immediately that Sally couldn't resist this opportunity either. They might well never see Katie again; they couldn't pass up this chance.

Katie had settled onto a seat at the bus stop, looking like a bag lady with her two swollen plastic carriers at her feet. She looked up in surprise as Sally spoke her name.

"Oh, hi," she said. The rims of her eyes were puffy and red and her face looked drawn, sunken in on its bones. She was painfully thin.

"Are you OK?" Jude asked clumsily.

"No," Katie said, a tinge of anger creeping into her voice. "Of course I'm not OK." She gestured to the bags. "I've just been getting my stuff."

"You should have borrowed some of Michael's duffel bags,

he's got loads," Sally said, concerned, looking at Katie's cheap carrier bags.

"I didn't want to take anything from him," Katie said shortly.

"Did you see Michael?" Jude asked.

"I told him not to be there. I never want to see him again."

"Oh, Katie, I'm so sorry," Sally blurted out.

"You're *sorry?*" Katie stared at her. "You did everything you could to break us up! I don't believe for a moment you're sorry!"

Sally was horrified. "Katie, I didn't!" she protested, knowing that this was not completely true. She hadn't actively tried to break them up; but she would have been happy, as she always was, if Michael and Katie hadn't made it. Not under these circumstances, though. That was beyond anything she might have fantasized.

"You were always round at ours!" Katie said. "Showing me you knew Michael better than me, you knew his flat better than me. You were like this awful reminder right across the street." She glanced momentarily at her bags. "Like saying I should have used Michael's duffel bags. You were always pointing out you knew everything he had in his flat."

"I didn't mean to make you feel bad! I was just trying to be helpful!" Sally said.

Katie snorted.

"I never came round without being invited by Michael," Sally protested defensively. "If you didn't like it you should have talked to him!"

"I tried," Katie said sadly. "I really tried. I should have known then that it wasn't going to work. Even before that girl."

She looked up at a noisy rattle in the street to see if a bus was coming, but it was Sunday afternoon, reduced service, and all that was coming down Caledonian Road was yet another lorry.

"Have you talked to him since then?" Jude said, sitting down on the seat next to Katie so they wouldn't both be standing over her as if they were conducting a cross-examination.

"He kept ringing me at Tash's, but I wouldn't talk to him. I switched off my mobile. I never want to see him again."

"But what about the baby?" Sally couldn't help asking.

Katie wouldn't meet her gaze. She looked up the street again, clearly desperate for a bus to come and take her away from this nightmare conversation.

"Should we call you a minicab?" Jude said.

Katie shook her head. "It's OK. I can get a tube at King's Cross."

"Are you staying with Tash?"

"Yeah. I didn't want her to come and help me with this, though. She's been so brilliant already. I thought I should do this on my own." She looked up at Sally. "I really hated you," she said, sounding very tired. "I felt I could never live up to you. Michael was always going on about you, Sally this and Sally that. It was like you were his ideal woman." She laughed, a short bitter spurt of breath that had very little amusement behind it. "And look what happened. I was so busy worrying about you that it never occurred to me he might be off with someone else." She stared down at her hands. "I never noticed anything," she said. "He was always so great . . . they say you notice when someone's having an affair. Well, that's bollocks."

The bags were both open, being too cheap to have any zips or buckles, and Jude couldn't help seeing a stuffed toy poking out of the top of one of them. It looked like a polar bear. She wondered whether Katie had bought it for the baby, or if it was her own. Either speculation was equally poignant.

"Mikey's terrible with relationships," Sally said. "It's not your fault."

"His mum's a bitch," Katie said, dragging the sleeve of her T-shirt across her eyes, scrubbing at them to hide any incipient tears. "She hated that I was having his baby. She's never let him grow up." She took a deep breath. "I just want to forget about everything," she said. "I want to pretend none of this ever happened."

The bus finally came, rumbling slowly down the street. Katie jumped up and stuck out her hand, flagging it down with such disproportionate eagerness that it showed all too clearly how keen she was to get away from Jude and Sally. She grabbed her bags and heaved them to the edge of the pavement.

"Can I help you?" Sally said. "Those look heavy—should you be carrying all that stuff by yourself?"

Katie brushed her away, already feeling in her pocket for her Travelcard. "I expect Michael didn't tell you," she said. The bus doors swung open and she hoisted her bags up the steps, fishing out her card to show the driver.

Jude knew suddenly that she didn't want to ask. But the word "What?" popped out of her mouth as if she had no control over her own speech.

"I had an abortion," Katie said. "No worrying about carrying heavy things for me. I'm surprised he didn't tell you. His mum's probably having a party right now to celebrate."

And she climbed onto the bus and made her way down the aisle, bags bumping along the floor, without looking back.

Chapter
Twenty-two

"Sal! Sal, let me in!" Michael pounded on the door. "Sal, I'm not just going to give up and go away! I have to see you!"

Jude had been chewing her fingernails for the past five minutes, wondering whether to intervene. God knew how Michael had got into the block of flats—probably waited till someone was unlocking the door, fumbled with his keys, smiled at them charmingly and got them to hold the door open for him. It wouldn't have been that difficult. In a smarter area of London, the scar on his head might have given someone pause, but in King's Cross it would barely raise an eyebrow.

"Maybe I should go out and tell him to go away," she said for the third time.

"Leave it," Scott said, equally repetitively. "If she doesn't open the door he'll get tired of it after a while and go away."

Jude pressed her eye again to the peephole. "No, he's sitting down," she reported. "Fuck. Thank God Sally wasn't seeing Paul tonight. Imagine if he was in there with Michael banging on the door like that . . ."

"If he was in there he'd have come out by now and told Michael to fuck off," Scott pointed out.

"Yes, I can see Paul coming over all manly," Jude agreed.

"Sal, I'm not going away!" Michael called. "I'm going to stay right here if I have to spend the night! You'll have to come out sometime!"

"Maybe the neighbors will ring the police," Scott suggested.

"Them!" Jude snorted. "They couldn't give a monkey's! Catch them worrying about something like that! People have screaming matches all over the place and no one's ever called the police."

"Not even if, you know, they think it's domestic violence?"

"Hah. It'd be nice to think so, wouldn't it?"

"*You* could always ring the police," Scott said.

"God, I don't know, that seems a bit much—it's not like Michael's going to do anything besides shout through the door. Besides, they'd take hours to get here, if they came at all. He's outside, she's inside—it's not like he's beating her up or anything."

"Well, Sally could ring them if she wanted."

"It'd never occur to her." Jude was struck by a thought. "Maybe I should ring her."

She dashed over to her phone and rang Sally's number. "It's engaged," she reported.

"She's probably taken it off the hook in case he rings her on his mobile."

Jude put down the phone. "I don't know what to do," she said helplessly.

"Leave them to it? Come back and watch the video?"

"I can't, Scott." She went over and hugged him. "I can't. They're my friends. And besides, if we turned the sound up loud enough to cover all the noise he's making, Mrs. Sagar next door'd start thumping on the walls. No one minds a bit of shouting, but she goes loopy if the TV's on full blast."

Scott sighed into her hair. "OK," he said. "What do you want to do?"

Jude felt a warm rush of happiness. Scott was supporting her. She hadn't expected that for a moment, given his previous comments about her over-involvement with the Michael-Sally situation.

"I thought you thought I should back off from all this," she said, raising her head.

"I do. But it's not exactly relaxing watching a video with some crazed bloke trying to beat down his ex-girlfriend's door, is it?"

Despite his bluff tone, Jude wasn't fooled. He was trying to help. She was hugely touched.

"I'll go out and talk to him," she decided.

"Well, I'll come too," Scott said firmly.

"Being all macho and protective in case Michael goes for me with a machete?"

"I want him to know you're not alone," Scott muttered gruffly.

Jude kissed him, feeling like the luckiest girl in the world. She crossed to the door and opened it, her heart beating fast. Now that she had actually decided to confront Michael, she was wondering if it was such a good idea after all.

"Michael?" she said nervously.

Michael, who had swung round at the sound of her door opening, looked up at her wanly. He was sitting at the base of

Sally's door, as if he thought that positioning himself any further away might somehow leave her enough room to make a dash for it. The scar on his scalp was bright red under the fluorescent strip-lighting in the hallway.

"Jude!" he said. "I just want to talk to her! It's really important! Tell her she has to talk to me!"

"I don't think she wants to, Michael."

"She has to! It's really important!"

"Why don't you write her a letter?"

"No," Michael said impatiently, "I need to *talk* to her, you have to understand—"

He pounded his fist on the door again.

"Sal, I'm still here! Let me in!"

Jude imagined Sally's eye pressed against the peephole, taking in this whole scene: Michael slumped against her door; Jude standing there awkwardly, her whole posture indicating embarrassment; and Scott, emerging from Jude's flat to lean against the door jamb. He nodded at Michael.

"You don't need to stand there like a bodyguard," Michael snapped. "I'm not going to start beating anyone up. I just want to TALK TO SALLY."

He raised his voice on these last words, completely unnecessarily: the walls were thin, and Sally, hovering as she doubtless was on the other side of the door, couldn't have avoided hearing everything that was being said.

"Why don't you come into Jude's and have a bevvy and talk it over, mate," Scott suggested nobly. "It doesn't look as if she's going to open the door any time soon."

So much for non-involvement. Jude shot Scott a glance in

which were mingled gratitude, appreciation, and the promise of some really good sex on the sofa later on. She wasn't sure if she'd managed to convey the last one successfully. Ah well, it would be a nice surprise for him.

Michael hesitated for a moment, probably at the offer of beer. Then he shook his head. "No, I'm not going anywhere. I've got to talk to Sally and it can't wait. Thanks, though," he added in a reflex of politeness.

"Michael, what's so urgent about talking to her now?" Jude said.

Michael set his jaw. "I've made up my mind," he declared. "Everything's going to change from now on. I have to talk to Sally."

He banged again on the door.

"Sal, did you hear that? Everything's going to change! I've been doing some really serious thinking! I need to tell you about it!"

Jude sighed, resigning herself. Michael wouldn't be persuaded away. He would stay there, shouting, for at least the next few hours, an atmosphere completely unconducive to her and Scott having wild animal sex on the sofa. They had rented *No Mercy,* a rather crappy thriller with Kim Basinger and Richard Gere, which however was supposed to feature some torrid sex scenes and a lot of Kim and Richard being handcuffed to each other wading through swamps and getting their clothes suggestively plastered to their bodies, and Jude had been looking forward to some hot shagging afterward as a nice culmination to the evening. She was still brown enough to make taking her own clothes off something she positively looked forward to.

Now Michael and his serious thinking were ruining all her lovely plans.

"We've got a fridge full of beer," Scott said persuasively to Michael.

How perverse Jude was: now that Scott was being supportive and helpful, she resented him for it. She had wanted to get rid of Michael so they could get back to *No Mercy,* not have him planted on the very sofa she had earmarked for a very different activity, getting drunk and beery and sobbing on their shoulders. She shot a repressive glance at Scott, but he wasn't looking in her direction.

Michael, however, had hardened his resolve. Having turned down beer once, he wasn't going to be tempted by it again.

"No," he said. "I've made up my mind. I'm not leaving till I've talked to Sal."

Sally had indeed been listening. The door clicked, and everyone fell so silent that the sound of it opening seemed magnified by the drama of the moment. Sally stood on the threshold. She stared at Michael, hardly seeming even to take in Scott and Jude's presence. She looked extremely tired, as if she had worn herself out with the effort of wrestling with herself to come to the decision to talk to him.

"You'd better come in," she said.

"Sal!" Michael clambered to his feet.

Her eyes flickered briefly to Scott and Jude. "It's OK, don't worry," she said, holding the door open for Michael. "I'll be fine."

"Do you think he's still in there?" Scott said, turning off the TV.

"Probably. They'll be making up. It was bound to happen sooner or later."

Jude reached for him as he came back to sit on the sofa. The lights were already dimmed; it was the perfect setting for a bit of hanky-panky. *No Mercy* had achieved the desired effect. Kim and Richard had shot it out with Jeroen Krabbé in a dramatic finale—lots of whirring overhead fans and picturesque balconies with white muslin curtains fluttering in the breeze—and Jude was all psyched up to recreate some of the crucial scenes from the film. Well, one of them. She wasn't planning to handcuff them together and stand underneath the shower till their clothes were soaking wet. Though that did stir up happy memories of a rousing bout of sex they'd had in a motel room shower in Florida. Naked, however. And with their hands free to grab whichever part of each other's bodies had seemed most appropriate at the time.

"Come here," she said lustfully.

"I sense you have evil intentions," Scott said, mock-nervously.

"Damn right I have. You'd better just make your mind up to submit to me. I don't want to have to hurt you."

"Oh no, you're turning me on, and you know *that's* not supposed to happen," Scott said happily, quoting an American comedy show they had recently watched on cable.

He sat down next to her. She grabbed at his T-shirt. The film must have had a similar effect on him, because two seconds later she was writhing underneath him, stretched full length on the sofa, and she could already feel his erection hard against her groin. They were just dragging each other's T-shirts up when the doorbell rang.

"*No,*" Scott groaned. "I don't *believe* it."

"Jude! It's me! Let me in!"

It was Sally.

"Let's just be quiet till she goes away," Jude hissed in his ear, running her hands over his bare chest.

"Jude! Let me in!"

"Fuck it," Scott said, sitting up, every fiber of his body expressing deep reluctance. "You won't be able to concentrate anyway, you'll get all worried there might be a crisis—"

"No, I will! I'll be fine! Honestly!"

"Jude? Please!" Sally yelled. "I wouldn't do this if it wasn't really important. I know you're in there!"

"Oh, *fuck,*" Jude said, sitting up too, as best she could, since Scott was still half on her legs. "Or not," she added sarcastically. She couldn't help reaching down and caressing Scott briefly through his trousers.

"Don't *do* that," he said in frustration.

"Ooh, that's a turnabout for the books," she said, kissing him. "You're usually begging me to pay it some attention."

"I don't have to beg," Scott said with hauteur. "You get it out sometimes before you even bother to kiss me, you sex-crazed trollop."

"I promise we'll get back to this once I talk to Sally, OK?" she said, heaving herself off the sofa.

Sally was lit up by some fervor of happiness that had Jude gaping. She had never seen Sally like this before. Her whole body was glowing as if she were radioactive. Jude almost imagined that she would get scorched if she got too close to her. It was like the way angels were presented in bad TV movies, surrounded by a flame of white light.

Sally seized Jude's hand. "You have to come to mine," she said. She sounded as excited as a five-year-old about to show off its birthday cake. "Scott too. Scott!" she called. "We're going next door!"

On Sally's coffee table were a bottle of champagne and four glasses. Michael was standing with his hand on the neck of the bottle, poised to open it as soon as they were all assembled.

"What's *happening?*" Jude asked, dazed by sexual frustration and a complete inability to grasp what might be important enough to summarily drag her and Scott away from their happy foreplay.

"We've got an announcement to make!" Michael said. He too was beaming as if he were about to pronounce that world peace had finally been achieved. He looked incredibly handsome, his big dark eyes glowing.

Jude had a really bad feeling about this. She reached for Scott's hand and gripped it tightly.

"Sally—" Michael stretched out his hand to Sally. She crossed to him and stood in the shelter of his arm, smiling shyly. He hugged her tightly.

"Sally," he announced, his chin resting uxorially in her hair, "has just agreed—Sally's made me more happy than I ever thought I could be—Sally and I just got engaged!"

And he reached for the bottle of champagne and in one triumphant gesture popped the cork. A white cloud of bubbles spurted all over the coffee table.

Chapter

Twenty-three

"It was like a premature ejaculation," Jude said. "Which is exactly what this fucking engagement is."

"I thought you'd be happy!" Scott said, baffled. "Didn't you always want to get them together?"

"Yeah, but not like this! Or not now! Not after Michael cheated on Katie like that!"

"But you always knew—I mean, you always said how unreliable he was," Scott pointed out.

Jude couldn't sit still. She was pacing up and down her living room. It made her realize how small it was. Only eight good strides between the wall on one side and the bookcase on the other.

"Yeah, but that was different! I thought it was because Sally was really the woman of his life and he was just messing up because he wasn't with her! But he seemed really convinced about Katie. There was a baby, for God's sake. And you should have seen Katie after the abortion, Scott, it was awful. He's really destroyed her. Someone who could do that'll do anything."

"You think he'll cheat on Sally too?"

"I wouldn't be at all surprised. Oh God, there they were, looking so happy—I thought that was what I always wanted, it was, you're right—and when it actually happened all I wanted to do was drag Sally off somewhere and just yell: 'Don't even *think* about it!' at her."

She came to a halt at the coffee table, which she had had to swerve around each time to pace properly.

"I don't know, maybe I'm being really negative. I just keep thinking that things aren't like before. Katie had to have an *abortion*. And he cheated on her with that Viliama nutcase. He was clearly desperate to fuck things up with Katie. I mean, can't Sally see all that?"

"She loves him," Scott said matter-of-factly. "And he really loves her. I never saw him looking at Katie like that."

"Really?"

Jude came to sit next to him, grasping at this straw of comfort.

"Really. He looked at Katie—more affectionately. Indulgently. No, that's not quite right. I'm not much good at this. Like a kid with a new toy he was mad about, but he'd get tired of eventually."

"And you don't think that was how he was with Sally?" Jude knew this was true, but still needed the reassurance.

"No. He looked at her like he really loved her."

"It just feels so *soon*," Jude said. "That's why I said that thing about premature ejaculation. I mean, it's only been a few weeks. He hasn't had time to think about what he's doing. I worry that he's rushing into something because he's fucked up everywhere else."

"He could just as well have rushed into shagging some other nutcase," Scott pointed out.

"Yeah, that's true." Jude cheered up a bit. "Maybe this has made him realize he needs to get serious."

"Exactly."

"He's never been engaged before," she continued, gaining strength from Scott's encouragement to see matters in a more positive light. "He doesn't just shoot around proposing to all his girls. He must have really thought about this."

"He did seem totally convinced," Scott said. "When he was outside the door, I mean. And when he was telling us, he looked like he was over the moon."

"Oh, I wish I could think it'll all be all right!"

"Well, even if it isn't—"

"I know. There's nothing I can do about it."

"Whereas," Scott said, taking her hand and putting it on his crotch, "there *is* something you can do about this."

"It's not in as interesting a state as it was before," Jude said a shade petulantly.

"Exactly. It needs help. I think you should concentrate on that. Take your mind off things you can't help and have some pity on it instead."

"You're not suggesting that for any selfish motives, of course," Jude said, cheering up a bit. "You're just being kind and trying to distract me."

"Yup. In a completely unselfish way."

She sighed a long deep sigh that felt as if she were dragging it up from the very bottom of her lungs.

"Well, if you think it would help me out—"

"I do."

"I'll give it a go," she said, unzipping his trousers.

*   *   *

There were wedding magazines strewn all over Sally's flat. Being, however, the thorough fashionista that she was, these were only the tip of the iceberg. She had bought a lavish coffee-table book called *Real-Life Weddings of the Stars,* which was already marked with a large quantity of bright pink Post-it notes.

"Look at Audrey Hepburn," she cooed. "Of course, I don't have the figure, and my hair wouldn't do that—I *wish* it was longer! Maybe I could get extensions—but doesn't she look lovely?"

There was no arguing with that one. Jude took the book from Sally's hands and started flicking through it. She couldn't help admitting there was something hugely touching about all those beautiful brides in white. It was very unfair: you hardly ever even noticed the groom. He might as well have been a celebrity walker, there solely to accompany the bride so she didn't look poignantly alone in her lovely flouncy dress.

"Elizabeth Taylor looks nice in this one," Jude commented. "That would suit you."

"God, don't even *mention* Elizabeth Taylor to an engaged woman! It's like saying 'Macbeth' to an actor!"

"Cross yourself and turn around three times," Jude suggested. "Isn't that what they do?"

"Damn, that *would* suit me," Sally said regretfully, looking over her shoulder at the glossy photo. "Well, never mind. It would be such bad luck."

"Suppose so." Jude turned the page. More Elizabeth Taylor. And then the page after that, and the page after that . . .

"Thank God you're not getting married in the sixties," she said. "Horrible pill-box hats."

"I don't even think I want a veil."

"Ooh, you should try some on first. They look so romantic."

"We'll have to do the rounds of all the wedding shops," Sally said happily. "The posh ones, of course. Money no expense. Mum and Dad said to push the boat out."

"You lucky thing," Jude said enviously. Her mother was so skint that if Jude ever got married, she'd be lucky to get a toaster as a present, forget any help with the wedding expenses.

"And there's our evening's entertainment," Sally said, gesturing at a large pile of videos.

"We can't watch all of them!" Jude protested, noticing the videos for the first time. "We'll be up till dawn!"

"No, silly. They're all films with people getting married. I thought we could scroll through them to see if there's anything nice I could get ideas from."

"Fun for me," Jude said dourly.

"Oh Jude, don't be mean! You said you'd help!"

"Yeah, I know."

"And you've seen them all anyway!"

"Have I?" Jude crouched down by the TV and looked through the pile. *"Runaway Bride,"* she read. *"The Wedding Planner."*

"Oh, we don't have to watch much of that. Jennifer Lopez's outfit is horrible. But I think there's another wedding in the beginning."

"Great. One down, three hundred and ninety-nine to go."

"You're exaggerating horribly."

"Father of the Bride, Seven Brides for Seven Brothers, Four Weddings and a Funeral, The Philadelphia Story, My Best Friend's

Wedding, The Princess Bride, High Society. Bloody hell, I never realized how many wedding films there were. *The Wedding Singer*—you don't want that, it's eighties. Horrible clothes. *Monsoon Wedding*—that's Indian, Sally, for fuck's sake! What are you going to do, pick up sari-wrapping tips?"

"I'm looking at everything right now," Sally said defensively. "I'm keeping an open mind. And some of the clothes in that were gorgeous."

"Well if you decide to go Indian, we can do the red dot on your forehead with a marker pen." She picked up another one. *"The Swan*—what's that?"

"Grace Kelly as a princess," Sally breathed ecstatically.

"Well, stay away from cars on steep mountain slopes if you're going to do that one. Talk about an omen. *Much* worse than Elizabeth Taylor." Jude came to the end of the pile. "You missed some," she said.

"Oh, what?" Sally reached eagerly for a pen and a Post-it note.

"Bride of Frankenstein, Bride of Chucky—"

"Fuck off," Sally said, but she couldn't help laughing. "Actually, there was one at the video store called *The Bride Wore Black*—"

"Ooh, very chic—"

"But apparently she wears black not because she works for *Vogue* but because her husband gets killed just after they're married and she hunts down all the killers and shoots them one by one."

"We'll put black on the bad omen list."

"And we have to think about your bridesmaid outfit."

"Oh Sally, *please no.*"

"Don't worry, no frills or pea-green gathered skirts. I thought a nice trouser suit."

Jude slumped to the carpet. "But it'll be in some kind of pastel, and I'll never wear it again!" she moaned.

She was also thinking that it would cost a fortune, but she couldn't say that to Sally. It would be too rude. Still, she would have to get them a nice present, and a trouser suit of the kind Sally would insist on—some trendy designer—would probably cost five hundred pounds at least. Jude was not blessed with rich doting parents. Five hundred pounds on an unbearable trouser suit was a huge sum of money for her.

Sally clicked her tongue reprovingly. "Trust me," she said, with a conspiratorial smile. "I've thought it all out. I thought something in a pale blue-gray, which will really bring out your eyes. And you can wear it for work, or posh dos. Nothing underneath the jacket, so it looks a bit sexy. *And*"—she paused for effect—"I'm going to pay for it. Or rather, Mum and Dad are. I'll put it on the wedding dress budget."

"Oh Sal, you don't have to do that," Jude demurred, hoping, however, that Sally would take this in the spirit in which it was meant.

"It's no problem. Really. Just think about it like this—you save more money you can spend buying us a nice pressie."

Sally was so tactful. She knew just how to present an awkward situation without any embarrassment. And she wasn't making Jude wear a dress that would show off her awful legs.

"We've got ages, which is good," Sally said. "Mikey and I are thinking of an October wedding. Then we can go on safari for our honeymoon."

"Ooh, lovely."

"Stephanie's friends with these people who run a safari company. They know this gorgeous lodge at the bottom of Victoria Falls with a treehouse you can stay in. It even has its own bathroom."

Jude couldn't help grinning: that was so Sally. Romantic treehouses by the Zambezi were all very well, as long as you had your own built-in shower.

The phone rang. Sally snatched it up.

"Hi, darling!" she said happily. "No, you can't come round now, Jude and I are looking at wedding videos, remember? No, it's bad luck. And I really need to get on with this . . . Yeah, Stephanie rang me too, she and Mum are going to look at hotels the day after tomorrow . . . I know. I know. It's all a bit overwhelming . . . No, sweetie, it'll be fine, we just have to think about things one day at a time, or we'll just drown in place settings and flower arrangements. Anyway, they'll do most of that, they're champing at the bit to get going . . . I know. I love you too . . . Well, why don't you come round at eleven, or eleven-thirty? We'll be done by then, or poor Jude will be, there's only so long you can talk about someone else's wedding dress without going insane . . . Yeah. Me too. I love you . . . See you later."

She made kissing noises into the receiver and hung up.

"Mikey's freaking a bit about all this," she confided. "All the arrangements. God knows I am too, but sometimes I feel that if I tell him that we'll both go into a spin. It's like when you get engaged, they strap you to this giant roller-coaster, and you can't get off."

"Are you having doubts?" Jude asked, thinking how formal

this sounded, as if she were a vicar giving the engaged couple a pre-wedding lecture about matrimony being a state not to be entered into lightly.

"No, not really," Sally said, but she took one of the throw pillows on the sofa and hugged it to her chest. "It's just so overwhelming. And it happened so fast. I just thought Mikey was coming round that night to make up, I had no idea he was going to *propose*. And he was much surer than me. He'd spent ages thinking about it, and then he talked to Stephanie when he went round to get the ring."

She stuck her hand out, contemplating this, in the time-honored manner of the new fiancée. It was an antique that had been in Michael's family for many years, a ruby flanked by seed pearls in an old gold setting, and looked as if it had been designed specifically for Sally's slender hand. Jude had tried it on and could barely get it over her little finger. She had big stubby joints.

"I *am* pretty nervous," Sally confessed. "I mean, I'm really happy, of course, but I'm really nervous too. So's Mikey. We spend a lot of time calming each other down."

Jude was enormously relieved by this. She would have been infinitely more worried to hear Sally and Michael announce blithely that they were one hundred percent sure they were doing the right thing. Doubts and nerves had to be part of the normal experience when you were engaged. Particularly under these circumstances.

"Right!" Sally said, in a tone that signaled she was putting aside any further discussion about pre-wedding nerves. "More coffee, and then we should make a start on the videos!"

*   *   *

Michael came round just after eleven. Jude had rarely been so grateful to see anyone. She felt as if she had spent the past few hours making herself sick by gorging on chocolate cake. One bride all dressed up in a cloud of white, tremulous and beautiful, appearing at the far end of the aisle on her father's arm to the oohs and aahs of the assembled congregation, was always a heart-stopping moment in a film. Scrolling to those moments, one after the other, so that they lost all their power of anticipation, and then pausing interminably to discuss the bride's bouquet, dress, and veil choices was not quite as moving.

Jude amended her previous reflection. It wasn't like gorging on chocolate cake; it was like watching your best friend do that while all you had to tuck into were some dry wafer biscuits. Not having Sally's sophisticated fashion sense, she was unable to offer much in the way of helpful comments. She was reduced to muttering "That looks nice" or "I don't like that skirt much," while noticing with horror the wide range of nasty bridesmaid dresses there were out there. Girl after girl in shiny unflattering pink satin, clutching inferior bouquets, trying hard not to look like the sidekicks that they were.

"Hey, fiancée!" Michael said, enveloping Sally in a long embrace. "How's the dress going? Picked out something gorgeous?"

"I'm going to have to sleep on it," Sally said, kissing him back. "I'm overwhelmed with choice right now."

"Bloody hell," Michael said, catching sight of the discarded videos strewn all over the living-room floor. "I'm not surprised. Did you watch all those?"

"We just fast-forwarded to the wedding bits. Well, I did. Jude made coffee."

"We needed it," Jude said, rising from the floor, where she had been lying propped on a pile of pillows.

It was still a novelty to her to see Michael and Sally exchanging passionate kisses. It felt oddly incongruous, as if she had been friends with a brother and sister whose sibling bond was much closer than it ought to have been. They turned to her, smiling matching idiotic smiles of happiness, and, despite the agony of boredom she had endured for the past few hours, she couldn't help smiling back at them. They stood now the way they had done when they had been announcing the engagement: Michael behind Sally, his arms around her shoulders, his chin resting in her hair, her small body looking as if it was about to be engulfed by his bulk.

"I should be going to bed," Jude said.

"Us too," Michael said promptly, kissing the top of Sally's head.

How to make you feel completely unwanted in one easy step, Jude thought as she said good night and crossed the corridor to her flat. That would settle down, once they were married, or once, even, they had got over the initial rush of having sex with one another—a few months, probably. But she was still very grateful that she had Scott. Observing this state of pre-marital bliss took its toll, even if you were in a relationship. She shuddered to think how awful it would make her feel if she were single.

Maybe that was why she had been concerned about whether the marriage would work: simple jealousy. It was hard to deny. It seemed as if Sally had miraculously skipped all the hard parts.

One minute she was single—well, she had been seeing Paul, but that had barely started. (Jude spared a moment to feel sorry for Paul, who had spent the past week at work looking as if he had been knocked over the head by a heavy object with nasty sharp corners.) And the next she was sporting a lovely ring and making plans to honeymoon in Zimbabwe. Or was it Zambia? Anyway, Sally had managed to avoid any of the usual, time-consuming stages: the decision to move in together, the first tentative discussions about who wanted children and when, the nail-biting period spent waiting for the man to get his act together and finally propose.

Jude had been, she was now aware, smug for the whole duration of her friendship with Sally. She had seen herself as better off, someone who was able to have relationships, while Sally sat there and waited for Michael. And now the whole balance was reversed. By some miraculous throw of the dice, Sally had jumped to the end of the board, and Jude was back in Stage One, with plenty of snakes and ladders still to negotiate. It didn't feel fair.

No wonder her resentment had expressed itself in doubts about whether Sally and Michael would make it. She determined to take a positive attitude to the wedding from now on. And who knew? Perhaps Scott would be subconsciously influenced by the wedding to suggest—not that they get engaged, that would be too soon, even by October—but that they move in together? Well, there was no harm in hoping. Or was it just women who got sentimental at weddings?

Chapter
Twenty-four

"*T*he salmon is wonderful here," Mrs. Gwynne suggested.

"Oh, is it?" Sally's mother said nervously.

She had clearly been planning to have something else, and now was swayed by the conviction of Mrs. Gwynne's manner. She consulted the menu again, looking flustered. Sally glanced from one to the other. Stephanie, she thought, would ride roughshod over her mother, in the nicest way, of course, when it came to all the details of the wedding arrangements. Well, Sally was fine with that. Stephanie had wonderful taste, and everything they had discussed so far was exactly what she herself would have liked. And her mother would be bullied gently into going along with whatever Stephanie wanted, convince herself that she had made all the choices Stephanie suggested, and end up happy and proud with the aesthetic triumph that the wedding would represent. It was exactly the same pattern she followed in her married life, and she was more than content with it.

Sally grinned at her father, whom no amount of persuasion would induce to order anything he hadn't chosen for himself. He smiled back at her conspiratorially; they both knew exactly what the other was thinking. His job was to sign the checks and give her away, and he was equally happy with his end of the bargain.

"Well, maybe I *will* have the salmon," Mrs. Masterson said. "It's terribly good for you, isn't it? All that fish oil."

"You should have whatever you want, darling," her husband said.

"Oh, but I *do* want the salmon, Geoff. Stephanie says it's wonderful."

"Were you happy with the hotel, Geoff?" Stephanie inquired.

"Very nice indeed," Mr. Masterson said.

"Oh *good,*" Stephanie said, quite as if she had been in any doubt that a hotel selected by her for the reception would fail to meet anyone else's standards of taste. "That's such a relief."

The waiter brought over their bottle of champagne and presented it ceremonially to Mr. Masterson for approval.

"Very good, carry on," he said, nodding.

Their glasses were filled and raised.

"To Michael and Sally," Mrs. Gwynne said, smiling all around the table. "Engaged at last. I couldn't be happier." She lowered her glass a little. "I've been hoping Michael would propose to Sally ever since I got to know her. And though it may have taken them a bit more time than usual—"

"Nine years, wasn't it?" Mrs. Masterson said. "I must say, I had completely given up hope by this time!"

"Oh, I always thought we'd see them together," Mrs. Gwynne said. "Despite everything. Michael knows how much I like to be right—don't you, darling?"

Michael snorted with laughter. "Understatement of the year,

Mum," he said, dipping some bread in oil and taking a large bite.

"Well, but I *was,* and nothing could possibly make me any happier," she insisted.

"We're very happy too," Mrs. Masterson chimed in. "We've always thought of Michael as a son, haven't we, Geoff?"

Geoff Masterson winked at Michael, deprecating the female tendency to exaggerate. "Well, if we didn't before, we do now," he said. "Michael, my boy. Welcome to the family."

He reached over and clinked glasses with Michael. "I know you'll make Sally very happy."

"I'll do my best, sir," Michael said, rising to the occasion.

"And I'll make him happy too," Sally pointed out firmly.

"You're doing that already," Michael said, squeezing her hand.

"Aah," Mrs. Masterson cooed.

"Drink up," Mr. Masterson said. "It's completely unnatural to be sitting around with glasses in your hands for ten minutes without so much as taking a sip."

"Oh Geoff, you always exaggerate," said his wife fondly, drinking her champagne, however, with relief at having been commanded to do so.

It was a love-fest, Sally thought. All it needed was for them to open their veins and hold wrist to wrist in a circle around the table for a ceremonial mingling of blood. She caught Stephanie's eye, and remembered an incident that had occurred a couple of days before, while she and Stephanie were going through quotes from flower shops. Sofie had wandered up from downstairs, on her way out to a meeting with the gallery that

was putting on her show of drawings, and been encouraged by
Stephanie to look at the various photographs of flower arrangements and bouquets.

"I find red roses very vulgar," Sofie had said. "They are so
rich. Me, I prefer lilies. One single lily, but perfect. That I think
would be very elegant."

"Oh, Sofie, she can't walk down the aisle just clutching a single flower!" Stephanie said robustly. "Just think how lonely that
would look! And then how can she throw it?"

"Throw it?" Sofie echoed blankly.

Really, Sally wondered, what planet did she live on?

"To the unmarried girls, of course! To see who'll get married
next!"

Sofie had made a moue of disinterest. Don't worry, you pretentious French cow, I won't bloody be throwing it to you,
Sally said to herself. I don't give a toss if you ever get married,
but I draw the line at cursing the poor bloke you might end up
with.

She had already planned to throw the bouquet directly at
Jude, conferring some of her own infinite good luck on her best
friend. Things seemed to be going so well with Scott. Sally had
warmed to him recently. He was still very quiet, but he did
seem to be making Jude happy, which was the important thing.
Ever since they had got back from Florida, Jude had been floating on air; she hadn't been in that state of anxiously waiting for
a phone call that had characterized the first months of their
relationship, and which Sally always considered a danger sign. A
man should make you feel reassured, not nervous. Paul had
always fixed a time that they would meet, or that he would ring

her, at the end of their previous date; he had been completely reliable. Guiltily she pushed thoughts of Paul to the back of her mind. Poor Paul, she had treated him so badly.

She glanced over at Stephanie, who was exquisitely turned out in a silk suit and diamond earrings, her makeup perfect. Not a smear of lipstick left on the champagne glass. Stephanie was, as always, perfectly in control. Sally thought with ironic amusement of the conversation they had had directly after Sofie had left for the gallery.

"Well, that all turned out exactly as I imagined," Stephanie had said with a smile of satisfaction.

"What do you mean?"

"Inviting Sofie to stay. She's a dear girl, and of course her parents are very good friends of mine. I would have had her to stay regardless. But I did have a little extra motive for being so keen she should come to London for a while."

Sally looked up from the brochures, a suspicion forming in her brain.

"Oh, you must have realized," Stephanie said. "I thought you would have. That Katie girl. She just wasn't right for Michael. And her practically moving in with him like that. I know she didn't have anywhere to stay in London, and Michael would have ended up letting her stay there indefinitely, and goodness knows what might have happened. It was before I knew she was pregnant, of course. That would have been a disaster." She shuddered. "But it's all worked out for the best now, thank goodness. I feel sorry for her, naturally, but it's better for her to have realized sooner than later that she and Michael just wouldn't have worked out. He was always meant for you, Sally, my dear. I was always sure he and you would end up together. He just needed some little pushes, didn't he?"

"And you inviting Sofie to stay was one of those little pushes?" Sally asked, still trying to work this out.

"Absolutely. Michael and Sofie—well, they were both very young. Sofie was only seventeen, I think, when they fell in love. And she's scarcely cut out to be a wife and mother, she's so tied up in her art. But there's always been a very strong tie between them. I thought at the time that having Sofie around would make Michael realize that Katie wasn't what he wanted. Much too young. And not really one of us. I mean, she never fitted in, did she? And naturally, even if he and Sofie had tried to start something up again, it would never have lasted. I thought Michael would leave Katie for Sofie, that would all fall to pieces, and then he'd turn to you. Well, it didn't quite work out like that, but it came to the same thing in the end, didn't it?"

Sally remembered Katie saying that Stephanie was a bitch. If she had had any idea what Stephanie had planned, she would have used even stronger language.

Stephanie pressed Sally's hand.

"You were meant to be my daughter-in-law," she said fondly. "Michael's just taken longer to realize that than I did! Of course, I couldn't say anything to him. Men are so difficult—if they think you're trying to push them in any particular direction they dig in their heels and won't budge. They need to be coaxed. But goodness, I was terrified when I heard Katie was having a baby. She certainly did her best to catch him!"

"It was an accident," Sally said feebly, feeling that as a fellow woman she ought to defend Katie against this accusation.

Stephanie raised her eyebrows.

"Oh come now. Young women today know it all, don't they? Hundreds of different contraceptive possibilities available to them, and still they keep having 'accidents.' I'm afraid I'm not quite as charitable as you are."

She shrugged. "Well, she finally came to her senses. She could never have competed with Michael's feelings for Sofie. And you, of course."

Sally realized that Stephanie didn't know about Viliama. How could she? Michael certainly wouldn't have told her. Stephanie had referred to Michael's scar a couple of times with deep concern, and told them never to go into that wine bar again, but she had obviously thought it just a freak bar fight with no personal relation to Michael. Stephanie thought that Michael had been having an affair with Sofie, and Katie had found out about it.

Stephanie saw the look of distress on Sally's face, but misread its meaning.

"Oh my dear, you mustn't worry about Sofie," she said reassuringly. "She's very much Michael's past. His first love, you know. But after all, when Katie left, Sofie was right here. He could have proposed to her, but it never entered his mind. You were all he could talk about. When you wouldn't see him, and he realized you were involved with someone else, he was absolutely desperate." She laughed. "You should have seen him that afternoon he came by to get the ring! He was frantic! I reassured him, naturally. I told him that you'd say yes. But he was in *such* a state. I've never seen Michael like that."

"He knew I was seeing Paul?"

"Yes, he saw you two go into your block of flats. He was terrified. He thought he'd lost you forever."

So that was what it had taken. I should have started seeing someone else years ago, Sally thought. Would that have done it? Or did it need Michael's disaster with Katie to make him realize he needed to settle down and stop messing around?

She reached over now and took his hand, needing reassurance. He squeezed it back, and leaned over to drop a swift kiss on her lips. The families cooed in pleasure.

"Just no more rescuing damsels in distress!" Geoff Masterson said to him jovially. "Unless it's your wife, of course!"

Sally froze for a second until she realized that her father was referring to the official version of the bar fight. They had told everyone that Michael had been trying to intervene between an angry guy and his girlfriend and got bottled for his trouble.

"Absolutely not, sir," Michael said, still holding onto Sally's hand. "I've learned my lesson."

"Really, Michael," said his mother, "I've never seen you looking this handsome. Being engaged obviously agrees with you."

"Wait till I'm married, Mum," he said happily. "You've seen nothing yet."

And he raised his glass to Sally, polishing off the last drops of his champagne in a toast to her.

Sally had told Michael about Paul, the evening he proposed, and Michael had feigned ignorance of Paul's existence. Of course, she had already agreed to marry him; there was nothing to provoke any insecurity in him. Still, Sally realized, he had done a damn fine job of seeming surprised. She had told him she would ring Paul the next day to tell him what had happened, and that she obviously couldn't see him anymore, and this was exactly what she had done. It had been surprisingly difficult. Though she and Paul had only just started to get to know one another, she had liked him much more than she had expected to. And, to her astonishment, she had been very attracted to him. Not just in a being-glad-to-hear-his-voice-on-the-phone, happy-in-his-company kind of way; she had found herself speculating incessantly about what he looked like naked, physically drawn, as if by suction, to placing herself as close as she could to him without actually touching him.

It had been a real shock to her. She hadn't felt this about a man since Mikey; had even been wondering if she would ever be attracted to another man again. It seemed ridiculous now, but for years she had been in sexual abeyance. Something must have snapped in her brain that night she saw Dragan bottle Mikey, or maybe more when Mikey wanted her to lie for him to Viliama. Some tie that had bound her to Mikey must have been fraying over all these years, and finally split in half under the pressure of that night. And perhaps it was only once that tie had been broken that she could create enough space between her and Mikey for him to feel its absence and miss her enough to realize that she was the one he really wanted.

She had been surprised to get a phone call from Paul just a couple of days before the family lunch, asking her to meet him for a drink. He knew she was engaged, he said, he didn't want to make her feel uncomfortable, but he would very much like to meet up with her one more time, just for a quick drink, no pressure. He had sounded so reasonable, so friendly, that Sally had found it impossible not to accept. He wanted closure, she imagined. After all, she had dropped him like a ton of bricks.

And she hadn't told anyone about their meeting. Not Mikey, obviously, but not even Jude. Putting on lipstick in the mirror of the ladies' loo at work, she wondered why. Was it a kind of mini-revenge against Mikey? He gets off with every woman in town, but I'm sneaking out to see an ex—well, a sort of ex—without telling him? That made sense, certainly insomuch as she was keeping it from Jude too. It added an extra clandestine touch to the encounter. Perhaps after all these years of such good behavior, Sally felt she was due a little harmless naughtiness.

Paul was waiting for her at the wine bar. He rose to his feet as soon as he saw her in the mirror; he had seated himself with his back to the room to leave the banquette free for Sally. He was such a gentleman.

"I ordered you a Pinot Grigio," he said, indicating the glass. "I remembered that's what you usually drink. Drank. But if you don't want it, I can easily get you something else."

"Oh no, that's lovely," Sally said, squeezing between the tables. She was pretty slim and even so her bottom almost rested on the table next to them for a moment; this wine bar crammed you in tighter than a mosh pit.

She settled her bag and jacket next to her and sat down, finding it awkward to meet Paul's eyes. She concentrated on her glass instead.

"You've got a good memory," she said, sipping at her wine.

"It wasn't that long ago, Sally," Paul said.

"No, it wasn't."

She took another, longer sip of the wine, feeling embarrassed and flattered all at once. She and Paul had barely dated for a fortnight—though they had spent a lot of time together, it was true—and though there had been a considerable amount of making out on each other's sofas, they hadn't actually had sex. Sally had wanted to wait a little and Paul had been very understanding. Memories of what they had actually done, however, now flooded up into her front brain, causing her to blush. A sudden vivid series of images of Paul licking her breasts, her hands buried in his thick fair hair—how sexy it had been to twist her fingers into his hair, she missed that now all she had was Michael's shaved pate—flashed before her like a slide show at Judgment Day.

"I'm very glad you agreed to come out for a drink," he was saying. "I've been thinking about you so much."

"Me too," Sally muttered to her glass. She could feel his eyes on her, but she was incapable of meeting them.

"I don't want you to feel uncomfortable," Paul said. "God, what a stupid thing to say. Of course you feel uncomfortable, we both do. I meant, I don't want to make you feel any more uncomfortable than the situation naturally, um, entails."

Sally peeked up at him. The highest she could go was his chest. Gray jacket, dark blue shirt with a dull satiny tie in almost the same shade of blue. Paul was always so well-dressed.

"But I did want to see you again, just one more time," he was saying. "I want you to know that I don't feel used."

"Used!"

This brought Sally's head up. She stared at him. His handsome face expressed nothing but concern; no rancor.

"Paul, I never meant to use you!" she said urgently. "Really! I was having a great time with you!"

More slide show. She blushed again, looking at his mouth and remembering where it had been.

"Me too," he said seriously. "I just wanted to say—I know you talked about Michael when we were seeing each other, I know what a big part of your life he was—I do understand that when he proposed to you it must have been impossible to resist—not that I mean you were resisting because of me or anything, I'm sorry, that came out wrong, I didn't mean to sound arrogant—"

"No, no, you didn't—"

There hadn't been any resistance, though. Once Jude and Scott had drunk a toast and gone back to Jude's, Sally and Michael had ripped each other's clothes off and gone at it all over her flat. Till dawn. It had been even better than Sally remembered, and she hadn't thought about Paul once. But now she was looking at him and her palms still had the memory of what his smooth naked chest had felt like, his biceps, and she was horribly confused.

"I know that things between you and Michael have been sort of—well, it was an odd situation for ages—"

Jude, Sally thought. Jude talked to him about me and Michael. There was an implied knowledge in the way Paul was talking that indicated he knew more about the peculiar nature of her and Michael's connection than she herself had told him. She didn't blame Jude: she knew how much Jude had wanted to see her happy. But she was sure Jude had filled him in on Sally's patient, seemingly hopeless long wait for Michael. It was there in his eyes; she could see it.

"And I—well, I hope you'll be very happy," Paul was saying. "I really do. You're a wonderful person and you deserve to be happy. But I wanted to see you just to say that if things go wrong, or don't work out for some reason—and I've got to be honest and say that I wouldn't be human if some part of me didn't hope that, I hope you don't mind my saying that—well, anyway, I'll be here. As a friend, at least. If you need to talk, or . . . whatever."

Sally couldn't speak. She was on the verge of tears.

"I don't mean to imply anything—and of course you and I had hardly got started—but I had feelings for you and I didn't want to let things go without at least meeting up with you once more and saying this—oh, shit, you're crying, I didn't mean to make you cry—"

Sally grabbed her bag and jacket, hardly able to see through a mist of tears.

"I have to go," she said, "I'm sorry to run out on you, I'm sorry for everything—"

"No, Sally, please, you have nothing to apologize for, it's me that's sorry, I feel terrible—"

Paul was on his feet, pulling out the table for her. She barely looked at him. Her head was ducked. She was afraid that if she did look him in the eye she would start sobbing hysterically. He was so nice, and so brave, to put himself through this, when he could just have dismissed her as some flaky chick who had been amusing herself with him till the man she really wanted came back . . . She practically ran out of the wine bar, aware that she was abandoning him, leaving him standing there with everyone around them staring. Fumbling in her bag, she reached for her phone and pressed the speed key for Michael's number.

"Mikey?" she said. "I'm really upset, I had a horrible day at work—where are you? I'm coming round right now—yes, I love you too, I love you *so much* . . ."

Chapter
Twenty-five

Sofie was clearly unhappy with the way the opening was going. Sally knew that she had been hoping—or assuming—that her exhibition would be shown at either a prestigious art gallery on Cork Street, or one of the cutting-edge trendy places in the East End. Instead she had been forced to settle for a small gallery in St. John's Wood, which had a wealthy and sophisticated clientele, but was not by any means fashionable. The people present were smartly dressed bourgeois locals, rather than the black-clad intellectuals with tight-fitting shirts, thick black-rimmed glasses, and artfully disarranged hair for which Sofie had doubtless been hoping.

Images of the sulking artist were everywhere: Sofie in black ink, sprawled across couches or beds, slumped at café tables, looking pouty and discontented and in the grips of a particularly bad existential crisis. Sofie herself was standing outside, smoking and refusing most attempts by the gallery owners to introduce her to prospective buyers; when a brave person did pluck up the courage to approach her, they found it impossible to get out of her more than a very Gallic shrug or a pouty "Moh," signifying her utter lack of interest in making polite conversation.

"Why won't she talk to anyone?" Jude asked, staring out of the front window at Sofie, who was slumped against it, a cigarette drooping from her lips, looking as aloof as a cat lying on a high shelf so that nobody could do anything as mundane as try to pet it.

"Says her art should speak for itself," Sally said. "Stephanie's doing her nut. She was the one who put Sofie in touch with the gallery in the first place."

"What?" Jude said incredulously, responding to the first part of this statement. "You can never get her off the subject of her bloody art normally! That's all she ever talks about!"

"Yeah, but that's when the work's not hanging on the walls," Sally explained. "When it is, she thinks people should be responding to that instead."

"Bloody hell. So why did she bother to show up at all?"

Sally pulled a face. "I think she was hoping everyone would just be wandering around staring at her drawings in reverent silence, rather than making cocktail conversation." She looked down at the contents of her plastic glass. "Or warm nasty white wine conversation, in this case. But that's just a guess. I have absolutely no idea what goes on in her head."

"Some of these aren't so bad," Jude admitted, looking at the drawing hanging closest to them.

"But it's weird to be looking at all these pictures of her naked," Sally said. "I mean, she's not somebody you look at and think, Cor, I'd like to see *her* without her clothes on."

"Meow," Jude said appreciatively. "Still, the blokes don't seem to mind."

"Her and her straggly pubes," Sally sniffed. "It's not exactly top-line porn, is it?"

"But it's artistically justified," Jude pointed out. "They can stare at Sofie's bare arse in front of their wives without any guilt."

A lot of the men present were happily doing just that. Still, none of the drawings had sold. There was a distinct absence of comforting red dots stuck onto their neatly typed labels.

"What do you think?" Jude said to Scott, who had just come up to them.

"I like girls with more meat on their bones," Scott said. "Oh, you mean what do I think of her artistic technique?" he added, poker-faced. "I haven't really thought about that yet. I was too busy looking at her bits."

Jude swatted him. "Very funny," she said.

"Well, you can't help it, can you? If it was some naked bloke you girls'd be standing around giggling about his willy."

"He's got a point," Sally admitted.

"Is she OK?" Scott asked. "She seems even grumpier than usual."

"She's pissed off that nothing's sold yet."

"It's early days," Scott said.

"Yeah, but apparently you do expect to sell stuff at the opening. I think Stephanie's going to buy one. She feels guilty about the whole thing, what with Sofie behaving like Greta Garbo and not even coming inside."

Sally looked over at Stephanie, who was chatting animatedly to one of the gallery owners, an expensively dressed woman married to a rich businessman. He had apparently given her a share in the gallery to keep her happy and off the antidepressants now that the children were grown up and gone to university.

"Did you hear Scott's sold some of the photos he took on

our holiday to this publisher who's doing a big coffee-table book on Florida?" Jude said to Sally.

"Oh, that's great, Scott! Congratulations!"

"It's a start," Scott said, shrugging modestly. Sally could tell, however, how happy he was. His reactions were much more subtle than most people's; only after several months had she learned to identify some of his moods.

"And they want him to do more pictures for them," Jude continued. "You're rubbish at this, Scott, no one would ever know all the nice things that were happening to you unless you had me to tell them."

"*You're* the nice thing that's happened to me," he said, kissing her cheek.

"Aaah," Sally cooed.

In her own pre-marital state of bliss, she wanted everyone to be as happy and coupled-up as she was. She was doing her best not to think about that awful meeting with Paul. She had felt so guilty and confused that she had rushed straight round to see Michael, distracting herself with a considerable amount of very good sex and the comfort of Michael's large warm body. Since then she had done her best to pretend that Paul had never existed, and it seemed to be working. Jude certainly knew better than to mention his name.

"Darling?" Michael came over to their little group. "I was thinking—Sofie's very upset that no one's bought anything so far, and I was wondering whether you thought we should—"

"Absolutely not," Sally said firmly. "We're saving for the honeymoon. She can give us a drawing as a wedding present if she wants."

Which I'll hang in the downstairs loo, she added to herself. The dark nasty one where you can barely see to find the toilet paper.

Michael was visibly disappointed. "Oh, I was hoping—"

"No, Mikey. She needs to make it on her own." Sally was struck by inspiration. "She'd hate us to buy one, it would be such an obvious oh-poor-Sofie thing to do. I think she'd find it very humiliating."

Michael's face fell. "Maybe you're right. I hadn't seen it like that."

Sally exchanged a brief glance of triumph with Jude as Michael wandered off, looking disconsolate.

"Only three weeks until she takes herself and her droopy tits back to Paris," Sally muttered to Jude and Scott. "I can't wait. Do you think I should give her a bra that actually fits her properly as a farewell present?"

Jude snuffled with laughter.

"I'd better follow Mikey," Sally said resignedly. "I don't want him losing his resolve and forking out five hundred quid on a naked picture of his ex's saggy bum."

"Very sensible," Scott agreed solemnly.

Sally peeled off into the crowd.

"Look, I have to get going," Scott said apologetically. "I've got a few more hours at work to do yet."

"Oh, Scott, not *again,*" Jude protested, her heart sinking. "We're all going out to dinner afterward. I thought you were coming."

"I'm sorry, I really am."

He was definite, though. Once Scott made his mind up, there was no shifting him.

"Is it always going to be like this?" Jude said hopelessly.

"I don't enjoy it, you know," he said, touched on the raw. "I'd much rather be coming out with you."

"Then why can't you? Couldn't you make the work up tomorrow?"

"No, I can't. I'm sorry, Jude, but you know my work's like this right now."

"I was hoping with those photos in that book things might be a little easier—"

"It'll take more than that. It's still a one-off. Until I get more commissions I have to keep going with the stock shots. You know that."

"Yeah, but . . ."

Jude tailed off. She didn't have anything left to say; it was a conversation they had had many times before. She felt very depressed. What was the point in having a boyfriend you never saw? Or who was so tired when you did see him that he just fell asleep in front of the TV? She knew she was exaggerating, but she had been looking forward to having Scott's company that evening, counting on it. Now that Sally and Michael were a couple, they were so absorbed by each other that she felt almost unimportant to them. Scott's presence would have balanced that out, given her someone of her own to share little jokes with, feel that she belonged to, go home with at the end of the evening, rather than returning once again in a minicab with Michael and Sally cuddled up on the back seat, planting little kisses on each other, all too clearly desperate to get home and be alone together.

"I thought maybe you could go back to mine, though,"

Scott said. "I should be back by eleven. We could watch a bit of TV, if you're not too sleepy."

Jude stared at him, puzzled. "But—"

"Here." He produced a set of keys. He must have had them in his hand all along; he hadn't needed to fish in his jacket pocket. "I got a set cut for you. That way, even if I've got to work late, we can still have the night together."

"Oh, *Scott* . . ." Jude's eyes pricked with tears.

"I've been meaning to do it for ages," he said awkwardly. "There you go."

He shoved them at her.

"The big one's for downstairs, and the Yale does my flat. You have to turn the downstairs one twice. Make sure you don't flick the button on the lock inside, though, or I won't be able to get in. The Yale, I mean."

Jude could tell he was covering the symbolism of this moment by a gruff series of manly instructions. It was oddly touching.

"That was really nice of you," she said, managing to sound matter-of-fact instead of throwing her arms around him and sobbing, "You love me! You really love me!" which she knew would be about as welcome to him at this moment as an announcement that she had pubic lice.

"It's purely self-serving," Scott said. "I like having you to cuddle with on the sofa."

"I'll get keys cut for mine too—"

"If you want," Scott said, sounding as if he were entirely indifferent about this decision.

They couldn't look at each other, too aware of and embarrassed by their own happiness at this shift forward in their relationship. A silence fell. Jude fiddled with the key ring.

"Oh!" she exclaimed, a nasty realization dawning. "Oh Scott, no, I can't come back to yours tonight! I'm so sorry! We have the monthly planning meeting tomorrow at work and I have to wear a suit—you know, look smart—so I'd have to go home and get that and then come round to yours, and it'd be really late . . ."

Scott lived in Balham, miles away from Jude and Sally's eyrie in King's Cross.

"I could try, I suppose—" she said.

"No, it's fine. Really. I understand."

"Oh, but it's, you know, the first time you—I mean, you just gave me the keys and now I can't—I don't want you to think I don't want to, but—"

"Jude. It's fine." He reached out and squeezed her hand reassuringly. "I understand."

"Do you? I feel terrible—"

God, she thought, I'm babbling like a moron. And I'm making too much of this, I'm making it more than it is, and that's going to put him off, he'll think I'm too keen . . .

"Maybe you should leave some more of your work clothes at mine," Scott said. "I know you've got your nightie, and things, but maybe you should bring some stuff round for work as well. That way you won't have this problem again. I'll clear some hangers and a drawer for you this evening."

"Oh, *Scott.*" Jude recovered. "Yeah, that does sound like a good idea," she said, getting her emotions under control. "I could do that over the weekend."

She had wanted to say "tomorrow," but "the weekend" sounded much less scary.

"That'd be great."

"And you could leave some things at mine too."

"OK."

They smiled at each other with a cautious excitement.

"Jude, dear, I haven't had a chance to talk to you yet," Stephanie Gwynne said, joining them. Jude hadn't noticed her approach, but in her current state of mind she would have been hard pressed to realize that the gallery had been entered by a dancing troupe of ballerina elephants.

"Oh, Stephanie, hello!" Jude said. She was always awkward around Mrs. Gwynne, who made her feel clumsy, large, and common. Jude would have much preferred to call her "Mrs. Gwynne"—it seemed almost like lèse majesté to use her first name, as if Jude were trying to pretend they were equals—but Stephanie insisted, and it would have been ridiculous for Jude to call her "Mrs. Gwynne" while Sally was happily "Stephanie"-ing her all over the place. It was one of the many differences between the working and the middle class that Jude had never been able to properly explain to Sally; when she tried, Sally would just say that she ought to relax more, because no one but her gave it a second thought. To Jude, this was precisely the point, but Sally would never see it.

"This is my boyfriend, Scott," Jude said, introducing him and looking nervously to see how he would react to the b-word. She knew she was being absurd; he had just given her the keys to his flat, for God's sake. But she still waited with bated breath to see his reaction.

"Scott! How nice. I've heard so much about you from Sally. Not Michael, of course, but then he never talks much about other men. Michael is such a woman's man. But you've probably worked that out for yourself by now."

Scott shook her hand, grinning at her comment.

"I do hope you're joining us for dinner," Mrs. Gwynne said. "I'm taking everyone out to a lovely French restaurant around the corner to celebrate."

"I'm sorry, I can't," he said regretfully. "I have to get back to work."

"Oh, that's such a disappointment! Can't you persuade him, Jude?"

"He's unpersuadeable about work," Jude said.

"Oh dear, what a shame. Well, maybe another time? I'm so fond of Jude, I was very much looking forward to getting to know you."

"I'm pretty fond of her myself," Scott said, kissing her. "Sorry—" He cleared his throat uncomfortably, wanting to use an endearment but not being very good at that, particularly with a near-stranger present. "I really should be getting going."

"You could always come round to mine if you finish on the early side," Jude suggested.

"Yeah. I'll give you a ring on your mobile. Sorry to miss the dinner," he said politely to Stephanie, pulling on his jacket.

"He's very good-looking, isn't he?" said Mrs. Gwynne as Scott left the gallery.

"Well, *I* think so," said Jude, flushing with pride.

"Sofie's *still* outside," Mrs. Gwynne fretted. "I think I might just try one more time to get her to come in and talk to people.

They appreciate that so much, you know, it's what they come to openings for, to meet the artist. Poor Monica's distraught. I must say, I'm baffled myself. Sofie's always so enthusiastic when she talks about her art the rest of the time, I can't understand why she's freezing up now—nerves, I suppose, she's very highly strung . . ."

She swept off in a wash of cashmere and silk and expensive perfume. Jude watched her go out the door and engage Sofie in conversation, or rather talk while Sofie smoked yet another cigarette and shrugged from time to time as Stephanie expostulated. Jude had the impression that Stephanie was becoming angry; her gestures became more and more impassioned, and she was leaning toward Sofie, her shoulders hunched, in a way that signified annoyance. The conversation became more heated. Stephanie started wagging her finger at Sofie, who responded by throwing away her half-smoked cigarette and launching into a tirade. Now it was Stephanie's turn to stand there while Sofie threw up her arms, gesticulating violently, her face becoming flushed. Her voice was raised; Jude couldn't hear what she was saying, just that she was almost shouting. Two people passing on the pavement stared at the little scene curiously, slowing down to get a better view.

"What's happening?" Sally said, coming up.

They moved as close to the window as they decently could and gawked at the spectacle.

"French Artist Throws Massive Wobbly at Art Opening," Jude said with relish. "St. John's Wood Shocked by Unrestrained Gallic Hissy Fit."

"Oh dear, oh dear—Sally, what's going on with Sofie?"

It was Monica, the gallery owner, highly flustered.

"I think she's upset," Sally said with impressive understatement. "Stephanie went out to try to get her to come back in, but it all seems to have gone a bit wrong."

"Oh dear, oh *dear* . . ." Monica wrung her hands. "I'll take her out a glass of wine, maybe that will help."

She joined Sofie and Stephanie on the pavement, holding out the glass of wine to Sofie with a pleading expression on her face, looking exactly like a hunted mother attempting to calm a screaming infant by producing its favorite toy. Sofie barely noticed her arrival; she was gesturing so passionately that she knocked the wine right out of Monica's hand and into the glass front window of the gallery. Being only a plastic glass, it didn't shatter, but the wine splattered the window at shoulder height and ran down it dramatically.

"Oooh," Jude said, "a modern art installation. Wine On Glass: a powerful symbol of the artist's—um—"

"Alienation from the modern world?" suggested Sally.

"I was going to say 'foul temper,' but yours sounds much better."

"It's a shame Monica took out red wine, isn't it?" Sally said.

"Nah. Red looks so much better than white dripping down the window."

The patrons of the gallery had become very excited by the goings-on outside. Being well brought up, they were discussing it in hushed tones and craning their necks to see the latest developments, rather than rushing to the window for a bird's-eye view, but Sofie's tantrum had galvanized the atmosphere. Phrases like "the true artistic temperament" and "how hard it is

for the genuine artist to engage with society" were being mur-
mured, together with a few "Bloody hell, did you *see* that?"s
from less sophisticated members of the party.

Sofie was now in floods of tears. She looked round her
wildly, then rushed into the gallery. The crowd parted to let her
through, all obviously dying to see what she would do next: tear
her drawings from the wall? Launch into a tirade against them
all? Jude had never heard breath being bated until now. Everyone was holding their glasses behind their backs, she noticed. A
really good scene of Gallic artistic fervor was one thing, but getting their nice clothes soaked and incurring heavy dry-cleaning
bills was quite another.

Sofie reached Michael, who had been at the back of the
gallery and was only just becoming aware of the drama in
progress. She threw herself on him, sobbing.

"Michel!" she wailed, clinging onto him. *"Michel! C'est pas
possible, tout ça! C'est affreux! C'est dégueulasse!'*

Michael put his arms round her and looked desperately over
her head for help.

"I think she should go home," Stephanie said, entering the
gallery, as grim as Sally had ever seen her. Pulling out her
mobile phone, she said, "Sofie? I'm calling you a minicab."

"Non, non," Sofie sobbed. *"Pas sans Michel. Je reste avec
Michel."*

"What's she saying?" Jude asked Sally.

"She wants to stay with Michael," Sally said angrily. "Bloody
cow, she's got a nerve. She's been even more annoying than
usual ever since we got engaged."

Sofie was now draped around Michael like all those old-fashioned poems about the woman being like ivy attached to the strong manly oak trunk. Michael tried to detach one of her arms but she clung on like a limpet. The gallery patrons were lapping this up: first an artistic temper tantrum and now an injection of thwarted romance. It was like being transported suddenly inside a scene from *Jules et Jim*. The closest anyone present ever got to that kind of thing normally was watching Truffaut at the local arts cinema. And this was free; not even a seven-pound ticket required. They were riveted.

"Maybe I should take her home," Michael said helplessly.

"Non! Non!"

"Or just for a walk, to calm down?"

Sofie didn't immediately protest at this.

"Sal, are you OK with this? I'll just walk her down the street. Get some fresh air into her . . . I'm so sorry," he said.

Sally summoned every ounce of will power in her body not to start screaming herself. The last thing she wanted to do was turn the situation into an even more dramatic love triangle, complete with a catfight, more wine spillage, and plenty of jealous, screamed accusations. She could feel every eye in the place on her, willing her to up the scene several notches by throwing herself on Sofie and dragging her off her fiancé.

"Yeah, I'm OK," she said, realizing how English and stiff-upper-lip she was being. Momentarily she longed to have that inhibition removed; if she were French, surely she would already have a good grip on Sofie's hair with one hand and be bitch-slapping her round the face with the other. Her palms were itching.

"It's just—" Michael looked down at Sofie. "We have to get her out of here—"

"Please," Monica implored, though to whom or about what was unclear.

Obviously nothing on this scale had ever happened in her nice elegant gallery before; she was completely unprepared for French pen-and-ink artists throwing hysterics. A gallery owner in the East End would have been over the moon about it, probably on the phone to the diary column of the *Independent* at this very moment to recount all the gory details and get some lovely juicy publicity. Monica, however, just wanted it all to go away.

"Come on, Sof," Michael said briskly. "We'll get you out of here."

Escorting Sofie to the door wasn't easy, as she refused to let go of her death-grip on him; their progress was slow and required a second parting of the crowd to make room for Michael's bulky body.

"I'll call you as soon as I can," he said as he passed Sally. "Love you, Sal."

He strained to kiss Sally, but it was impossible to reach her with Sofie attached to his chest, and he finally gave up the effort and made for the door instead. Sally touched his arm briefly, seething inside. Her stomach was boiling with acid like a mad scientist's chemistry experiment; she half-expected to see froth and smoke bubbling out of her mouth.

A deep silence fell as Michael and Sofie exited the gallery and walked down the street. The crowd watched them till they vanished from view, hoping to see Sofie break from Michael and throw herself under a car, or some other gesture of the high dramatic standard they had come to expect from her. Then there was a collective exhaling of breath, and they all turned as one to poor Monica, standing in the middle of the room. The Red Sea flooded back, but Monica wasn't drowned in anything but eager—and, judging by her expression, entirely unanticipated—requests to buy Sofie's work. St. John's Wood patrons of the arts were no different from any others: they wanted excitement and bad behavior from their artists, and Sofie had just provided that in spades. They were practically waving checkbooks in her face. For her, at least, it was a very happy ending.

Chapter
Twenty-six

"*T*hey must have sold every drawing in the place!" Sally fulminated. "I can't *believe* that cow actually conned them like that!"

"Come on, Sal, I don't think it was a con, do you? She was really upset."

"Milked it for all it was worth, though. I still can't get over everyone going mad trying to buy her drawings because she behaved *badly*. There's no justice in the world."

"Oh, a nice bit of drama they can tell people about over dinner parties—make them seem like they hang out all the time with temperamental French artists, raise their cred points with their investment banker friends . . ."

Sally sighed. "I suppose so. Still, it pisses me off."

What Sally was, of course, really pissed off about, Jude knew, was that Sofie and Michael were still AWOL. It was over two hours now since they had left the gallery, and apart from a brief call from Michael a while ago saying that Sofie was still very upset and he was taking her for a drink, they had heard nothing. Mrs. Gwynne had insisted on taking Jude and Sally out for dinner—"We have the reservation, after all, we shouldn't let our plans be completely ruined"—but it had been an awkward meal. By mutual consent they had only ordered one course, to get things over with faster, and Sally had jumped every time someone else's mobile rang, imagining that it was hers. Stephanie Gwynne was furious with Sofie; Monica's having sold practically every drawing in the gallery was no compensation to Stephanie for the vast social embarrassment Sofie had caused. Sally had never seen Stephanie in this kind of bad mood before, and it was impressively intimidating.

"I know exactly why Sofie didn't want to go back to Hampstead," Sally said now. "The thought of Stephanie in that kind of temper with me makes me shiver all over. She's going back there right now to sit in wait for Sofie and rip her head off."

"Well, she deserves it," Jude said.

"I know. Still, I'd almost feel sorry for her if it wasn't my fiancé she'd latched on to."

"Michel! Michel!" Jude did her imitation of Sofie, hoping it would cheer Sally up. "I am too fragile for zees cruel world!"

Sally smiled automatically, but was still too annoyed to be much amused.

"She'll be out of here tomorrow," Jude predicted. "I bet Stephanie's packing her suitcase right now. She'll have her on the Eurostar quicker than you can say 'psycho French artist with droopy tits.' "

"You really think so?" Sally brightened up.

"Yeah, don't worry. You saw Stephanie's face tonight. There's nothing that kind of woman hates more than being embarrassed in public. Sofie just bought herself a one-way ticket back to Frogland."

"Oh, Jude, I love you." Sally hugged her. "You always say the right thing."

Jude hugged her back.

"Oi, lesbos!" yelled one of a group of boys loitering on the other side of the road. "Give us some, eh?"

"God, this area really pisses me off sometimes," Sally said, linking her arm in Jude's as they walked on. "Mikey and I are thinking of selling up and buying somewhere together, did I tell you?"

"Oh Sal, no! I thought you'd be moving into Michael's! You can't go! What will I do without you two?"

"Only in Kentish Town, or somewhere close. Anyway, Miss I-have-keys-to-my-boyfriend's-flat, what are you worrying about? You and Scott'll be living together in a year."

"Touch wood, touch wood—" Jude veered to a shop front to touch its wooden door.

"I'm so happy things are going so well for you, Jude," Sally said, squeezing her arm.

"Me too. He's really great, Sal. You just need a bit of time to get to know him."

"Yeah, I'm warming up to him, honestly. I see what you mean about his sense of humor. He's so dry sometimes it takes me a while to see that he's joking. But he can be very funny. And he appreciates you, which means that he's got excellent taste."

"Or he's desperate."

"Yeah, that was the other option."

"I've got some ice cream at mine, why don't I bring it over to yours and I can keep you company while you're waiting for Michael to ring?"

"Oh, *would* you? That would be brilliant. Mmn, ice cream. I really wanted to order dessert at that restaurant but I was too twitchy to feel like it."

"Another thing to hold against Sofie. You get taken out to a really posh place with someone else paying and you can't go mad over the lovely free food because the atmosphere's all weird and everyone wants to be somewhere else."

"Oh well, like you said, she'll be packed off soon." Sally had cheered up tremendously. "I expect we'll have to have her back for the wedding, but Stephanie will keep an eye on her and make sure she doesn't try to mess things up."

Jude had chocolate chip and strawberry swirl ice cream in the freezer. She trotted over to Sally's and put both containers on the kitchen counter to thaw out a little. Her fridge was old and, despite being turned down to the lowest setting, the freezer hardened everything left in it for more than twenty minutes to the consistency of granite.

"Here you go," Sally said, handing her a glass of wine. "Shall we see what's on TV?"

She started flicking through the channels. Jude strolled over to the window and pulled back the curtains to see if there was a light on at Michael's.

"I checked already," Sally said. "He's not back. He would have rung."

"I know, it's just automatic . . ."

Jude's voice tailed off. She had just seen two familiar figures walking down the far side of the street, toward Michael's. They passed under a street lamp and in the orange flare her recognition was confirmed: Michael's shaved scalp, shining in the light, was unmistakable. He was opening the little gate in the wall now, holding it open for Sofie. She watched them walk up the short garden path and pause as Michael unlocked the front door. It had closed behind them before she had fully thought about whether to say anything to Sally or not. She knew how angry Sally would be at Michael for having brought Sofie back to his: going out to a pub for a few calming drinks was one thing, but entertaining her when Sally wasn't there, and Sofie had ruined their evening, was quite another.

Jude decided to remain silent for the moment. Probably Michael was, even now, reaching for the phone to tell Sally he was home, and ringing for a minicab to take Sofie back to Stephanie's. The light came on in Michael's sitting room, not the overhead one but a small lamp by the side of the sofa. With that and the light he had turned on in the hall, there was enough illumination for Jude to see both Michael and Sofie, as the latter followed him into the living room.

"There's a repeat of *Friends* at eleven," Sally was saying, flicking through the TV schedule in the paper. "Not much on before that. Ooh no, wait, there's *Frasier* at ten-thirty! Cool!"

Sofie was taking off her coat. She threw it on the back of a chair in the casual way that always annoyed Sally, who liked everything in its place and had recently got Michael to put up more hooks in his hallway so there was plenty of room to hang coats. Sofie's cardigan came off too, chucked over the coat. Michael had disappeared from view. Sofie lit up a cigarette. Then she placed it in an ashtray and started unbuttoning her blouse. Jude blinked in disbelief, half-expecting that when she re-opened her eyes, the world would have righted itself again and the brief hallucinatory flash of Sofie's bra would have disappeared, magically hidden once again under her blouse. But she knew already what she would see. Sofie was standing there in the middle of Michael's living room in her bra, the blouse cast over the chair. She took another drag on her cigarette, replaced it in the ashtray, and then her hands went round her back, her head tilted to one side, the classic position every woman assumed when unbuttoning the waistband of her skirt.

Maybe she's sleeping over on Michael's sofabed and she's just getting changed, Jude thought desperately; Michael's gone to get her a T-shirt to sleep in. The skirt fell to the floor. Sofie, in bra and panties, reached for her cigarette again and stood there, smoking, quite casually, as if she were fully dressed. Jude assumed that if you had spent years sketching yourself in the nude you had absolutely no embarrassment left about standing around in a state of partial undress.

Michael re-entered the living room. Jude waited, her teeth clenched tightly together, for him to throw Sofie the duvet and start making up the sofabed. Despite her previous speculations about how much it would grate on Sally to have Sofie sleeping over at Michael's, now she found herself praying for this eventuality. Anything but the other possible scenario.

But Michael's hands were empty. He laughed, said something, walked over to Sofie and began to kiss her, his hands roving up and down her narrow back. At the point that they focused on her shoulder blades and started to work at the fastening of her bra, Jude shut her eyes again. She couldn't bear it.

Her brain spun in frantic circles. To tell Sally, or not? She had to, she had to tell Sally, but she couldn't bear to do it.

Maybe it was just a one-off, a last fling of Michael's before the marriage, maybe it was better to leave things as they were with Sally in happy ignorance. But then Jude thought of Katie and Viliama, and knew she couldn't make that easy assumption.

"Jude? What are you staring at? Is someone being mugged? God knows that's the only thing we ever have to look at outside."

Jude heard Sally standing up. She would be over to the window in a couple of seconds. Jude's heart was pounding so fast she thought she might choke. She let the curtain fall, her hand shaking.

"My God, you're white as a sheet. What *is* it?"

Sally pulled back the curtain. Jude couldn't help looking again at the scene in progress across the street. Michael and Sofie were on the sofa now, Michael pulling his sweater off his head while Sofie unbuttoned his shirt. Jude was incapable of speech. Sally, too, remained silent for what seemed like minutes, though it couldn't have been more than thirty seconds. Enough time to take in, comprehensively, what was happening in Michael's living room. He hadn't even closed the curtains, Jude thought suddenly. Did he want to be caught? Because he and Sofie could so easily have gone upstairs to his bedroom, whose window didn't overlook the street; kept off all the lights till they got up there, so Sally couldn't see that he had got back home, and then done whatever they wanted without any fear of Sally finding out. And instead he had chosen to fuck Sofie on his sofa with the light on. He might as well have sent up flares.

"Jude—" Sally turned slowly toward her.

Jude couldn't bear to look at Sally's face. It was too raw. So instead she pulled Sally toward her and buried her head in her shoulder, hugging her, rubbing her back, as Sally cried and cried as if she would never be able to stop.

Epilogue

The barman uncapped a bottle of beer and handed it to Michael. Most of the women here were drinking the night's special cocktail, a blood-red concoction in a Martini glass, but Michael, like practically every man he could see, had chosen beer. A scattering had been brave enough to try the cocktail, but they were all designer types in French or Italian suits, in whose hands a fragile Martini glass didn't appear completely ridiculous. And even if Michael hadn't known how silly he would look drinking a Martini, he drew the line at any red mixture that the bartender had described to him with a wink as a "Halloween Horror."

He walked away from the bar and stood, drinking his beer, surveying the room. The hosts of the party—a graphic design company—had really pushed the boat out. He hadn't been expecting anything this posh. It was being held in their offices, which would save them some money, but the accoutrements were lavish. Presumably it was an attempt to reassure their clients how well the company was doing, even in these difficult times. The bartenders were all in costume, with scars painted down their cheeks; the room was lit by hundreds of pumpkins, carved into scary faces, with votive candles flickering inside their hollowed-out centers; and hired actors circulated through the room dressed as serial killers out of films. So far he had spotted Freddy from *A Nightmare on Elm Street,* Jason from *Friday the 13th,* and Frankenstein's monster. Not exactly a serial killer, this last one, but it fitted in with the Halloween theme well enough.

The guests hadn't come in costume; that wouldn't be appropriate for a business party. Practically all the women were in black, but that was less any tip of the hat to the fact that it was Halloween, and more the perpetual, obsessive need of women to look as thin as possible. Michael could never understand it. They were mostly wearing tight black trousers, little asymmetric tops and high heels, with their hair pulled back from their faces, and they looked like an endless variation on a single theme. No originality. Michael wasn't interested in a girl who looked like a clone.

His eye fell on a girl standing by the window, talking to a couple of men he didn't know. He couldn't walk over and let them introduce him; he would have to wait till the group broke up. She was small and sleek, her dark hair cut short to her head, dressed in an op-art printed dress with knee-high boots, and the way she was laughing and gesturing indicated a lively personality. Michael watched her, intrigued. She was drinking beer, too. No Halloween Horror for her. The more he saw of her, the more he wanted to go up and talk to her.

"Michael?"

He turned to the man who had spoken. It took him a few seconds to realize who he was.

"Scott?" he said.

"Yeah." Scott gave a small smile which indicated that he

knew Michael hadn't instantly recognized him. "Didn't expect to see you here."

"My company did a lot of work for them this year. Big design revamp on their computers."

"Me too. Not the computer part, of course."

"Oh yes, that's right." It was coming back to Michael. "You work for a photographic company, don't you? Stock shots?"

"Not anymore. I went freelance a few months ago."

"Did you? That's great."

They stood in silence for a while, drinking their beers. Michael had never liked Scott much, but he did have to admit that Scott had that ability to let a pause happen naturally in the conversation, without feeling the need to rush into speech, which was much more common in men. Women couldn't do it; they always needed to fill the conversational gaps. Though Michael always preferred the company of women, there was no denying the restfulness there could be in hanging out with men. He had been doing that a lot since the break-up with Sally: going to pubs and sitting at the bar, the kind of quiet pub where no one bothered you if you didn't feel like talking. Usually he would have been looking round the pub, seeing if there were any women he could talk to, but recently he'd been a little off his game. He was feeling ready to start again, though. He wondered if Scott might by any chance know the girl in the op-art dress, and then discarded this thought regretfully. Even if he did, under the circumstances Michael could scarcely ask for an introduction.

"So, everything good with you?" he said finally.

"Yeah."

"You're still with Jude?"

"Yeah. We're moving in together at the beginning of the year. She's going to rent out her place."

"That's great."

"Yeah. I'm sure it'll be a bit of a shock, but I'm really looking forward to it. All the back and forth between each other's places was knackering us out."

Michael had always liked that part: going to a new girl's flat, seeing how she lived, a window into someone else's life. Moving in with someone would have made that much more difficult. But he nodded as if he understood and drank more beer.

"She would have come tonight, but she had her own work party. I'm going to meet her there later."

"Oh, right."

Scott looked at Michael curiously, as if wanting to see how Michael would take what he was about to say.

"We're all going out afterward," he said. "Me, Jude, and Sally and Paul, I mean."

Michael just stared at him.

"You know Paul, don't you? Works in Jude's firm. He and Sally are seeing each other now."

Scott was clearly trying to get some sort of response out of him. Michael determined not to give him the satisfaction. He missed Sally horribly. Not so much as his fiancée; that hadn't been such a good idea, when he thought about it. He wasn't cut out for marriage. It had been the only way he could get Sally back, and look how that had turned out. But he hated not having Sally across the street, always there for him. He had moved out after the Sofie fiasco; he was staying at his mother's now while he rented out his house. Sally had insisted. He had never seen her like that before, so determined on something, and he hadn't been able to fight her on it. Now he regretted it; maybe if he'd stayed on, things would have settled down, back to the happy balance they had had for all those years.

He knew that wouldn't really have been possible, but it was a lovely dream. His beer bottle was empty. He drained the last drops wistfully, remembering how happy he and Sally had been. It was Katie who had messed up everything; that was when the rot had started. He was deliberately not thinking of Sally and Paul, that wanker in smart suits he had seen those few times escorting Sally into her block of flats. One of those men who always walked on the car side of the street when he was with a woman, and insisted on opening doors and hailing taxis. He couldn't believe Sally had fallen for anything that obvious.

"Well, I'd better be getting on," Scott said, looking at his watch.

"Yeah, sure."

"Bye then."

"Bye."

Scott was a wanker too. A different kind of wanker, with his goatee and his cooler-than-thou attitude. All too clearly, he had been trying to make Michael feel bad. Well, he hadn't succeeded. Michael went to get another beer, and this time he noticed that one of the offices leading off the main reception area was illuminated with a dull purple glow, spotted with the fainter moving speckles of a revolving mirrorball. Intrigued, he moved over to get a closer look. Two girls came out of the door, giggling to each other. He poked his head in.

"Come in!" said a woman's voice.

Michael never needed asking twice.

She was sitting at a table covered with a purple cloth, a crystal ball in the center. Since this was a fashionable party, rather than a booth on Brighton Pier, she didn't look anything like the conventional fortune teller: she was wearing a tight black dress and her long blond hair hung in ringlets to her shoulders. Red lipstick, unpainted nails. She could have been just another party guest, if it weren't for the props that immediately identified her profession.

"Want your fortune told?" she said. "Sit down and give me your hand."

"Don't you look in the crystal ball?" Michael said, pulling up a chair.

She laughed. "No, that's just for show. I read palms, mainly."

"Do I need to cross yours with silver?"

She smiled. "All taken care of by your gracious hosts."

Her voice was the one element that fitted: it was a low husky contralto, perfect for revealing intimate secrets. Already Michael felt as if they were in some sort of conspiracy together. He reached out his right hand to her. Her fingers were cool as they turned it over, running one nail down his palm. How erotic this was, alone in a room with a strange woman touching his hand so intimately. Michael was enjoying himself already.

"Long life line. Very good. No marriage here. You're going to stay a bachelor. Though I do see something—a little break— perhaps you were engaged once?"

Michael started to speak.

"No." She held up one hand. "Don't say anything. I like just to give a reading, without the client chipping in. It can influence me."

She was still gazing at his palm, running her nail down one of the lines.

"No money worries. Probably never. This is looking good, you have a very solid wealth line. No big fortune, but no financial problems either. Romantically . . . hmn, this is interesting. One girlfriend after another, right?"

This time he knew not to respond when it sounded as if she was asking him a question.

"And sometimes overlapping. You're a busy boy. This is very interesting . . ." She studied his palm even more closely. "There's a lot of similarities here. I think your girlfriends are all very much alike."

She paused for a moment.

"This is a strong pattern. I do see one, one girl I mean, who's more defined. She was very close to you for a long time. I can't tell whether she'll be close to you in the future or not. But the pattern will keep going, for as long as I can see. Hmm. This is quite unusual."

One of her hands flickered out and rested on the ball for a moment.

"Brunettes," she said. "That's just an intuition I'm getting. But that's what I see."

She looked up at his face for the first time since she had taken his hand, and smiled.

"Lots of brunettes, I think. Lucky you."

The girl in the op-art dress was by the bar when Michael returned to the main party area. She was getting another beer.

"No Halloween Horror for you?" he said, smiling at her.

"God, no. No offense," she said to the bartender. "I expect I should, it would go with my dress. But I'm not a cocktail drinker."

"You don't like spirits?"

"Oh, I like my vodka! But it doesn't like me."

"Well, here's to happy beer drinking."

They clinked bottles.

"I'm Michael," he said. "Michael Gwynne."

"Natalie Jackson. I do PR for the company. I'm afraid . . ." She lowered her voice mock-confidentially. "I'm afraid I'm responsible for the Halloween Horrors. Indirectly. I booked the catering company."

"And Freddy and Jason and Frankenstein's monster?"

"Me too. All me. Feel free to hate me if you want."

"I just went for a palm reading," Michael said.

"Oh good! I was worried people would be nervous! But I've been keeping an eye on things and it looks as if quite a few people have been in there. I wanted them to stumble across it, you know, let the word just trickle through the party. It's always more exciting if you feel you've found something yourself, rather than have a big sign above the door. Was she good?"

"Very good."

"Dark handsome strangers and trips across the sea?"

"Dark beautiful strangers," Michael corrected, smiling at her. "I didn't think it would come true quite so quickly."

Natalie Jackson laughed and drank some of her beer. "You're very smooth, Michael Gwynne," she said, looking up at him flirtatiously.

"I do my best," Michael said.

Up Close and Personal
With the Author

IN YOUR ACKNOWLEDGMENTS, YOU SAY THIS BOOK IS FOR YOUR FRIEND AARON, WHO ALWAYS WANTED YOU TO WRITE ABOUT HIM. IS HE A MAIN CHARACTER IN THE BOOK?

The character of Michael is based on Aaron and his wild ways. He also looks very like Aaron, right down to his build, his eyes, his charisma, even the ridge on his forehead. . . . I had been wanting to write about Aaron and his serial dating of youngish brunettes for years, and, when I was thinking about what my new book would be about, Aaron said to me: "I want you to put me in a book. Say anything you want, I don't care what you write about me!" This was an unprecedented thing to say, because people always want to appear in your books, but only from a flattering perspective! So Aaron's saying this was really exciting, because it freed me up to write about—and obviously fictionalize—his situation. Michael in the book is a lot nastier than Aaron—his behavior is much more manipulative and careless of other people's feelings than Aaron's, who's a lovely guy. I took a lot of license with Aaron's dating life! But he's read the book and really enjoyed it, so luckily I don't have to feel guilty. Phew.

DON'T EVEN THINK ABOUT IT REALLY HAS THE FEEL OF A COMEDY OF MANNERS, WITH THE FOCUS SQUARELY ON HOW THE MAIN CHARACTERS INTERACT WITH EACH OTHER. WAS IT A CONSCIOUS CHOICE TO DO AN UPDATED VERSION OF NOVELS BY THE LIKES OF JANE AUSTEN OR SOMETHING THAT WAS DISCOVERED IN THE PROCESS OF WRITING THE BOOK?

Honestly, these questions have been sent by my fans—I didn't make them up to flatter myself! I would never compare myself to Jane Austen, it would be sacrilege! (Though I have just written a book on Jane Austen, see the last question for more details. . . .) Perhaps the reason for the comparison, though, is that this is the first book I have written in the third person—it had to be, because I needed to give multiple perspectives. The reader had to enter the mind of every protagonist one by one to tell the story effectively. We start with Katie, and then switch back between Sally and Jude, and end up with Michael. I was pretty scared of doing a third-person book—it's always scary to try something new. Because of that, this is the first book I've ever outlined in detail before I started writing it. There were going to be a lot of plot twists and turns, and I needed to work them out carefully beforehand. It's structured like a play—prologue, three acts, epilogue. And, because it's in the third person, that gives it much more of a comedy of manners feel, rather than first person narration, which filters everything through the perspective of the central protagonist. Here, we empathize—I hope!—with Katie, Sally, and Jude by turns, back and forth. We can understand Sally and Katie's mutual hostility, for example, while sympathizing with both of their situations. And though we want Michael to get his comeuppance by the end, I hope that during the book we also want him to be redeemed. The best comedies of manners, though funny, are rooted in reality; people behave badly and let you down, trust is hard to build, a rake will rarely change his ways. I wanted to give the book a core of seriousness. Michael hurts Sally and Katie badly, and they have to move on from him to recover. Without serious potential consequences, a comedy of manners is all froth and no substance.

three girls struggling in their very different ways with their issues about love and commitment, but it needed my editor to really get into the manuscript and advise me on the central plot issues to pull it all together. I learned a lot from that experience and now would NEVER write a romantic comedy without having a good strong outline in place!

IF, AS YOU SAY IN THE ACKNOWLEDGMENTS, THE CHARACTER OF MICHAEL IS BASED ON YOUR FRIEND AARON, DO YOU YOURSELF IDENTIFY WITH ANY OF THE FEMALE CHARACTERS?

This is the first book I've written where there wasn't a central character who shares some of my own weaknesses—and hopefully, strengths. In my Sam Jones mystery series, Sam was definitely like an alter ego of mine—to the point that my sister confuses her and me on a regular basis!—and Juliet, the heroine of my first romantic comedy, *My Lurid Past,* shared my own fear of commitment, which was very much what the book was about. It dealt with three women working through their own very different feelings about committed relationships—admittedly, one of them was a dominatrix, but I've always enjoyed pushing the envelope! In *Don't Even Think About It,* I had to take a different approach, because I didn't have a first-person narrator, and put myself in the shoes of Katie, Jude, and Sally by turns. I wouldn't say I identified with one of them more than the other, but I do share emotional experiences with them. We've all fallen madly in love—like Katie—or clung onto a past love long after we should have let it go—like Sally—or struggled at the beginning of a relationship with insecurities about where it's going—like Jude. So I drew on my own memories to make what they were going through as true and honest as possible.

YOU'VE MOVED AWAY FROM WRITING YOUR SAM JONES MYSTERIES TO FOCUS ON ROMANTIC COMEDY. WAS IT A HUGE CHANGE FOR YOU, AND DO YOU MISS WRITING MYSTERIES?

No, it wasn't a huge change. What interests me as a subject, more than anything else, is people—the way they relate to each other, the weird dynamics they set up, the situations they get themselves trapped in, out of love or hate or custom or family ties. And that's always been a huge part of the Sam books. It's crucial, in fact, to explaining why someone would be driven to kill another person! So when I started writing *My Lurid Past,* I didn't feel that I was making a leap into the unfamiliar. I don't miss writing mysteries at the moment, though I am planning a psychological thriller. But it will be very tightly based around a love story. I adore writing about love—falling in, falling out, getting addicted to a new person, with all the risks and excitement that entails. I can't imagine writing a book where a love story of some sort didn't play a prominent part.

WHAT ARE YOU WORKING ON AT THE MOMENT?

I've just finished a new romantic comedy, called *Exes Anonymous,* about a girl who starts up a self-help group to help her get over a really bad break-up—she's still clinging onto memories of her ex, and needs help to let go of him and move on. And I've also written a dating advice book, called *Jane Austen's Guide to Dating.* It uses examples from Jane Austen's books and ones from modern life to show how she sets out really good, healthy rules for dating that can be used to find the match of your dreams—and yes, I'm using them myself, and they really do work!

ONE OF MY FAVORITE SCENES IN *DON'T EVEN THINK ABOUT IT* IS WHERE KATIE AND HER FRIEND ARE TEXT MESSAGING EACH OTHER, IN THE STORE, EVEN TO THE POINT WHERE THEY ARE ALMOST FACE-TO-FACE! I ALWAYS WONDERED IF THAT WAS BASED ON SOMETHING YOU'D WITNESSED. . . . SO I GUESS HERE'S MY QUESTION: *DON'T EVEN THINK ABOUT IT* HAS A LOT OF SOCIAL COMMENTARY ALONG WITH THE HUMOR. DO YOU HAVE ANY SYSTEMATIC WAY OF COLLECTING SUCH ITEMS AS THE TEXT MESSAGING SCENE (WRITING THINGS IN A NOTEBOOK AS YOU COME ACROSS THEM AND HARVESTING LATER FOR NOVEL SCENES, FOR EXAMPLE) OR DO THEY JUST OCCUR TO YOU AS YOU ARE WRITING?

Both! I really should carry a notebook with me everywhere I go, and I am regularly kicking myself for forgetting when something funny pops up—a friend makes a great comment or I see something hysterical on the street—and I can't write it down. I always have a notebook on plane flights or train travel, because that's when my brain relaxes and lots of ideas pop into my head. But also things will very often come to me while I'm writing. With practice—this is my ninth book, after all—you get into a really fertile mode where your conscious and unconscious brains mesh together and become extremely productive. The conscious brain is working on the mechanism of plot and characters—where do I need this scene to go, how would these characters react to this given situation—and the unconscious is in a very fertile state, adding all those details of observations and character quirks which make a book rich beyond the basic plot structure and give it its uniqueness. . . . But my advice to aspiring writers is always to carry a notebook. Then of course you have to remember to read through it regularly for observations you've made that you might need for stuff you're writing! The act of making notes, however, actually putting it down on paper, means that it enters your subconscious more fully, and hopefully will allow it to 'pop' things out when you need them. . . .

DON'T EVEN THINK ABOUT IT HAS INTERWOVEN PLOT LINES—
DO YOU DO AN OUTLINE BEFORE YOU START WRITING, SO
THAT YOU KNOW IN ADVANCE WHAT'S GOING TO HAPPEN?
OR DO YOU HAVE A METHOD FOR KEEPING TRACK AS YOU
GO? (OR ARE YOU SO INCREDIBLY BRILLIANT THAT YOU
ACTUALLY JUST WRITE THIS STUFF OUT OF YOUR HEAD WITH
NO PLANNING AND WRESTLING OVER RECALCITRANT PLOT
POINTS, AND IF THE ANSWER IS YES TO THAT ONE, I HATE
YOU WITH AN ARDOR NORMALLY RESERVED FOR WOMEN
WITH FLAT STOMACHS AND SLEEK THIGHS WHO ARE ALSO
FABULOUS MUSICIANS . . . JUST KIDDING . . .)

Like I said, I used to be very nervous of writing an outline because I thought it would impede the creative process. Actually, I found out with *Don't Even Think About It* that having an outline in place made it the easiest book I have ever written. I think putting down a page of the plot bones before you start is a damn good idea. I wouldn't do it in too much detail, unless you're writing the kind of tightly crafted thriller that's all about plot twists and turns and therefore has to be plotted down to the last millimeter—but for a novel like this, a good old three-act structure is incredibly helpful. I recently attended the Robert McKee screenwriting lectures, and the part where he talked about how to structure a screenplay was very interesting and thought-provoking. I did *Don't Even Think About It* way before the lectures, and figured out that I needed a three-act structure on my own, but the way he talks about the need for big, character-transforming punches at the ends of the acts, and the heightened jeopardy of the protagonists as the plot cranks up, was very helpful. I used to write mystery novels, and when you have a dead body near the beginning of the book, this kind of tension is a given—you don't need to work at creating it, as the existence of a corpse and the need to find out whodunnit before more people get killed provides its own propulsion of the plot. But when I started writing romantic comedy, I needed to learn plotting skills even more than writing a mystery, because the tension comes out of the characters' interaction with each other, not out of having a killer on the loose! *My Lurid Past,* the first romantic comedy I wrote, is about

Like what you just read?

Then don't miss these other great books from Downtown Press!

Scottish Girls About Town
Jenny Colgan, Isla Dewar,
Muriel Gray, et al.

Calling Romeo
Alexandra Potter

Game Over
Adele Parks

Pink Slip Party
Cara Lockwood

Shout Down the Moon
Lisa Tucker

Maneater
Gigi Levangie Grazer

Clearing the Aisle
Karen Schwartz

Liner Notes
Emily Franklin

My Lurid Past
Lauren Henderson

Dress You Up in My Love
Diane Stingley

He's Got to Go
Sheila O'Flanagan

Irish Girls About Town
Maeve Binchy, Marian Keyes,
Cathy Kelly, et al.

The Man I Should Have Married
Pamela Redmond Satran

Getting Over Jack Wagner
Elise Juska

The Song Reader
Lisa Tucker

The Heat Seekers
Zane

I Do (But I Don't)
Cara Lockwood

Why Girls Are Weird
Pamela Ribon

Larger Than Life
Adele Parks

Eliot's Banana
Heather Swain

How to Pee Standing Up
Anna Skinner

Look for them wherever books are sold or visit us online at www.downtownpress.com

down tOwn press

Great storytelling just got a new address.

PUBLISHED BY POCKET BOOKS